D1355776

THE KING
OF MONEY

THE KING
OF MONEY

Jeremy Scott

W.H. ALLEN · LONDON
A Howard & Wyndham Company
1982

Printed and bound in Great Britain
for the Publishers, W.H. Allen & Co. Ltd,
44 Hill Street, London W1X 8LB

ISBN 0 491 02677 3

Words from the lyric 'Help Me Make It
Through The Night' reproduced by permission
of Combine Music Corp., copyright 1970.

With acknowledgements and thanks to Jane Knocker who has
made sense of and typed this and the manuscripts of two
previous novels.

For Peter Mead, and for
my brother Hamish

Prologue

The man crouched within the closet, bound and helpless.

He was blindfolded. His hands and feet were tied. He was hunched in the foetal position, his knees drawn up to touch his chin.

How long, how many hours, how many days had passed while he had squatted here he had no idea. Feeling, sense, and even terror had decomposed into a dull and timeless fog of pain.

In this close upright coffin was no sight, no touch. Sound there was, a muffled vibrating drone. At times his prison lurched and shook. He guessed it was in movement. But how? Where? By whom was he held and for what reason?

Smell there was, his own. Trapped within this narrow space its stench rose to choke him. And into this foul grave madness leaked and filled the stifling air he breathed with dread and horror.

Food there was – of a sort and intermittent. At random intervals a teat was shoved between his lips. He sucked on it greedily and tasted the sugared milk of life, cut off too soon. Following each feed his disordered mind slipped and staggered further down those shifting unsubstantial slopes where nothing held, the ground and reason crumbled, spectres grinned or clutched and all that was most real, most dear, dissolved to narcotic dream. There was nothing to hold on to.

All that specified his life had decomposed. He did not know where he was; now the sense of *who* he was had slipped away. In last efforts he struggled to recall his name, but it was gone.

In the rancid darkness of his cell the shell of flesh once known as Adam Lupus broke down and wept, lifted up its muzzle and howled at the surrounding night . . .

Chapter one

On the first day of April, the day before his fortieth birthday, Adam Lupus flew to Zurich to visit his money.

Founder and chairman of a multinational conglomerate whose interests ranged throughout the world, he was accustomed to travelling widely and often in connection with his work. Then he went by private jet or scheduled airline accompanied by a staff of lawyers, accountants, architects and aides.

On those occasions he travelled with a staff. Today nobody was with him.

The reasons for a Swiss bank account are secrecy and the evasion of income tax. A citizen of unblemished moral character, on this visit to Zurich Adam flew alone.

Dr Liebl and the others were already in place and waiting when he was shown into the room.

'Gentlemen,' Adam said, 'My plane back leaves at a quarter to six. Shall we begin at once.'

He was a tall blond and handsome man who possessed that elusive gift of presence. Around the conference table in the panelled room at the head office of Credit Suisse no one could fail to be aware of it. Though he spoke seldom, his bearing and manner dominated the assembly. Gravity is a precious element in the conduct of a successful life; it had served Adam well in his journey to where he was today.

The three Swiss in dark suits who sat across from him knew exactly who Adam Lupus was. The business section of the newspapers and the financial magazines which reported his activities formed their daily study. They were fully aware of his identity and the share price of his company and what were its current and intended ventures and a great deal else about him as well.

They knew, and Adam knew they knew, yet no one betrayed this fact on either side. Here he was protected by a wrap-around conspiracy of discretion.

The reason that brought Adam and most others to Credit Suisse was unlawful in the narrow restricted terms of their own countries, yet here, in this hushed air-conditioned place, the rules of the confessional applied. In Swiss banking, secrecy is an article of faith. The professional training of these men was to respect anonymity. Here Adam Lupus had no name, merely a numbered account. Nothing distinguished him from all other men - except that he was a good deal richer.

Sitting in that secluded room whose double glazed windows insulated it from the world outside, Adam listened in silence to the liturgy of investments held on his accounts. As they were read out he catalogued them on a sheet of paper and jotted down their nature ... the Swiss and American bonds ... Treasue bills ... German industrial ... Commodity and Eurodollar positions ... Against each item he noted its value of that day.

Dr Liebl's voice rose a shade as he came to the end of his summary and looked up, ' ... so this then, sir, together with the fifteen kilos of gold you instructed us to purchase on your behalf forms the present disposition of your funds. '

Adam asked, 'What's today's price of gold?'

Kilograms into ounces, ounces multiplied into money. Adam did the sum on a calculator no thicker than a wafer and wrote down $974.000.

'And the state of the current accounts?' he questioned.

The man in the dark suit checked his file. 'Swiss francs today 25,442. Dollar account 15,600. In Deutschmarks 4,252.'

Adam noted the amounts. He said, 'There's a transfer on its way to you from Monaco, 1.7 million French Francs. You should receive this tomorrow.' As he spoke he added the figure to his list.

'It is understood. You will take coffee?' the banker asked.

Adam glanced at his watch. 'No thank you,' he said. 'My plane ...' Beside his notes lay a copy of the Herald Tribune, folded open at the pages which showed the day's exchange rates. From habit he converted into sterling the values written against his various investments. His fingers flicked delicately over the tiny buttons as he tapped in the calculation and read the result.

It totalled five million and four pounds.

Then he was on his feet and those accross the table were standing up and shaking hands with a small polite bobbing of the head, saying 'Good day ... Good flight ... ' in ugly Switzerdeutch accents and he was walking away across the room and down the corridor and into the elevator and pressing the button to descend.

He had five million pounds in the bank.

He was a rich man in England but this was something else. The money in this account was absolutely and only his, squirrelled away. No one knew about it, not the tax authorities, not his associates, not even his wife. It was Adam Lupus' secret stash.

All the way down in the elevator he was waiting for the surge and rocket rush to get to him, and his heart to leap in answer to the hit, and his blood race and for elation to bubble through him like a rill of laughter. He waited for the money hit.

And instead he felt nothing. Nothing at all.

Chapter two

The first flakes of snow were beginning to fall as Adam left the solid edifice of Credit Suisse and stepped into the taxi waiting for him in Paradplatz.

Bahnhofstrasse was already illuminated. In the shop windows he saw the sparkle of jewellery, gleam of polished leather and of furs, the modish trappings of prosperity. The light was failing in the late afternoon and the lake was the colour of slate, hinged without horizon to the sombre sky beyond.

Adam's cab skirted the water, crossed the bridge and followed the tramrails up the hill towards the zoo. By the time the car had reached the outskirts of Zurich and turned onto the motorway which led to the airport it was snowing heavily.

Adam sat back in his seat and looked out at the suburban landscape sliding past the window, blurred by the storm, and wondered if his flight would be delayed and why he felt neither excitement nor triumph nor delight, and why there was no hit and what the hell was wrong with him.

He looked rich. He looked the success he had become. He was dressed in a grey suit, white shirt, dark tie, black well polished shoes. He wore no jewellery except a watch. There was neither opulence nor show in his appearance yet there was about him a certain private glamour, a suggestion of affluence and ease in the way he handled himself which told the observer that life had been good to him.

Low cloud scudded across the gloomy sky but the airport was open; planes were still flying. He heard one coming in before he saw it blundering down from the murk with flaps extended and bright noselight scouring out the runway in its final approach. Foul weather for flying, he thought again.

Paying off the taxi outside the terminal he waited, briefcase in hand, for the driver to give him change. A woman dismounting from the cab behind glanced at him curiously and wondered who he was.

He was a handsome man. Tall and well built, his suit concealed that thickening of the waist which had come with idleness and indulgence. His blonde hair was bleached by the sun and his skin had a golden glow. During the seconds that she watched him through the chill murk of a stormy evening the woman saw health and well-being beneath the gloss of good living which had protected him from the harsher weathers of the world. Then he had pocketed his change and turned away, strode into the bright antiseptic air of the airport concourse and was gone.

He checked in at a First Class desk.

'Any baggage, sir?'

'Nothing,' he told the girl.

She handed back his ticket, cool and dark with neat breasts buttoned away behind the trim jacket of her airline uniform. 'We regret there is a forty minute delay on all flights due to adverse weather conditions,' she told him. 'Swissair is pleased to offer you a complimentary dinner in the restaurant while you are waiting.'

He stood at the bar and stared out through the glass wall at the swirling whiteness of the storm which hid the runway. Then he turned, commanding the barman's attention with a nod. He ordered a quarter bottle of champagne.

As it was put before him he raised his eyes and caught sight of someone watching him from the crowd across the bar. There was something particularly intent about the look, that hard set face, the blank level gaze and deadness of the expression. It was the regard of an enemy. He flinched – only to see the movement exactly repeated by the watcher. With a shock he realised that it was himself, his own reflection in the mirror behind the bar.

His hand twitched upon the counter. He took up his glass, defiantly he raised it to that other reflected man in salute and celebration of what he had achieved.

To a secret, he toasted, to five million pounds. Then he tipped back his head and drank down the golden wine. He waited.

And still he did not feel a thing.

From the entrance the restaurant looked full. The Swiss are a thrifty race, not about to refuse a free meal even at this unchic and early hour. No, Adam answered the maitre d'hotel, supressing a stab of irritation, it did not disturb him to share a table.

But what was it, he asked himself as he was led across the room, what was it that caused this strange dulling of the appetite and dusty lack of joy? Was it age, or familiarity and habit which had spoiled his palate and the thrill he always got from making money? Was it being forty tomorrow? Was it that, or something else?

The man seated at the table by the window had been engrossed in his book, eyes fixed upon the page while the fingers of one hand fiddled with a lighter which lay beside his drink and pack of cigarettes. The dark stranger looked up startled at the headwaiter's question.

'What's that?' he said. His glance moved to Adam. 'This seat free? Sure. Help yourself?'

He was American and glad to have company, it seemed, for he laid aside his book and smiled. 'Another orphan of the storm?' he asked.

'Aren't we all?' said Adam as he took his place.

With his hand the stranger indicated the table whose crisp white cloth sparkled with cutlery and several sorts of wine glass. 'I've got a dinner date in Rome but waiting makes me nervous and nervousness makes me hungry. What's a man supposed to do?'

He was in his early thirties, Adam judged, round-faced and short-haired, wearing a lightweight suit. Salesman? he wondered and glanced at the title of the book.

'Know him?' the American enquired, turning it toward him. 'Graham Greene?'

'Of course,' Adam answered. 'How strange a writer so intelligent should believe in God.'

14

Beside them a flurry of snow battered the window as the other laughed and Adam too picked up the menu. 'I suspect we don't have to rush this meal,' he said.

In silence both men studied the extensive choice while outside, inches away, raged the silent storm. 'Well, what do you think?' the American asked at last.

'For me foie gras,' Adam said.

'And then?'

'Venison chasseur.'

'Yes?' The other sounded doubtful.

'Or tournedos,' said Adam. 'Beef in this country is excellent.'

'No, I'll go with venison,' the stranger agreed. He took up the wine list.

Adam summoned the waiter. When he had completed ordering, the American said, 'Listen, the storm's not about to end yet. How about we share a bottle of something good?'

'A burgundy?' Adam suggested.

'Right. You select it.'

'A Richbourg,' Adam ordered and suppressed a smile. In the younger man he recognised something in his own early days. He settled back in his chair and studied his companion with pleasure as he finished his drink and waited for dinner to be served.

The weather showed no sign of improving. This turn to an evening, this sort of encounter, delighted Adam. Travellers' tales and the random accident of a stranger's company. A state of transit and escape.

The American leaned forward. 'Can I ask you a personal question?' he enquired.

'What?'

'Where did you get that suit?'

Adam laughed. 'London, but it's ancient.'

'I'd be grateful if you'd tell me where to go. While I'm based in London, I thought I'd get myself a couple of suits.'

Adam asked, 'Based in London?'

'Yes.' The American was lighting a cigarette. 'Just been posted to our Embassy there. And you?'

Adam made a small self-deprecating shrug. 'I suppose I'm

15

a businessman,' he said.

The wine waiter appeared, proffering their bottle wrapped in a napkin and cradled in a basket. Adam indicated his companion's glass, and the sommelier poured a half inch then stood back, attentive, waiting for judgement.

The American performed the full ritual. He took it up, swirled and held it up to the light. Doing the whole cinema, he tasted, sucked in air chewed and savoured the mouthful then swallowed, nodded in approval and said, 'Yes, that's wine.'

It was poured for both of them 'What kind of business?' he asked Adam.

'Management, shipping, construction, real estate. The group's involved in a number of things.'

'Where?'

'Europe, the Middle East, South Africa,' Adam told him. 'We're pretty widely spread'

'So you get around. What's your star sign?' he asked.

Adam smiled. 'Aries,' he told him.

'You are? Me too. What date?'

'The second,' said Adam. 'Tomorrow.'

'No!' The man seemed astounded. '*No,* that's not *possible.*'

'Why so?'

'It's my birthday too. Tomorrow.' Excitedly he bent beneath the table to fish in the flight-bag by his feet. He surfaced with a magazine.

'Why that's some coincidence.' He turned the pages. 'Listen . . . "a crucial and decisive phase in your career but storm clouds gathering over family relationships where you are badly aspected . . . A turning point in your life . . . Allow nothing to hold you back . . . Fortune favours the bold and luck is on your side . . ."'

'Well, well,' said Adam, smiling still.

The foie gras was served, to each a glistening segment upon a bed of chopped lettuce. Adam found it excellent. The American sliced into the pâté with unaffected pleasure.

The venison was set before them and proved superb, tender, ripe and rare. The wine was gone by the end of the first helping. The blizzard gave no hint of abating, so they ordered another bottle.

It was a warm well-lit place they sat in, an island in the storm. There was no coming or going, none of the change and bustle and activity of a restaurant in normal operation, no urgency of hurry to fret the nerves or agitate the digestion, for all there were prisoners of that storm and captive to the meal. Time out of time, thought Adam in a pleasant glow.

The earlier feeling of deadness left him while he ate. The disappointment of before was forgotten. As he ate, his mood improved and subtly there stole over him that special warmth engendered by a perfect meal, that sense of benign comfort and goodwill, a repletion and philosophical detachment, a wise well-nourished calm.

His dinner companion was called Drury Sheldon, and at that table, linked by chance for the duration of a meal, the two talked freely, each finding the other's company agreeable and speaking with a certain intimacy, that shared candour permissible between strangers who will never meet again.

Sheldon was not only a decade younger than Adam but very different in appearance. Broad and powerful of build, forceful and overloud, yet there was a warmth to him and charm. He was a listener too, not just a talker.

'Do?' asked Adam in answer to the question. 'I told you, I run a company.'

'Yeah, but do.' Sheldon insisted. 'Not what you *are*, what you do. Me, I sit in meetings, fly on airplanes and answer the telephone. That's not my job designation, but it's what I *do*.'

Adam nodded. 'Yes, I do that too. Also I sit too long at table.'

'Yes? Good stimulating conversation?'

'Would it were,' said Adam.

'You have kids?' the other asked. 'How's your marriage?'

Adam was taken aback by so direct a question. 'It's fine,' he said after a moment.

'Any material worries?'

'None' The answer this time was immediate.

Sheldon said, 'Ninety-nine point nine per cent of the people in this world would envy you to hell.' He laid down knife and fork upon his empty plate. 'Envy me too, I guess.'

'I know,' Adam said. 'I know.' He glanced away. Beyond

17

the window the snow whirled across the glass with diminished frenzy. The storm was passing.

'Listen,' Sheldon demanded with sudden urgency. 'Listen. If that door opens and a broad comes over dressed in tinsel and carrying a wand and stops and says, "Mister, you've scored. You've just got yourself three wishes." How do you answer?'

Adam considered the improbable scenario. 'Goodness,' he admitted when a few seconds had passed. 'I can't tell you.'

'Why not?'

'I don't know. Not exactly.'

Sheldon seized upon his answer. 'Nor me. But sure as hell know what I *don't* want.'

Adam gazed at him thoughtfully. 'Yes,' he conceded, 'So do I.'

'Brandy?' Sheldon asked.

'Why not?' Adam did not speak again until it came then, 'I've got everything I set out for,' he said.

'I'm happy too,' Sheldon agreed quickly. 'I'm *happy* but . . .'

Adam smiled. 'Exactly,' he said. 'But.'

'So?' the other demanded keenly.

'Well . . .' Now that he had to put it into words it was hard to pin down. 'I feel there's something wanting.'

'Wanting?'

'Lacking,' said Adam with greater certainty. 'Something absent.'

'What?'

Adam took a sip of brandy. ' . . . Well I suppose its the chance that something, something *different* might happen.' His own candour surprised him.

Sheldon did not let up. 'Like what?' he demanded.

'Different,' Adam repeated vaguely. 'Just different. How should I know.' He paused and in that moment the public address system crackled and came stridently to life, '*Meinen Damen und Herren* . . .' The airport had reopened.

With effortless Swiss effiency bills for the wine were appearing everywhere as if by magic. In the space of a few seconds the peaceful atmosphere of the restaurant had changed entirely. Suddenly everyone was repacking their briefcases, standing up, putting on coats.

A continuous list of departing flights streamed out over the address system. Adam heard his own called for London and felt for his credit card. 'Well, that was an excellent dinner,' he observed.

The other, too, was reaching in his pocket. 'Yes, it's been a real pleasure . . . '

Sheldon thrust something at him. 'My card . . . ' drew it back to scribble down a number, 'my direct line.'

Standing, coat over his arm, Adam flicked through his wallet. 'And mine . . . my office.'

The American reached out his hand. 'Good trip then. Most interesting to talk with you,' he said.

'With you too. I enjoyed our chat. Maybe we'll meet again one day.'

A grin split Sheldon's face. The light flickered in his eyes. 'Whatever you say, sir. Maybe we will.' They shook hands.

Then Adam turned about and walked from the restaurant. Portrait of a successful businessman, Gucci briefcase in hand, he descended the escalator to the departure gate and the plane which awaited to take him home.

The atmosphere within airports is different from the air of the country in which they are situated. Rebreathed through foreign lungs, purified, disinfected, it is the climate of other places and of nowhere. Adam walked steadily through the antiseptic corridors, down the covered ramp into the plane, and took his seat.

He had always loved to fly. From his early twenties he had used airplanes with fluency, but always with a special pleasure. Wherever he was headed, the moment of take-off brought a thrill of stimulus and change.

He buckled his seat belt. His fingers fumbled on the catch. A fat drop of sweat formed between his shoulder blades and started slowly down his spine.

Suddenly a cold hand touched Adam; a fist squeezed around his heart.

The note of the jets mounted in a whine of terror. The plane taxied toward the runway. What the hell is happening

19

to me? he thought as panic throttled him. He knew with fatal certainty that Death rode upon this very flight. He looked wildly at his neighbour, a balding businessman slumped in the seat beside him. The man glanced back, then swiftly looked away.

Adam gripped the seat, his knuckles white. His mouth was parched, his shirt drenched with a mess of sweat. He had the sense of losing balance, of being about to tip clear off the edge.

Poised upon the start line the engines roared to full power. The huge airplane lumbered forward, gathering speed, the runway consuming beneath its wheels as it rushed toward lift off . . . too late to abort, too late to stop now . . .

It heaved upward. Adam felt it check and lurch. He sensed the fall, the impact, the obliterating wall of crash . . . Then they were up and soaring to the sky.

He sank back into his seat, fumbling for his cigarettes. It was past, whatever it had been. Terror left as swiftly as it had come. Yet nothing would ever be quite the same again. Death had touched him, had tweaked his ear 'I am here. Live,' she whispered, 'I am waiting.'

Chapter three

Two weeks later, on the morning of the 15th April, Adam woke at home in London.

It was 8 a.m. and the start of a perfect day. The light was cool and clear, the air fragrant with the scent of spring. Outside, the garden's trees were clothed in delicate young leaf; framed in the bedroom window the tops of the acacias shimmered against a steel blue sky.

The room where he lay was airy and bright, decorated in pale tones and furnished with elegance and taste. Not Adam's doing but his wife's, and she was not there. The covers of the twin bed had been thrown back. The room was empty. he was alone.

The Honourable Mrs. Vanessa Lupus sat straight-backed at breakfast in the morning room, a long stemmed English rose.

Adam came downstairs. He took his place opposite and picked up the folded paper. He touched the bell beside his foot.

'You were up early,' he remarked.

'Yes darling. Freddy and I have a meeting with the advertising people to promote the club.'

The manservant entered with orange juice and coffee, wished Adam good morning and set them before him. Vanessa's and the man's reactions were as usual. Clearly he looked normal. Yet it was as though all he saw was distanced behind a thick glass wall. He raised the *Financial Times*.

Adam's cool blonde wife put down her coffee cup, rather loudly. 'You do remember we're invited by the Huxtables this evening?' she asked.

21

'I'd forgotten. Dinner?'

'Drinks. But I said we'd go on with them afterwards.'

'That's a big bore.'

'Yes darling,' said Vanessa drily, 'But try not to tell them so.'

'Do I ever?'

'Yes darling,' she told him. 'Nowadays rather often actually. I'll join you there, I too have a very busy day. Do your best not to be *too* rude.

Adam left the house at 9 a.m. precisely as he always did.

His car awaited him outside, a Rolls Royce of unusual size. Only fifty of this type were built each year for it was a model normally reserved for Royalty and Heads of State. It had cost the company not only £95,000 but influence to acquire.

The chauffeur closed the door. Adam settled into the womb-like comfort of the back and reached for the telephone. '935 2434,' he instructed.

The big car drew off smoothly from the kerb. 'Dr Ransom please,' he said when the receiver was picked up in Harley Street.

'I'm sorry, Mr Lupus, the doctor isn't in here yet. I'll get him to call you back as soon as he comes in.'

'Please do' he said.

The Rolls eased into the Old Brompton Road and turned toward South Kensington. Viewed from inside it, the world looked reassuringly unchanged. Sunlight dappled the street. The day was warm and all in sight were dressed in summer clothes. At the bus-stops the queues waited patiently in line. The terrace houses were painted white and cared for, their lawns trim and gardens neat and colourful with flowers. The streets were clean. There was a pleasant orderliness to all he saw.

Yet Adam did not feel the same way, not orderly at all.

'The name of the game is winning.'

So Adam most firmly had believed. It was the fundamental principle of his success, the creed on which he had built his life.

The Lupus Building in Knightsbridge commemorated that faith, both monument and shrine. The first high-rise building to be put up in London, since the age of twenty-two it had been his ambition to own it. It had taken him ten years. Renamed, it became his corporate headquarters, a twin-towered bridge of concrete and glass which straddled the roadway to soar above Hyde Park.

The three commissionaires touched their foreheads as Adam went through the marbled lobby whose main wall was engraved with the names of the companies which the group had taken over. He nodded back and stepped to the annexe which contained the directors' lift. He fitted his key to the panel. The doors slid wide and he entered an interior of blue Venetian leather, tooled in gold. He pressed the single button and, soundlessly, the express elevator swept him up to the executive suite on the topmost floor.

This plushy eagle's nest with views over all of London was the very cockpit of his domain, the throne where he reigned comfortable and in command.

The two secretaries were already at work in his outer office. Wishing them good morning, he passed through and gained his desk.

His opened mail lay neatly stacked before him. He lit a cigarette and forced himself to go through the pile ... the minutes of yesterday's meeting together with a note from the chairman of the GLC ... invitation to a luncheon at the Guildhall ... a report on the Colombian resort development he was interested in acquiring, and a schedule of his visit to South America next week ...

'Do you have a moment?' His Managing Director stood in the doorway.

'Of course, Tony. Come in.'

The young man entered and, unasked, took a seat. Two years ago Tony Carvel had been an executive in a real estate agency which the Lupus Group had obtained almost accidentally as by-product of a deal. Adam had spotted his potential in a conversation which lasted less than ten minutes but he marvelled still at how fast he had learnt; not even the accent now betrayed him.

23

'So?' Adam asked, 'What's on your mind?'

'I had a call last night from Nigel Dempster.'

'The columnist?' said Adam sharply.

'Yes, but it's not the usual sort of thing. It seems he's had an appeal from Help the Aged, the charity.'

'Dempster? How very inappropriate. Whatever for?'

'The earthquake in Yugoslavia. They asked if he knew anyone with a private plane who might agree to a mercy flight ... medical supplies and blankets and stuff for the victims.'

'Can't an airline help them?'

'Well, not immediately it seems. It has to be something small to land on the local strip. He asked if we could do something.'

'You want to send the Lear Jet?'

'Well, if you're not intending to use it yourself, the company has no need of it this week. It would be a nice gesture and we can get mileage from it.'

'*Can* we?' Adam demanded. 'You know Dempster?'

'Yes' the other answered. 'I trust him.'

'Do it then,' he said.

'Shall I ask the Board?'

'No, what do you think this is,' asked Adam, 'A democracy?'

The telephone rang. 'Dr Ransom,' he heard.

He waited till Tony had left the room before he spoke, 'Mark, I'm off to South America and my secretary tells me I need a couple of shots.'

'Of course. Get her to fix an appointment anytime.'

'Today,' said Adam.

There was a beat of silence. 'Well today's a bit ...'

'It'll take ten minutes,' said Adam. 'Say one o'clock?'

'Well ... say one fifteen.' The suggestion was reluctant.

'I'll be there.' He set down the telephone and lit a cigarette. He drew on it heavily, then took up the instrument again. 'The Foreign Secretary,' he ordered and waited for the call.

It clicked through. 'Lupus? Is this you?'

'Sir John, I'm sorry to do this but I can't make your lunch party, I'm afraid.'

'Foolish boy ... ' the voice drawled back full and rich and ripe. Irritably Adam pictured the politician lolling in customary pose of exhausted langour within that Common's office where of late he had come to be accepted as a familiar.

But now the tone grew petulant. 'Inconsiderate, I *need* you,' it continued. 'Nigel Broakes is coming, and Tiny, *and* Maxwell Joseph. *All* the oldies. I was *counting* on you for the younger blood. Dear boy, I *insist* you come ... '

It was folly to refuse. This was a regular monthly event of advantage to all who attented, an informal Think tank where good wine oiled the wheels of conversation.

It was flattering to be invited, pleasurable to sit so close to the centre of influence and power, to express opinion while others listened and deferred. Such intimacy promised favour; it signified advancement, a step towards his K.

'I'm sorry Sir John, I can't. Something just came up.' He rang off, knowing what he had done to be unwise.

He lit a cigarette and sat there smoking. Worse still, the way he had done it was clumsy and badly handled; he had *spurned* the old fool by suggesting that something else was more important. Idiot!

He jerked the chair closer to the desk and started to deal with the rest of his correspondence. His hands were trembling. He was in a furious temper. He did not feel well, not well at all.

'Actually,' said Adam Lupus to his doctor, rolling up his shirtsleeve, 'While we're at it you might as well give me a check-up.'

'Of course, Adam.' Dr Ransom's exasperation at the request was imperceptible. His patient had already obliged him to cancel a lunch date.

There was nothing clinical about the place which they were in. Furnished with leather chesterfield and chairs, the consulting room resembled a study or small library, a place such as may be found in a gentlemen's club as a den for reminiscence or smutty stories, for frank man-to-man disclosure and confidence that would go no further than these walls. Glassed cases of books surrounded them and the examination table was hidden behind a Chinese screen.

Dr Ransom wore striped trousers with a black jacket. Perfect waves of white hair swept back above his ears, like wings. Coiffure and man were faultless. Dr Ransom did not believe in illness; he considered it indulgence.

Adam undressed and stepped onto the scales.

'Smart bastard,' Ransom observed. 'You still have a tan.'

Adam was irritated by such irrelevance. 'Vanessa and I had two weeks in Bermuda, you remember.' He lay upon the table. A rubber armlet was wound around his upper arm.

'Everything all right there?'

'In Bermuda?'

'With Vanessa.'

Unwillingly Adam found himself responding, 'Fine, she seems better now she's got this club she's starting with Freddy Reynolds. It was boredom, I think. I was at work and there's not much to occupy her during term.'

'Prosper's doing well?'

'Head boy,' Adam told him.

The mercury danced up the scale to find a level. The pressure from the cuff released with an expiring hiss. 'What is it?' he asked at once.

'150 over 100, the same. You've stopped eating salt?'

'Never touch it,' he said. It was reassuring to be here and in such capable hands. Ransom exuded calm; for years he had been his physician and his friend.

The groomed head was bent over his chest, faintly smelling of expensive oils. 'Breathe in.' The stethoscope shifted across his rib cage 'Out slowly ... again ... How many are you smoking?'

'Less.'

Firm fingers explored Adam's stomach and probed his liver. ' Any pain?'

'Not really,' he admitted.

Ransom's face suspended above his own. A sharp beam lanced through his eye seeking the dark spot, the flaw within the brain. 'What are you drinking?'

'Not much. Wine with lunch and dinner.'

'And spirits?'

26

'A couple of drinks before dinner. Possibly some brandy afterwards if we have guests.'

'Which you normally do?'

'I suppose so, or go out.' He added, 'Somehow just the two of us now . . . '

'Quite.' Ransom nodded, testing his reflexes, then told him to get dressed.

Still knotting his tie, Adam joined him at the desk. The doctor took an ashtray and a pack of cigarettes from a drawer, offering them, then lit one up himself. He exhaled luxuriously. 'Well, what really brings you here?' he asked.

'I told you, I wanted a check-up,'

Ransom smiled. 'Reassure yourself Adam, you're fine. I can't find a thing wrong with you. You're slightly overweight, your blood pressure is marginally high but still in the safe zone. You should watch your diet and take more exercise. You smoke and drink too much, you work too hard. You're in perfect health.'

After a moment Adam asked, 'So why do I feel like shit?'

'Just now or all the time?'

'All the time.'

'Like shit?' Ransom examined the end of his cigarette. 'As a symptom it's not very precise.'

No. But Adam's disease itself was inexact, not specific but general, a malaise which poisoned his entire body, his mind, his life. He was sogged by lethargy. His skull was packed with straw. He was without zest; in the mornings he had to force himself from bed. The work he loved now exasperated and bored him. He had no drive for business or for sex; he felt sapped, stagnant, flat and dead.

Ransom heard him out. 'You're drinking more than you admitted,' he remarked without censure.

'You felt that in my liver?'

'No, but are you?'

'I'm not . . . I don't *like* it,' he protested. Alcohol's never worked for me as it does for other people. It doesn't stimulate but slows me. It makes me dull and stupid. At best it is an anaesthetic and I hate it.'

'You should be grateful,' Ransom said. 'That's one tempta-

27

tion less.'

'There aren't enough temptations,' Adam told him bitterly.

'No? How did Shelley put it, "You crave for louder music, stronger wine?"' The doctor put out his cigarette and crossed the room to open a window. 'So tell me about work,' he said.

'Work? It's very good. We go from strength to strength.'

'That ought to be very satisfying.'

'Yes,' said Adam. 'It ought.'

It should. The company grew steadfastly more profitable. Even in the adverse economic climate its share price had not wavered. Invested across the world, the giant multinational corporation ran on rails now. It was established, and it was safe. Hope and fear - twin forces to a life - were absent. A man's drive is what he yearns for and Adam yearned for nothing - since Zurich not even money. Ambition was his mistress but he had tired of her. She had failed him.

The doctor listened to his confession with sympathy and understanding. 'Of course you're something of a special case,' he observed. 'A wonderboy, a tycoon, a millionaire, you've achieved it all and the dream's come true . . . so what do you do now?'

Adam reached across the desk for another cigarette. 'Don't think I haven't asked myself that question.'

'Politics?' Ransom suggested.

'What?' Adam's nerves jumped as he remembered the lunch he was not at.

'Politics, wouldn't that interest you?'

Ransom seemed to be staring at him oddly. He forced his attention to the present. 'I don't know. The people seem as mediocre as everyone else but more pretentious. The issues which concern them are paltry. There's nothing very noble about hanging onto office.'

'It would make another game for you. You've spent twenty years working very hard. Slow down a bit, get to know your family, play tennis with your son, enjoy the pleasure of old friends.'

Adam said, 'Old friends are greatly overrated as a pleasure. One grows as bored of them as of cold turkey in the week after Christmas.'

The doctor laughed. 'Then maybe you should find a new one to restore your blood.' He was writing something down.

'What's that?' Adam asked. 'A telephone number?'

'That you must find yourself but these may help your mood.' He passed over the prescription and glanced surreptitiously at his watch.

'Shall I tell you something absurd?' Adam asked as Ransom walked him to the door. 'If I go out at night without my car I have to explain not only to Vanessa but to the chauffeur.'

Absurd it was, yet so. He had no time that belonged to him alone. Too many people depended on him. Two decades of discipline and habit had led him inexorably into a trap. He had built himself a palace and found it was a jail. He was captive to a golden life. Where once he had been trapped by poverty so now he was by wealth. He was caged by responsibility and, even more inexorably, by a sexless worn-out love.

'There's not a thing wrong with you,' Dr Ransom repeated as he laid an arm across Adam's shoulders and eased him from the consulting room. 'Not a thing. You're in tip top health. You're not sick, Adam, you're forty. What you've got is called the midlife crisis. Take the pills and come to see me when you're back from South America.'

Fifteen minutes later the Rolls delivered Adam back to Lupus House.

'Any calls?' he asked as he went through the outer office.

'Just the one,' his secretary replied. 'A few minutes ago. An American who wants you to lunch with him next Tuesday.'

'An American? Who?'

'He says you know him,' the girl answered, 'A Mr Drury Sheldon.'

Chapter four

It was three days later. Tony Carvel came fast into Adam's office carrying a newspaper. 'Look at this,' he suggested, spreading it upon the desk.

Adam focused his attention on Nigel Dempster's column:

'The generous and charitable nature of millionaire Adam Lupus has ensured that medical supplies arrived safely in Yugoslavia yesterday for earthquake victims.

'A few days ago Help the Aged rang the column to ask ... mercy flight ... plane ... put in touch with Mr Lupus ... within hours the operation was under way.

'Chairman of the group of companies which bears his name, Mr Lupus is one of the most generous of men ... His beautiful wife, the Honourable Vanessa, daughter of Lord Waterfield is better known socially than her husband. Now associated with restauranteur Freddy Reynolds in his new club-venture, HERE, she is a prominent hostess whose dinner parties are justly celebrated for their excellence.

"Mr Lupus' speedy action was tremendous," say Help the Aged.

"Now we have five more tons to go and need other people with planes." What offers, readers?'

Adam laughed, laying aside the paper. 'Well, Freddy and Vanessa will be pleased. I'm glad we could be of use,' he said.

Tony nodded enthusiastically. 'Yes, it's a good story, the kind we'd never get through buying space. I've asked Dempster to lunch. Look, it's none of my business, but have you ever thought of a biography?'

Adam's hand waved off the suggestion. 'It's the corporate image which counts, Tony. I have no ambition to become a personality.'

The other's enthusiasm was causing him to pace rapidly

between the window and the desk. Adam watched him with affection and remembered how it felt to be so young and keen. One of these days he'll have my job, he thought.

'You needn't write it yourself,' Tony said. 'We could find someone to write it, someone you get on with.'

'It would be dull reading,' Adam told him. 'Hard work, one wife, no scandals, no defection, no jail; that's not the kind of story people want to buy.'

'Success is,' said Tony. 'Will you consider it and meet Dempster?'

'No,' said Adam. 'Definitely not.'

At one o'clock Adam was seated in the Sovereign restaurant in Hertford Street waiting for Sheldon.

He had asked for him on coming in and been shown to a table at the far end of the room. He ordered a gin and tonic and when it came, lit a cigarette and sat there without impatience in the sequestered privacy of the stall, assembling what he remembered of the man who had invited him to lunch.

When Sheldon arrived a few minutes later he looked exactly as Adam recalled him. He entered in a manner entirely American, finding his way across the restaurant unaccompanied, fast and without fuss.

'Sorry to be late but a call found me just as I was leaving.' He sat down opposite Adam and looked round impatiently for attention, needing a drink. 'You know an old guy called Bailey?' he asked. 'Sir Michael Bailey?'

'I don't think so.'

'Runs your Intelligence Service here. I've spent all morning with him. Whee!' He blew out his cheeks and rolled his eyes heavenward in disbelief, then turned away to snap his fingers at a passing waiter. 'Man! I swear he's modelled himself straight out of a spy book and I'm trying to remember which.'

'James Bond?' Adam suggested.

'Shit, no. Talks about church music and gets off on playing the organ somewhere at weekends. Where's that drink?'

'You discussed church music?' Adam asked amused. The

31

idea was incongruous.

'I think so, but who knows. I understood one word in three. That accent! If that guy gets any more British he won't be able to talk at all.'

Sheldon's whisky sour was placed in front of him. He picked it up and downed it in one thirsty gulp. His hand shot out and caught the departing waiter's sleeve. 'Another,' he ordered.

'And apart from that?' Adam asked, indicating his own glass as well.

Sheldon grinned. 'Apart from that working in this country is like wading through mud.'

'I don't know exactly what you do.'

'Liaison. Liaise with European intelligent services.'

'Yours sounds like a fascinating job,' Adam said.

'Yeah, can be,' Sheldon admitted. 'When I'm not talking about Gregorian plainsong. So tell me about *your* life.'

'It's not that interesting.'

'Come on! I've learnt what a big wheel you are. Tell me where to make my next million.'

Adam shrugged, 'Personally I'm thinking of South America.'

'Right on,' Sheldon said. 'What'll you eat? Lobster?'

'Sole,' said Adam who had studied the menu while he waited.

'Grilled sole and Lobster Americaine,' Sheldon ordered. 'And to start?'

'Smoked salmon.'

'Right, two smoked salmon. Now you're my guest but you select the wine 'cos you got that European "savoir faire".'

His accent was appalling. Adam suspected this ingenuousness to be at least partially an act on Sheldon's part yet it was refreshing to meet him once again, this easy stranger who knew no one that he did, to share with him an atmosphere so displaced from both domestic life and work. It was an interlude from real life, a two hour holiday upon an island of difference and good cheer.

'Montrachet?' Adam suggested.

'Whatever you say.'

An island; a holiday encounter with an incongruous yet agreeable fellow traveller. It seemed Sheldon felt something of the same as, for the second time, these two men enjoyed an excellent meal together, eating well and drinking two bottles of wine then lingering over coffee and brandy in the comfortable seclusion of a near empty restaurant where no one hustled them to depart.

'I must say,' Adam remarked finally, leaning back in his chair and lighting a cigar. 'I must say it's pleasant to meet like this and all the more so for being a pleasure which I thought was lost to me.'

'Lost? How so?' Sheldon asked.

'Well, for years I've not enjoyed a meal unless I wanted to get something out of it, a girl, a deal, to bring someone around to my point of view. It's a long time since I found enjoyment in a lunch for no reason, just for the hell of it.'

Sheldon nodded. 'I know what you mean,' he said. 'Yes . . .' He dropped his eyes and fiddled with his glass. 'Yes, I think that too but, well . . . ' He paused. 'Well, the bitch is I got to admit there *is* a reason. I *do* want something.'

Adam's heart shifted minutely. He said nothing.

'International Construction,' Sheldon went on. 'That's one of your companies?'

'It's part of our group, yes.'

'Yes, our people checked it out. Well . . . ' He picked up the coffee pot and refilled both cups. 'Well, five or six years ago you put up a building in Tehran, right?'

'The Peacock Centre, yes, that was our development. Why?'

But Sheldon was not to be rushed. 'Obviously a pretty funky place,' he observed. 'The Russians want to take it over.'

'The Russians?' Adam was baffled. 'Whatever for?'

'For their embassy. Their staff's gone from 150 to 400 there. They're buying your building to move into.'

'Well, that shows taste.' He waited. 'Go on.'

But Sheldon had picked up his pack of cigarettes and was slowly extracting one. He set it in his mouth then hitched back his chair and crossed his legs with a maddening deliberation. He lit the cigarette and behind the movement

33

and the flame Adam saw his glance shift left then right to the adjoining booths. Then he looked at Adam.

'You were in the military?' he asked quietly.

'National Service. Years ago. The last draft.' Adam refused to drop his voice. 'Why?'

'You had a commission. Lieutenant in the Artillery.'

'Second Lieutenant. How do you know that?'

'We checked you out. What I need to know is if you signed the Official Secret's Act.'

'What do you mean "checked me out"?' Adam demanded.

Sheldon shrugged, indifferent to the sudden anger in the other's tone. 'Background stuff. Standard procedure. That Act, did you sign it?'

'Of course. We all did. What is this, Sheldon?'

'All right,' After a moment the American answered. 'All right, I'll tell you. But what you got to understand though is you can't talk about it to *anyone*. *Anyone*, Adam, not even your wife. This is national security, and that Act still binds you. If you break it you can go to jail.'

All at once it seemed very quiet in the restaurant. 'What is this?' Adam said again, but his voice was lower now and he did not sound angry any more.

'OK,' Sheldon sat forward and fixed his eyes upon his listener's face. 'You understand what happened to us out there was the pits, Adam. It was the diplomatic equivalent of Pearl Harbour. We lost face, national confidence . . . and an entire intelligence network in Iran. Now we're halfway through rebuilding it, and if we move fast we can bug that new embassy whilst it's still being redecorated. What I need from you are the original construction plans. You dig, Adam?'

He dug. But at the same time he felt a stab of the keenest disappointment. The blueprints, was that *all* which was required of him.

'I suppose I can think up some reason to get you those,' he said after a while. 'You said "we", are the British in on this too?'

'Are they ever!' Sheldon spoke with a bored weariness which suggested that his patience had been sorely tried that morning. 'Man, are they ever!' Do you think you can get something by the weekend?'

'I suppose so. What do I do then?'

'Call me at the Embassy,' Sheldon told him. 'You have my direct number. Don't go through the switchboard, it's not secure.'

Adam sipped on his brandy, his mind racing. 'Well, well,' he said at last. 'In mid-life am I making a career switch? Are you recruiting me? Am I becoming an agent, Sheldon, is that what the job's called?'

The American placidly lit another cigarette. 'You're getting your feet wet.'

'Is it paid, this job?' Adam asked and the other replied with more than usual promptness.

'It's a service for your country. I wouldn't insult you,' he said crisply. 'How about a brandy?'

'Why not?' Adam answered with a laugh. 'Why not indeed, Sheldon. It's a fair price for a beginner, I suppose. Make it a large one.'

On his way back to the office after lunch a thought came to Adam. He had no belief in the occult, the idea of astrological influence he considered nonsense. But memory of the horoscope which Sheldon had read him in Zurich airport came back to him.

'The Great Sun passing through Aries ... A turning point in your life ... Things begin to happen very suddenly and unexpectedly ... '

'A turning point.' Was this it? he wondered.

Chapter five

That evening Adam and Vanessa ate at home in Kensington. Unusually they dined alone.

The table could hold twelve. The dining room was formally arranged, rather heavy in its furnishings, rather dark in the colour of its walls. The lighting, controlled by dimmer switch, was turned low for daylight still lay outside. The curtains were pulled back and the windows open on the gardens and the Boltons' church which stood opposite the house.

Dusk fell while they ate. The evening closed in, windless and still heavy with the threat of storm. The dense greenery of the trees outside hung sombre in the humid lull. There were no voices in the street; no passing traffic disturbed the quiet which enveloped them.

Filled with people the room worked perfectly. For a dinner party it was ideal. The carpet and thick drapes sopped up the discord of so many voices prattling together and rendered each intelligible. With a crowd it worked; on two alone the hush dropped in a stealthy pall.

'How was your day?' Adam enquired and the words seemed to echo from a distant land.

'Hectic! I don't see how we can conceivably be ready on time.'

'I'm sorry I won't be here for your opening party.'

Vanessa sipped game soup from the side of her spoon. 'Quite honestly darling, I don't think it will be your kind of thing.'

Silence followed for the space of three spoonfuls.

'How's Freddy?' Adam enquired.

'In great form,' answered Vanessa.

Both would have continued the conversation but the

36

subject seemed exhausted. The silence crept back.

They had been together for eighteen years. It was not passion which had united them; their reasons for marriage had been more considered than emotion and more sound.

Each had chosen a partner who fulfilled a need. Even as a young man starting out in business Adam had the aspect of a winner. Vanessa had thought it, and so had her family. Their judgement had proved accurate.

Those had been her reasons; his were different. As a choice she was impeccable. Attractive, sophisticated and adept, marriage had brought an improvement to his social position which it would have taken years to achieve otherwise. Her family and her background were her dowry. Aristocratic but poor, through them there opened to Adam a world of privilege and connection, an insider's club of which he became a member.

Each had delivered on the bargain: Adam gained advancement and Vanessa obtained the life to which she would have liked to have been accustomed. In their union they were content.

Until recently they talked together easily, agreeing on practically everything. They discussed politics, people and the popular novels which they read on holiday. Strangely, the one subject which they had never gone into was themselves yet each believed they knew the other very well and, to a certain point, they did. Beyond that point stretched the unknown. In all its years their marriage had not been threatened; it had never fallen under strain. Crisis had not put them to the test. Who knew how they might react if confronted by tragedy or disaster? Yet one bond was amply proven, they were skilled in uniting to eliminate inconvenience.

Adam and Vanessa talked together less often now. Familiarity breeds constraint. Unadmitted, each found evenings such as this, passed together without company, to be something of a strain.

Tonight their unaccustomed state of intimacy was purely temporary. Help was on its way. Help in an unpremeditated, most unexpected form. During the afternoon Adam had received a call from Sir John Doff, the Foreign Secretary. Sir

John wanted a word before Adam left for South America, had forthrightly proposed himself for a drink that very evening. 'A social call,' he had explained, 'A notion I'd like to try on you.' Following so soon upon his rejection of the Minister's lunch party, Adam had been amazed.

While they sat at coffee in the drawing room they heard a ring upon the bell.

'Sir John . . . I'm sorry you weren't free to dine with us.' Adam greeted the portly figure who entered behind the man-servant. 'My wife' he introduced.

Vanessa had also risen as the Minister came in. A mark in her favour, Sir John concluded as he took her outstretched hand.

'We met once at the Streethams,' she reminded him, 'When I was with Daddy.'

'I remember well,' he answered. 'At the Club your father is sadly missed. A certain style is gone from us.'

'Yes,' said Vanessa, 'he did get very rude. What will you drink?' she asked.

'A whisky please.'

Adam poured and served it. Sir John's eyes were looking past him. 'Is that what I think it is?' he asked, staring at a picture above the fireplace.

'A Renoir? Yes.'

'Stunning,' he said, moving closer to examine it.

'You might be interested in this,' Adam remarked. Taking Sir John by the arm he led him to a small canvas in a gilt frame wired for both light and theft.

'Fascinating,' said the Minister. 'Seurat?'

Adam confirmed it.

'But how do I recognise this?'

'You know "Les Baigneurs",' he explained. 'This was a pre-liminary sketch; the arrangement of the figures and the bridge section is the same.'

The two returned to the fireplace which burned the exact replicas of real logs and beside. which Vanessa sat in a wingback chair, a blonde handsome woman of thirty-seven, well-dressed and poised and slightly drunk – a fact undetect-able to anyone but her husband.

'You men want to talk?' she asked.

'If you'll forgive us,' said Sir John.

'Lah!' exclaimed Vanessa, rising. 'You see before you a woman who knows her place.' She made a small mock curtsy. 'Goodnight, Sir John. Lock up, will you,' she told Adam. 'I shall retire to my needlepoint.'

'Good-looking girl,' the Minister remarked when the door had closed. 'Father was mad as a hatter of course.' He looked at Adam sharply.

'Drink,' said Adam. 'I don't think it is hereditary.'

'Well,' began Sir John, 'You're probably wondering why I have called.'

He stationed himself before the fire, legs apart, warming his haunches, left hand deep in the pocket of his blue striped suit, right grasping his crystal goblet. 'Well, the fact is, the PM and I, we've just brought off something of a coup.'

He looked at Adam levelly, expecting a response.

'That's excellent,' Adam heard himself replying.

'Summit,' said Sir John, raising his glass as though to indicate a distant peak. 'The word "summit". It conveys a certain picture, an achievement in diplomatic terms. We maintain that very concept is an error. Together with our friends the Americans, we have proposed that we shall meet without *intention* of achieving a result.'

'Who's "we"?' Adam asked.

'The Russians and the Western Heads of State,' Sir John paused, his glance again on Adam, 'together with a small selected group of personal advisers.'

'I see,' said Adam.

'Geography is what links us,' Sir John resumed, 'Together with expedience, trade and the need for growth. The idea is this meeting should be as small as possible. Each country will field a team of not more than twenty-five. Discussions, dinners. Deliberate informality, an itinerary but no agenda. Novel, no?'

'It's a fascinating idea,' Adam said.

'It is,' said Sir John. 'I came here to tell you I've put forward your name to the PM.'

Adam was baffled. By refusing to come to lunch he seemed

39

only to have made himself more desirable in the minister's eyes. Denial had turned him on.

' ... And that you are invited to attend,' Sir John concluded.

'Why?' Adam enquired after a long moment.

'Why? Because I value you,' the other replied. 'Because your companies represent a significant proportion of Britain's export earnings ... and because I trust you,' he added.

'I am honoured,' Adam said, 'But bewildered.'

'Come, come,' Sir John said sharply. 'We speak the same language, we understand each other. I know that you are loyal.'

He was staring at Adam very quietly and intently. His look conveyed a meaning beyond words.

Sir John set down his empty glass. 'It's understood of course that all this is off the record and not to be released until the timing of this conference is decided and announced.'

'Of course,' said Adam.

'Politically we must move while we hold the initiative. Call me when you're back from South America. We'll lunch.' Sir John drew his left hand from his pocket and glanced at his watch. 'Now you will excuse me. I have one more call to make tonight.'

'You keep late hours,' Adam murmured.

'And so do you,' Sir John replied. ' That is only one of the things I like about you.'

Adam walked him to the front door and opened it.

Whilst in the curtained living room the two within had been aware that the storm which had been gathering all evening had finally broken. As they stepped out into the porch they heard the hiss and spatter of the water and saw the night beyond curtained by falling rain.

Without waiting for his chauffeur, who was already coming up the path with an umbrella, Sir John ran for shelter. Clutching the man's arm he hurried him back to the waiting car. Adam heard the thud of two doors closing. The sound of the limousine's motor as it drove off was inaudible above the storm.

Adam remained in the open doorway, staring at the rain.

He felt profoundly flat, flatter than ever in his life.

It had been an eventful day. Recruited to the CIA he had performed his mission. The job had lasted less than five minutes. He had asked his secretary to fetch the Iran file and make photocopies of the architects' blueprints. Having done so, the girl rolled these in a tube and packaged them for him. He telephoned Sheldon on his direct line to say that it was ready. He addressed the parcel himself then had his chauffeur deliver it to the Embassy in Grosvenor Square. Five minutes, less than five minutes, then it had been over.

That was the afternoon. This evening he had been propositioned by the Foreign Secretary, presented with a blind contract which he was expected to sign at once – indeed Sir John's manner on departure clearly indicated an assumption that he *had* signed it. Adam's role had been spelled out clear, token tycoon on England's team ... and the Foreign Secretary's obedient bumboy.

Once Adam would have been flattered. Now he felt only bordeom and disgust at the charade of both events, the big nothing that was the truth of life. He gazed out at the sodden garden and the dark shrubs beaten by the storm. He moved to go inside and, as he turned, saw a ragged figure beyond the flower beds standing against the wall.

After the first second of startled shock he felt a rush of pure compassion surge into his veins. That *I* should be so discontented, he thought. What weather to be homeless in! 'Wait!' he called out. 'Don't be afraid.'

But the tramp was already slipping through the gate. Adam hesitated a moment, shrinking from the storm, from a flicker of good sense, then pity drove him on.

He ducked out into the night, hurried down the path, through the gate, and stood there indecisively on the pavement in the downpour, not a soul in sight.

The lamplit street curved away, the great trees drooping over it, sheeting rain. He was drenched within seconds. He looked about him, then set off in blind pursuit.

The torrent cascaded down, dancing on the black road. The district was deserted. There was no one about, no cars. The dark houses stood back behind garden walls, their gates

41

locked, their doors and windows closed tight against the storm.

He hastened on, peering about him into the shadows for the tramp, seeking where he lurked. A short street connected the Boltons to the Old Brompton Road, one side of it occupied by an immense Victorian house, the other by a courtyard and ornamental pond. Beyond it, the stark outline of a modern school lay part hidden behind trees.

Adam sensed the figure even before he saw it. In the still and soaking night, against the black slab sides of the building the darkness moved. The form of a man stood there observing him.

Adam halted, straining into the murk. 'Come here,' he ordered, his voice stifled in the hiss of rain. 'Come,' he called out louder.

The figure, if it was figure, made no move. Now Adam had begun to doubt. Was it a man who stood there or the play of shadows on the wall? He started towards it.

A shape detached from the surrounding dark and slid around the corner of the building.

Adam ran forward, reached the angle and peered beyond.

Cut off from the street lights by the building, here the darkness was more dense. A playground stretched away from him, bounded by high walls, its surface a black lake flickering in the downpour. At his side a run of plate glass reached into a wall of mist.

Adam stood absolutely still, holding his breath. He knew the man was there, lurked close to him. He felt his presence.

He shrank back against the glass. It was crazy to be here, he told himself. No sane, law-abiding citizen would roam abroad at such an hour in weather such as this. It was lunatic to follow. This was a night for violence or sudden death.

Easing away, he backed around the corner of the building ... then all his breath left him in a gasp of terror. He stepped against something soft. A shape reared at him, huge and formless. A blow struck him upon the shoulder as a figure rushed past, thrusting him aside. He reeled away.

'Stop!' He sprinted after. The thing dashed across the courtyard. Its overcoat flapping, like a half-shot bird it broke

42

toward the street.

Adam raced to overtake. Cutting the corner he vaulted a low wall, saw his error even as he leapt and tensed to take the fall. He came down heavily in the pool, crashing to his knees into waist high icy water.

Dazed, he shook his head, clearing water from his eyes. The shock had numbed him; he felt no pain yet when he tried to rise one leg would not bear his weight. There was no sign of the creature he had chased.

He dragged himself to the edge and sat there, feet still trailing in the pool. His sodden clothes clung to him in clammy folds. The storm sheeted down, he felt it soaking through his skin to dilute his blood. The rain beat on him; he saw himself lying dead in it. Was he utterly insane? A damp wad of money was still clutched in his hand.

He drew himself abruptly to his feet and clambered out.

He took the weight on his good leg and stumbled across the road. What in God's name had come over him? Furious at himself, he limped home through the beating storm.

Adam re-entered his house, bolted and double locked the door. Passing through the hall he switched on the burglar alarm system.

Instantly the air was blasted with the raucous jangling of bells. The circuit had been broken.

The system connected with the local law. Within minutes a police car was outside. Accompanied by four officers Adam searched the rudely woken house.

In his dressing room they came upon the reason. A window had been forced and opened.

But nothing was gone, nothing disarranged. Adam's cufflinks, his studs, a chequebook and gold watch still lay upon the dressing table. The intruder had taken nothing. The man had been disturbed, the police concluded. But *what* had alarmed him, Adam wondered, no one had come upstairs.

When, finally, the police had finished their whiskies – which, after a token refusal, they drank standing awkwardly in the living room making stilted conversation and clearly

43

overawed by their surroundings – when finally they departed, it was after 2 a.m.

The household had already returned to bed when Adam at last made his way upstairs, wet and chilled.

In his dressing room while he was peeling off his sodden clothes, his keyring fell from his trouser pocket and, bending to retrieve it, he spotted something on the floor, glinting beneath the bureau where it had rolled.

He reached to pick it up. Light and small it lay in his hand and he looked at it, bewildered. A flash cube, burned out on all four faces.

The burglar's? Why?

He laid the flashcube on the dressing table. He went through the interconnecting door to the bedroom. He lay down. Vanessa was asleep.

The storm had passed. Through the window glass he looked up into the cold infinity of the heavens and the new moon glittering behind a tattered wrack of scudding cloud. He could not sleep.

Why should someone have broken into his dressing room to take photographs, he asked himself. The only things he kept there were his clothes and his suitcases.

What had happened made no sense.

Chapter six

By the time Adam at last fell asleep it was 4 a.m. in London. In Florida it was eleven o'clock at night, and as the programme ended and NBC went to commercials the old man extinguished his fortieth cigarette of the day and leaned forward to turn off the set. The tests would be waking from their sedative. It was time to make his round.

He rose carefully from his chair for he was stiff. He was seventy-years-old and his Palm Beach shirt and unpressed trousers hung loosely on his frame. His bones showed through the skin, his features pierced sharp with age.

He moved slowly to the door of the small prefabricated house. He wore thick lensed glasses and walked bent forward in the shuffle of the defeated. He stepped outside.

It was like entering a warm wet sponge. The soaking air closed around his face, hot and stifling. Eighty-five degrees with ninety-six per cent humidity. His skin began to sweat even as he turned to close the door behind him. He plodded down the path toward the hangar.

Fifty yards away from his prefabricated dwelling, the windowless single-level building stood upon a raft of concrete raised above the surface of the surrounding Everglades, an island in the marsh. Not a light, not another building could be seen. The sodden dark stretched for miles around and, as he went toward the hangar, the old man heard the night noises of the swamp, the electric rustle of cicadas, frogs, a distant splash, silence.

He opened the door, reaching for the switch. The lights came on.

The wide bleak space was illuminated sparsely by hanging bulbs. He spent the minimum on electricity. Aisles of crates

45

stretched away from him, shadowed corridors into the darkness. Wooden crates, lined in tin, the front of each covered by a flapped glass door. Row upon row of cages.

When he switched on the light the place had fallen quiet. Now in the noxious air a furtive shuffling and rustling began again. The smell was nauseating. The old man no longer noticed it. He had lived with that stench for years, the complaints of neighbours at last forcing his move here where there were no people, no complaints.

The hangar contained 2,000 rats. They were isolated within each cage in colonies of ten. A galaxy of red eyes gleamed around the old man as he shuffled down the aisle, headed for the test cage.

There, the colony lay asleep within, a furry pulsing pile draped by scaly tails. They had eaten the additive ten hours ago and soon begun to exhibit the customary behaviour patterns it provoked. He had allowed them to continue these for two hours, then shot them with a sedative to break the cycle. Only when unconscious had he injected Test Antidote 107.

He shone his torch into the cage, examining the sleeping heap. Roused by the light, one rat stirred. It raised its head, squirmed from the pile of bodies and staggered to the glass. Rising unsteadily to its haunches it looked at him. Man and rodent regarded one another.

The old man waited he did not know how long while he stared into those bright intelligent eyes. Waited, hoping.

The shrill whine of a mosquito disturbed his attention. He felt it settle on his cheek, even as he raised his hand felt the insect sting him. He scratched the spot.

Watching him, the rat's paw raised to its muzzle and twitched. It began to scratch its furry snout.

It was not dismay the old man felt, just disappointment. He was used to disappointment. The antidote had not worked; still he watched for a while, knowing what would happen.

Now the other rats woke and looked around them. They struggled from the heap, sat back, regarding their first woken still industriously scratching his muzzle.

46

First one paw came up, and then the another. The movement was repeated. Soon all were copying the example of the first in scratching at their snouts.

The old man sighed. He went to fetch the hose, dragging it back to the test cage.

He slotted the hose into the cage and turned on the jet. Imperfectly constructed, the cage leaked, spilling water from its seams. Yet the jet was powerful. Rapidly it filled up and forced their heads under. They struggled then ever more frantically, and then they died.

The old man unplugged the bung and drained the cage. The water splashed upon the concrete floor and flowed away down the tracery of guttering chipped across its surface.

At one time he had killed them by injection. Now he had no money to spare for that. Left, they would have continued till their sharp claws had torn away the fur, the flesh, the eyes. Till their faces were raw flesh. Till they bled to death. Drowning was the most humane method the old man had been able to devise.

He unplugged the hose. He switched off the lights, closed up the hangar, returned slowly on the path towards his house.

The night was still and stagnant, the air close, a damp membrane wrapped across his face. The cry of an animal screeched across the swamp. The new moon was coming up out of a band of fog. The naked trunk of a palmtree reared above the mist, its leaves a frozen starburst silhouetted against the paler sky. A distant smear of light on the underside of the clouds was Miami.

As he came into the house the old man heard the telephone start to ring and his spirits lifted. Since the widow in Fort Lauderdale had died there was only one person who called this late at night. He hurried to the table and picked up the instrument. 'My son, it's you?'

'Hi Dad. You got the money?'

'You send money, you can't come yourself?' he asked.

'I'm working Dad.'

'How's business? So *I* should ask.'

'You've done a test?'

'So I've done a test,' he answered. 'And it hasn't worked.

47

Why don't you come to see me? Where are you, still running around with that German shicksa?'

His son ignored these questions. 'Did my messenger come?' he asked.

'Yes,' the old man answered after a while. 'Your messenger, *that* you call him. He came.'

'And?'

'Who is this man? I did not want to give it to him.'

'But we agreed . . . ' his son began.

'Yes. But when I saw him I did not want to give it to him.'

'You refused?'

'I refused.' There was silence on the line. 'I was frightened,' the old man said in another voice. 'I was too frightened.'

His son's tone raised, 'he didn't threaten you?'

Exact memory came back to the old man and his heart shrank from it. 'No, not threaten. No.'

'What did he do?' his son asked.

'He didn't do anything.'

'What did you say?'

'I didn't say anything.'

'Why didn't you say anything?'

'I was too scared,' the old man said. 'I just looked into his eyes.'

'His eyes scared you?'

'His eyes are the most frightening thing I've ever seen,' the old man said. 'I gave it to him.'

Far away on the other end of the line his son breathed out slowly. 'It'll be all right, Dad,' he said at last.

'All right I don't know. I don't know anything anymore. Why don't you come and see me?'

'I will, Dad. There'll be more money in a month.'

'Forget money. Bring yourself.'

'I will,' said his son. 'I must go now.'

'Call me soon. Look after yourself my boy.'

The old man waited till the connection was broken, then he replaced the receiver. He crossed slowly to the TV set and switched it on, picking up his cigarettes. The thought of those eyes was still with him; he shuddered. It was out of his hands now, gone from his control. He lit up. Two packs, three

48

packs, what did it matter now? It was out of his hands. He could not forget those eyes.

Chapter seven

Cruising at a height of 6,000 feet and speed of 180 knots, the Beechcraft flew towards the glittering ice wall of the Andes which towered to twice the altitude of the aircraft, fifty miles ahead.

Adam peered down from the window over a limitless jungle of dense green, a vast landscape of awe-inspiring monotony without road, habitation or signs of life.

This was his third day in Colombia. He had flown to Bogota from New York with the attorney from his Manhattan law firm who had uncovered this deal in South America and proposed it to the Lupus Group.

The lawyer had introduced him to Jose Vincente, a local millionaire who headed a corporation which owned hotels on the country's Carribean Coast, plus this ski complex high in The Andes in an area of year-round snow. It was here they were headed now. The lawyer did not accompany them. For the moment his job was done and he had left that morning on a flight to New York.

Aimed toward the ice wall, there were only three passengers aboard the Beechcraft, Adam, Jose Vincente and Gretchen, his Swiss girl friend. The plane banked and began to climb. Below, the tops of the mountains were white with snow.

'Gets pretty crowded at weekends,' Jose Vincente remarked. 'The beautiful people fly from Panama and Nicaragua.'

'There's no road?' Adam asked.

'Sure there's a road,' he answered. 'But pretty much everybody on this continent owns their own plane. You have a Lear Jet, I understand.'

'You've done your homework well.'

The other laughed. 'I'm a businessman,' he said.

His manner belied it. He was a small, balding man who acted with a bouncy and defiant youthfulness. His model girl friend was in her early twenties. Blonde, sensational to look at, she was of a type which rarely mated with its contemporaries. Her taste for clothes and jewellery could be understood more easily by older men.

The note of the engine changed. The plane banked again then straightened and started to descend as the pilot cut his speed and applied full flap.

It was all white below, the light dazzling. Knife edged crests of mountains rose up on either side, cutting off the sky as they wobbled down towards the valley floor.

With a showy flourish the pilot feathered his propellers and dropped down fast and short onto a narrow tarmac strip miraculously clear of snow.

'Heated,' Jose Vincente explained, reading the question in Adam's mind. 'And it doesn't cost a cent, we pipe it from the hot springs.'

They taxied towards a hangar where a Range Rover awaited them.

'What do you want to do now?' he asked when they were in the car and driving up a road enclosed between high banks of snow. 'Rest? Have a drink? See the place over?'

'What would be best of all would be to get a couple of hours skiing,' Adam said. 'That is if you can lend me the clothes.'

They stopped in front of the hotel. Their luggage was unloaded by two Indians incongruously dressed in striped waistcoats and green baize aprons, the staff uniforms of another continent and era.

Adam looked around as he followed and was impressed by what he saw. The hotel had been designed imaginatively and well. With dark planked walls, the tiled floor scattered with Indian rugs, a huge fireplace containing a roaring blaze of logs, the effect was both rustic and modern.

'Simple and clean,' said Jose Vincente, dismissing the place with an airy wave, 'And *very* expensive. I'll show you over

51

later. Let's find some skis and get it on.'

Adam had passed a week at Gstaad with his family over Christmas but that was the only skiing he had done this season. He was out of training.

Looking across the cable-car during its ascent, he realised that Jose Vincente and the girl were certainly more skilled than he. Their boots were Caber, their skis Rossignol, the best. Being Swiss, Gretchen had to be an expert, and it was most unlikely that her middle-aged lover would practice any sport at which he did not excel.

This proved to be the case. The cable-car swayed to a halt and its dozen passengers stepped out onto a wooden platform where they put on their skis.

The sun struck across the snow and the light up here was blinding. Adam pulled down his yellow visor to cut the glare.

'Ready,' the South American asked.

He nodded, then watched as man and girl dug their sticks into the packed ice at the edge of the platform and flipped off the edge, crouched over their skis and twisting in controlled shallow turns without loss of speed.

Adam sighed and pushed off from the platform. He sank toward the slope, riding the skis and waiting for them to become one with him as extensions to his muscles and his will.

All around him range upon range of mountains reached to the horizon. The air was very cold and thin and clean. He swept down and his heart beat faster, his blood quickened to the speed. His body felt light. His nerves kindled with excitement and a fine electricity of fear prickled across his skin.

He was going fast. Expert terror and excitement purified his blood and purged all vile humours our of him.

The man and girl were waiting for him halfway down the run. He joined them, stopping in a wrenching turn with skis broadside to the slope and his leg muscles screaming in agony of protest.

They were off again at once. Jose Vincente allowed him no time to recover his breath, he was set to win. He was showing off before the girl, Adam realised. It was stupid to respond, childish to be lured into competition. He could break a leg and prove nothing.

He skied then with deliberate control, determined to take no risks. He found them waiting by the cable-car with scarcely concealed impatience.

'You go ahead this time,' he told them at the top. 'I'll find my own way down.'

He saw the South American smile in satisfaction.

The afternoon was late. Only four others had come up with them in the car. This was the day's last ascent.

The binding of one of Adam's skis was loose. On the platform he paused to tighten it while the others started down.

Far as the eye could see, the peaks rose around him. Colour was draining from the sky. The mountains were gashed with shadow and the white slopes which had glittered so brightly when he had stood here less than an hour before had faded to become sombre and ghostly in the dying light. Beyond the snowfields the sun, like an enormous bubble of blood, sank toward the horizon.

Adam drew on his gloves and moved to the edge of the platform. At his feet the piste glistened as an icy road, snaking down into the treeline.

The points of his sticks squeaked as they bit on packed snow. He thrust off, flexed his knees and hit the slope. Far, far below he could see the tiny buildings of the development in deep shadow at the bottom of the valley.

The temperature had dropped. The piste was frozen now. He went swiftly, keeping his weight low and edging his skis into the ice for grip. He rushed down, zigzagging across the beaten swathe.

He was alone. Those who had been with him in the cable-car were hidden now among the trees below. The glittering slopes were empty. He came down fast, the cold air ripping past his face, his will and concentration focused on the turns.

Then, where the moguls ended and he straightened his track, he became aware that he was not the only skier on the slope. A hundred metres behind him another figure was swooping down the mountain. Fast, choosing a line much steeper than his own. An expert skier, he noticed in that

53

glimpse, who was serpentining down the fall line with no pause between the quick supple turns.

A girl, he realised, bringing back his attention to the path, and out to overtake him. He sharpened his angle to aim more steeply down the slope.

He raced down. It was fifteen seconds before he glanced back and in the time she had gained thirty metres on him. She was out of the broken ground already and on that smooth highway which curved toward the dense wall of trees.

If he reached them first he could beat her. There the piste ended in a single track sliced through the wood with no room to overtake. He increased his angle and his speed.

Ahead were the firs. He could see the narrow gap which was the path. He heard her behind him now, the hiss of skis on snow and the sharp clatter of their metal edges across the ice.

He could sense her right behind him as they reached the trees. He thought for a panic second that she would try to take him there, right at the entry to the path, and crowd him off to smash into the trunks.

Then he was on the path with skis set in the icy furrow of the track. For a second he turned his head. The figure was on top of him, the tips of its skis almost riding on his own. What he saw was horrible. His gaze slammed straight, his mind skittering from the sight. His muscles melted as he staggered and almost fell.

The creature was scaly black. In the broken light beneath the trees its quick crouched body glistened with an insect's sheen. It had no face. What was set upon the shoulders in its stead was horrible.

The speeding figure shifted in its rush, stepped to the jagged rim of snow which edged the path, stooped and cut past, its clothing scraping against his own. He reeled away.

A skull had turned and leered at him. For a second he stared into blank sockets from which the eyes long ago had rotted. Black holes gaped in yellowed bone where tufts of hair clung in grey and greasy wisps to stream behind the creature's swift descent.

As it went by it turned its face to look into his own. Foul

54

teeth grinned at Adam from the lipless mouth in recognition and ghastly promise.

The figure of Death flashed past while he rocked in its passage with mind spinning into nightmare, flashed past and away, flicking into a turn which carried it into the trees, plunging down in a wild jinking course between their trunks. Then it was gone.

It had been dreadful. He was shaken by mortal terror and that sense of weakness and panic stayed with him up to the moment that he saw, at the bottom of the valley by the towlift, the horror ski mask pushed back to reveal a lovely face and Death became the slender figure of a dark haired girl.

Chapter eight

Adam ordered his second drink of the evening in the hotel bar, feeling better than he had in a long time. A hot bath had soaked away all aches, his muscles were warm and tired. His body glowed, at peace from the unaccustomed exercise, but his mind was very much alive.

It was 8.30 and the bar was crowded. People kept Spanish hours here; no one had moved through to the dining room to eat.

Jose Vincente and Gretchen had not yet come down to join him. Certainly they were getting laid, he thought, but he was in no hurry for them to appear. The girl who had passed him on the slopes sat four stools along from him at the bar.

Only hours before their eyes had crossed at the bottom of the towlift, crossed and held. For an instant they had looked at each other down slick tunnels while, leaned upon her skistick, she held that laconic stance, that cool disdain of youth for age.

Full-faced, dark-haired, green-eyed, she was vividly attractive. Spotting her as he came into the bar he had felt a thump within his gut and the brush of wings light and delicate as a moth's along his nerves. The touch and whisper of it was rare as almost to be forgotten. The flicker of a pulse both dangerous and thrilling was a sense he had thought was atrophied and lost for him. It was years since he had experienced that same sharp sting of curiosity and desire. But she was not alone.

The man beside her was unusually short. Black-haired, handsome, flashily dressed in blue suit, dark shirt, white tie, he looked inappropriate and small. Standing, his head was on a level with her own as she sat upon the barstool. With face thrust close he was talking rapidly in a low angry tone and Adam strained to hear the words and what language was being spoken.

In the hubbub which surrounded him he was unable to distinguish it. Among the crowd the man's was the only tie in sight, the only suit. That mean and stupid face could belong to no one but a villian. Others at the bar were dressed with premeditated unconcern in aprés-ski wear, the men in cashmere sweaters, the women in trousers with silk shirts or velvet tops, the simplicity of their attire offset by the jewellery which gleamed on their tanned flesh. Central Americans, all spoke Spanish, their voices loud, their gestures vehement and expressive. Jose Vincente had not exaggerated, Adam thought, it was a lively bunch who came here. Lively and rich. All exuded that disdain and effortless assurance which comes with wealth.

Under cover of lighting a cigarette he threw another glance into the mirror, scanned it with a passing look - and held there startled, for the girl now looked directly back into his eyes. It was not a come-on. It was no sly burn or sultry appraising gaze which reflected from the mirror, but an urgent message. It was an appeal for help. He read it as clearly as if it had been spoken.

He held his glance, her own dropped away then lifted to the tense and angry man beside her as she tried to reason with him. He cut her off, his hand raised in threat. He turned and strutted from the bar.

The girl stared after him for a moment, dismay and fear written on her face. Then she picked up her purse and cigarettes and slipped down from the barstool. For a moment Adam thought she was about to run after her companion but she did not. Instead she came directly up to him.

'Senor, perdone me por molestar le,' she said to Adam.

'I'm sorry,' he answered. 'I'm afraid I don't speak Spanish.'

'I said I'm sorry to speak to you like this.' Her accent was German.

'That's all right. You have a problem?'

'That man ... ' She drew heavily on her cigarette and he

57

saw her hand was shaking.

'Your boy friend?'

'No, I never saw him before. He threatened me. He says he knows the man I'm waiting for. Would you please talk to me for a few minutes so it looks you know me.'

'It would be a pleasure,' he told her. 'Can I offer you a drink?'

'It is not necessary,' she said. 'I do not wish to make expense for you.'

Adam smiled. It was a long time since anyone had said *that* to him.

'In that case you can buy me one,' he told her. 'You owe me that. You scared me half to death and I damn near wrapped myself around a tree.'

Her hand flew to her mouth in consternation. 'It was you?'

'Introduce me, Adam,' Jose Vincente's voice spoke behind them.

Adam turned to where he stood with Gretchen. 'She's Death,' he said. 'I met her on the slopes.'

'Not Death,' stated Jose Vincente with exhuberent conviction. 'Death does not stay at *my* hotel.'

Unsmiling the girl thrust her hand out like a man, 'Jutta Metz,' she said.

The South American snapped his heels together, raising it to his lips while he looked at her with velvet eyes. Adam experienced a flash of irritation.

'Ja, I am seeing these ski masks,' Gretchen told her. 'But why you wear?'

'It was a present. From New York, I think.'

'From Bloomingdale's,' Gretchen informed them. 'I too am seeing but I buy not. Not attractive, I think.'

'Who are you meeting here?' Jose Vincente asked.

'A man called Guttierrez. I have a date with him.'

Jose Vincente's face had changed on mention of the name. 'He does not come,' he told her.

'But yes. He is meeting me here.'

'No, he does not come,' Jose Vincente repeated flatly. 'These are bad people, you must not be seeing them. You will have dinner with us.' As though the arrangement were

58

decided he gave a nod to Gretchen and led the way toward the dining room.

Adam was at a loss. He said. 'I don't know what this is about but I'd be delighted if you'll eat with us.'

She shook her head, clearly disconcerted.

'Please do,' said Adam. 'If your friend comes you can join him. Till then we'll look after you.'

She hesitated before accepting. 'Thank you. You will explain where we are to the barman, please?'

When they joined him at the table Jose Vincente did not at first allude to the incident but began at once advising them on the menu. He was very much king of the castle here. Nodding, greeting, blowing kisses, his had been a royal progress across the restaurant to their table.

'What I suggest,' he said, directing his words to Adam but speaking to them all, 'is to begin with something simple. The plane has come today which brings us smoked salmon from British Columbia.'

The remark made Jutta laugh. 'This is simple?' she asked. 'That our fish flies 5,000 miles to table?'

'But yes,' he assured her. 'Simplicity is hard to find and always expensive, is that not so Adam?' Without waiting for a reply he continued, 'You are on holiday here, Fraulein Metz? Alone?'

'Alone yes, but I am not on holiday. I am doing a piece about this country.'

'A piece?' he questioned.

'I am a journalist.'

'Yes?' Jose Vincente's look had hardened remarkably. 'And you write about drugs and Mr Guttierrez?'

'About drugs . . . and other things.'

'Like skiing? Like this place I hope? Yes indeed, drugs are a most interesting subject but it is not good you write about them.'

'No?' she stared back at him coolly. 'Why not?'

'Because you will be . . .' he paused, searching for the word, 'whacked out.' Then he turned again to Adam. 'I know this Guttierrez,' he explained. 'He asked to be my partner in this place. It is known I look for fifteen million dollars to expand.

59

With ski lifts and more hotels here will be more famous than Aspen Colorado, than Megeve.'

'To achieve that,' Adam said, 'you must also put it on the map.'

'Of course. For that I look to journalists like Fraulein Metz to write about movie stars who come here and the excellence of my smoked salmon.' He made a small ironic bow in her direction. 'But I am not short of offers for this money, Adam. Here in Colonbia it is available. Many wish to invest with me.'

'Why not?' Adam observed. 'The scheme looks attractive.'

Jutta said innocently, too innocently, 'This is a rich country Mr Lupus. You have noticed this.'

The tone was lost on the South American. 'Yes there is an economic boom, six billion dollars in reserves. The country is democratic, conservative and stable. The future here is good.'

'So stable,' said Jutta, 'that if the US legalised marijuana the Colombian economy would collapse.'

Adam realised he was staring at her, lost in a private blaze. He shifted his look and saw that Jose Vincente's face had changed; hard lines tightened it and his eyes were angry. Pointedly ignoring her he said, 'So you see, Adam, money is available but frankly I prefer yours. I hope we will be partners.'

Adam remarked lightly, 'By the sound of it, I'm less dangerous perhaps.'

'Yes, I am admirer of the English. You are gentlemen. But it is not only the colour of your money and my esteem for you personally which makes me say this. What I like about you very much is the line of cruise ships which you operate.'

Adam's attention sharpened. 'It had occured to me,' he said as the smoked salmon was put upon the table, 'but how do you see it?'

Food was of no interest to Jose Vincente at this moment. 'To make package,' he explained. 'Summer as well as winter cruising. To bring younger people to Cartagena for the sun then fly them here to ski. Liners, hotels, skiing, we put them . . .' he slotted his fingers together, 'into mesh.'

Adam nodded thoughtfully. 'What do you think?' he asked

Jutta. 'Would your readers be interested in a holiday like that?'

'I think,' she said after a moment, 'people are well paid in West Germany. Yes, with publicity people will come I think.'

'Thank you,' said Jose Vincente a shade sarcastically. 'This is what I think also, there is a market.'

Gretchen, the Swiss girl, had played no part in this conversation. Since they had sat down her partner had not addressed one word to her. Sulkily she had picked up her fork to eat. Now, in what all took to be an attempt to draw attention to herself, she pushed back from her plate with a startled cry, 'Heiss! This is hot!'

Jose Vincente twitched with anger. He touched his plate, sharply drawing away his hand. 'Cabellero!'

The Indian waiter was at his side immediately, 'Senor?'

Jose Vincente showed a countenance hard and mean and black as fury. He abused him in a harsh contemptuous voice, suddenly thrusting aside his plate so it fell and shattered on the floor. After a second, in silence the waiter knelt to gather up the pieces.

'Dumb idiot,' he said savagely. 'Stupid fucking peasant.' Then he looked around his guests and sensed at once that he had gone too far. 'You don't understand,' he told them passionately. 'You don't know this country. I have to speak to him like that or he will not respect me. Here if a servant feels he is being treated as a human equal he will despise you for it.'

'Do you keep staff in your apartment in New York?' Adam asked.

'Rules there are different,' the South American conceded in a calmer tone. 'When in Rome ... But I do not have them resident. Why pay an enemy to live within your house?'

'We go dancing after?' Gretchen asked in the pause which followed as new plates and fresh fish were set before them.

'Personally I like Indians,' Jose Vincente said to Adam. 'I think everybody should have one.' He stole a sly glance at Jutta. Only after a moment did his smile tell them it was a joke.

After smoked salmon came steaks. More than a pound of

meat filled each plate and Adam protested at the daunting size of it.

'It is normal,' said Jose Vincente. 'Meat is plentiful here. It made this country into a paradise. I remember when a labourer working on the roads would build a grill and cook twice this much for his mid-day meal. Meat was cheap as bread.'

'But not now, I think,' Jutta said and he stared at her challengingly.

'Every country has problems, Fraulein Metz. Even West Germany, no?'

Whatever it was she had been about to say, she checked herself.

The meal continued without further incident. Unable to tear his eyes away, Adam studied the German girl and attempted to draw her out. Clearly intelligent, with political beliefs he suspected to differ radically from his own, she intrigued him. He had heard such views expressed before, of course, but seldom by a woman and never by one so young, so lissom and so smoky-eyed. And he had never met a girl who skied so well. All her movements were controlled and graceful; slender and tall, she had perfect body ease both on the slopes and here. A bubble of heat throbbed within his groin.

After dinner they went downstairs to the hotel's discotheque. Gretchen had insisted, and when they stood at the bar in that obliterating thud of sound Adam noticed the Swiss girl began to move her feet and jerk her head in an absurd and self-conscious manner, exaggerating the pleasure she received. 'Komm tanz,' she called to Jose Vincente.

He shook his head and watched with irritation 'as she flounced to the floor by herself and started to dance in a fashion wildly exhibitionistic, as if under the spotlights of a TV show, getting off on the attention and applause.

Jose Vincente put his mouth close to Adam's ear. 'The best thing about Gretchen,' he confided with his glance bent sombrely upon her, 'is the way she looks.'

'Yes?'

'I tell you that bimbo's big time dumb,' he said. 'But she

amuses me for now.'

After a few minutes Adam asked Jutta to dance. He kept his feet close together and his movement small. Opposite him, equally controlled, she shifted her supple body to the rhythm.

The sound was deafening, stunning the ears. It was impossible to talk. The music caught up all there within its driving beat.

Beside them on the floor, Gretchen was flinging herself about in showy abandon. Jose Vincente's bad humour had not lasted long, or perhaps he did not care to be seen alone and sulking at the bar, for he had come to partner her. All signs of irritation had disappeared; his snapping fingers and rapt face demonstrated that he was having the grandest time. In another era, Adam thought, he would be ordering champagne for the band. His deft feet twinkled nimbly about the floor, his little legs encased in silk jeans so tight they might have been painted on him. At fifty plus he seemed to parody his own style, as though having once discovered a manner that worked for him he had come to believe it more effective through exaggeration.

Ridiculous, Adam thought and saw Jutta's eyes upon him. Her expression was inscrutable. He caught his breath and all consideration of Jose Vincente went from him. The electric guitar wailed in on-heat ecstasy. The music exploded and crashed around them. Her look threw a claw into his heart and dragged him to the bottom of the sea . . .

The evening wound down. They danced, then drank, then danced again. When they finally came off the floor Jose Vincente was longer at the bar but sat with Gretchen at a table of friends.

Adam proposed to join them but Jutta shook her head.

'No, I must ski tomorrow and I have drunk enough. Also I think your friend does not really want me.'

They left the club together. 'I have whisky in my room,' he said, 'if you'd like a last one somewhere more quiet?'

'It is kind. But thank you no.'

They rode the elevator together. He walked her along the passage to her room.

63

'Will you work with him?' she asked.

'With Jose Vincente? Probably. You thought it a good idea?'

'It will make money, yes.'

'But . . . ' he prompted.

'It is not right to put money here, to support this government.' She turned on him impulsively. 'You have seen Bogota? The gangs of four and five-year-old children who sleep in cardboard boxes in the street and live by stealing. I was held up by a seven-year-old with a knife. Can you imagine what that does for you? It makes you weep for the whole world.'

They were standing outside her door. 'It's ghastly, of course it's ghastly,' Adam agreed. 'But one may also argue that with capital and a prosperous economy they can afford to improve these unfortunate conditions.'

'Unfortunate,' she repeated bitterly and fitted her key into the lock. 'Yes, it is "unfortunate". You want one more drink?' she asked him.

It was freezing in her room. The curtains were pulled back and the French windows stood wide open to the snow-covered balcony.

'You Germans are very Spartan,' he remarked.

She laughed, closing the windows, 'No, not so Spartan.' She tore the duty free wrapping from a bottle of Scotch and poured two drinks.

'Here,' she said abruptly, holding one out to him. She took one long deep swallow from her glass then set it down and suddenly she had taken a pace forward and was in his arms.

It was totally unexpected. He held her to him, her slender body pressed against his own, trembling from nervousness or cold.

He led her gently to the bed and sat her down. He took up the duvet and wrapped it around them both, like a rug. He passed his fingers through her hair, tightening his grip upon the nape. She looked him in the eyes and it was as though she had touched him between the legs. He reached over to the bedside table and switched off the light.

He caressed her throat, her shoulders, her breasts. With his

64

thumb he traced the outline of her lips, he kissed her. Suddenly she shivered and clutched him to her. They fell back upon the bed.

It was not making love, it was fucking. It was a commerce of the flesh, urgent, sharp-edged and passionate. There was a fierceness in their hunger; Adam grabbed at sex as a starving man at the pleasures of a banquet, with no restraint. There was desperation in his hunger.

He felt heat flare and race through his body. There was no technique in what they did that first time, nothing of the subtlety and impure cunning that informed their lovemaking in the days that followed. For Adam these seconds were brutal, consuming, total. It flushed through the glands and all the secret chambers of the flesh and swept him forward in delight. It whirled him beyond the edge and hurled him down the dizzy drop. He held back nothing. It wiped him out.

He lay there, drenched with sweat. The cold struck sharp as a knife at their naked bodies. Adam gasped and dragged the duvet over them. Warm peace stole back to wrap his flesh in the balm and langour of satisfied desire.

He held her close. She said nothing and nor did he. He wondered what she was thinking. Had she come? In the haste and passion of his long deprivation he did not know. He had been a selfish lover, certainly. He glanced at her. Her eyes were closed, she seemed asleep.

Beyond the window the snowfields unfolded from the night. Washed by moonlight, the ghostly landscape reached into the distance, hushed and muffled by snow. The mountains looked like gleaming spires holding up a dome of night brilliant with stars.

Within his arms he held her slender, sleeping body close.

Chapter nine

Normally so dark blue, so placid beneath the glaring tropic sun, the sea at Cartagena heaved in the aftermath of a distant storm.

The three children were playing in the line of surf thirty yards offshore, shouting with the exhilaration of their game as they leapt to ride the breaking waves. The fact that these excited cries had changed to screams of terror just after Adam and Jutta left the hotel beach to go up to their room was not at first apparent to the sunbathers who remained. It was some time before anyone noticed that the childrens' lively play had turned into a flailing and frantic thrashing to stay afloat.

In the bedroom the shutters were closed against the heat and light. Unconscious of the drama taking place outside, Adam threw off his clothes and went to shower.

After a few minutes Jutta entered the bathroom wearing only a towel wrapped around her waist. She walked to the basin and he watched her haunches shifting beneath the white material. She took a sponge to wash her face and, as she bent to the mirror, the towel rode up and he saw the soft shadow between her legs. His sex throbbed once, like a pulse.

She straightened up. Dropping her towel, she came to join him in the shower, The hot jets beat on them both in the steaming cubicle. She reached for the soap he held. Refusing it, he started to lather her shoulders. The foam slithered down her body. Her breasts were taut and full, their tips prominent and very dark.

He turned her about to soap her back then slid his hands around her body. The nipples came erect at once beneath his touch. His fingers glided down her flat belly and across her

mound. He drew his hands back to work up more lather. The
soap shot from his grasp, hit the wall and fell by Jutta's feet.
She bent to retrieve it, her long legs straddled. The foam
streamed down the valley of her buttocks, mingling with the
tender curls.

The sight of it was like a thud into his groin. An erotic
frenzy stung his nerves. He was hard at once, his flesh hot
and swollen. He stepped forward and rubbed against her,
seeking an opening. He found it, slick and soapy, and drove
in.

'No!' She cried in pain, starting upright, rigid from his
thrust. 'No, please!'

She struggled, but he gripped and held her still. Neither
dared to move. He felt her breasts crushed beneath his hands.
Imperceptibly, she loosened in his grasp. Her thighs heaved
under him.

Her eyes blurred as if she were drunk. Very slowly she
swayed away from him and back. She staggered and reached
up to hold the shower-rail. With infinite tenderness he
withdrew a half inch then eased forward. He heard her catch
her breath. She twitched and pushed back on him. He felt her
clench and sensed her turmoil. He came back, without pause
drove in again.

Water cascaded over both of them. His face was in her
streaming hair. Wildness seized him. He bit her shoulder,
demanding and insatiable. Pain flared down the pathways of
her nerves then all control fled from her. It was like a
sacrifice, a rite enacted in the white tiled cubicle. He the
tyrant, she the victim powerless to resist. Her face became
transfigured, ecstatic and almost sacred with intensity as
though she were witnessing a vision.

Her hands gripped the rail. Her body clenched and tightened; it cramped as a spasm grasped and held her, held them
both. Then all at once she shuddered as her insides coiled. He
felt her soften, melt, as though she flowed apart, nothing in
her struggling or holding back. As she came free she
screamed as if he had murdered her.

The drowned bodies of the children had been recovered. The

ambulance and police cars had departed by the time Adam and Jutta came downstairs. The small sodden corpses laid out upon the sand had been removed and no sign or flavour of the tragedy reflected in the hotel lobby or outside.

They took a taxi into town.

Adam had suggested the weekend here the day after he had met Jutta. In the morning he had woken before her, had watched her face swollen with sleep, her cheeks flushed, lips parted. Nothing was visible of the sophisticate of the night before. She looked like a tousled child. A swelling wave had travelled through Adam's body, lifted up his heart and flung it toward shore.

Now, together, they strolled the cobbled streets in the old walled town of Cartagena. They drank in several bars. For Adam this weekend was stolen time; illicit pleasure charged the content of every minute as it clocked by. Tomorrow he must fly to New York and continue that same night to London.

Meanwhile, it was pure pleasure to be here. From the start Adam had felt marvellously at ease and well with her. In the sun and in her company he had sensed the sap flow back into his loins, freeing him from the long winter of age and doubt.

At dinner outside a restaurant on the old port she left him as they sat down to eat, returning with a package, crudely tied.

He unwrapped it while she watched and recognised a pair of naif paintings in carved wooden frames. Hunting scenes, innocent in their cruelty, he had remarked on them in a gallery window as they passed by.

'I can't' he protested for he had also seen their price, but she stopped him with a hand laid over his.

'Please,' she said. 'I know you liked them.'

He accepted, wondering what he would give her in return. Jewellery? He was inexperienced in these matters, the legacy of eighteen years of marital fidelity.

It was time out of time here, sharper and more sweet than anything he had known before; he was bewildered by the depth of his delight. He had never tasted it before, this spontaneity and trust and openness and ease.

68

He had feared in London that he had contracted some fatal weakness, for so long had he lived within an unchanging, hollow, dusty emptiness of feeling. Now immodest passion had put its wild mouth all over him and he had become another man. The rich juice of life coursed through his veins. An overwhelming sense of wholeness and of harmony possessed him.

Her glance was like a warm caress. He looked into her green eyes across the table and closed his mind to the thought of anything beyond tomorrow. He lived in a breathless present. Only now was real.

Midnight and they stood upon the balcony of their hotel room.

The moon, rising from the sea, threw a path straight to them across the waves. It looked like a silver road into the night and the unknown.

'Tell me who you are,' he said.

Her body quivered. 'What do you mean?' she demanded sharply.

'I know nothing about you,' he said.

Her rigid muscles slackened. 'Not so interesting,' she said when a moment had gone by.

'Tell me.'

'Why?' she demanded. 'Isn't this what every man wants? Love with the proper stranger? I am what you make of me, your fantasy.'

'Tell me.' he persisted. 'I want to know.'

She shook her head, then raised her hand to indicate the view, the place they stood. 'It's strange,' she said, 'as a girl I was taught that this was how it should be. My father brought me up to believe that I would spend my life upon a beautiful beach with a host of handsome men paying court to me.'

'Glamour? Romance? It's only what you deserve,' Adam said.

She pulled away from him abruptly. 'Don't be a fool,' she told him. 'That doesn't work for me, it never did. Even then my idea of glamour was meeting with Che Gueveara in some jungle clearing.'

69

She turned and went into the room. He followed. Standing behind her he kissed her neck, lifting the hair to do so.

Her head came back. Holding her shoulders he moved her to the bed. There, instead of turning her to face him, he pressed her forward. She tensed. He pushed her so she stumbled, falling to her knees. She recovered at once and tried to rise, arching her back. His hand, gripping the nape of her neck, forced her head down. She struggled. 'Hold still,' he ordered. Lifting up her skirt, with his other hand he began to stroke her stretched bare thighs, to caress her full bottom beneath her knickers.

A queer lethargy overcame her. Her struggle slowed. He played with her sweet wetness and her trembling fire. He put his finger there. She twitched. He held her, wet himself against her and eased in. She gasped in pain, locking rigid beneath him. He held her still for an infinity of time, felt her muscle loosen, and slid in ... stayed, slipped back, and in again, deeper now.

The pain gone, she quickened pressing back on him. Deliberately he kept slow, giving less than her body asked. Face down, she writhed, thrusting back. He controlled his own excitement as she threshed and reared, gasping like a runner coming to the tape.

At the last moment he grasped his fingers in her hair, pulled back her head, turning it so he forced her to look back into his face. He held her still. His stare pierced through her muddy eyes and looked straight into a dark closet within the brain. And, staring back at him, she saw he saw her shameful secret clear.

Her own gaze blurred then, her mouth came open. She groaned. He turned her head away and forced it down, drove into her long and hard. She bucked, out of all control now as he went at her. Suddenly she screamed. A spasm threw her forward. She collapsed face down upon the bed. Her thighs twitched in a last throb of ecstasy, then she lay still.

They were not the same couple as they had been before. The event had dislocated and revised their relationship, transforming it. Something had happened to alter and define them, a havoc which short-circuited the intellect to rampage in tumult through baser fleshy cells – as if those cells had been swept up, shaken violently together, then spilled back into their owners' bodies only now rearranged in their proper pattern, so close together in the night that their two bodies felt as one.

She woke before he did in the early light. When he opened his eyes she was busy about the room, a towel knotted around her waist.

'There's no need to *pack* for me,' he protested sleepily from the pillows. 'I'll do that.'

'Don't worry,' she told him. 'This is not my role but it is late. The paintings, I cannot fit them in your case. I will wrap them and get the hall porter to mail them to you.'

'To my office,' he said. 'Not my home.'

She nodded, knowing what he meant. 'You had better get up and dress, I think.'

Suitcases, porter, the taxi ordered to the airport, Jutta took care of everything with the same crisp efficiency. She dealt expertly and fluently with the whole transaction of departure. He did not know if he would ever see her again.

When they were in the car on the way to the airport he asked casually, 'So where do you go from here?'

'Back to Bogota. I have interviews with businessmen and a minister. Very difficult to arrange. They move only between their home, the office, the club; two cars, guns and always bodyguards.'

'And after that?'

'New York, then Los Angeles. My next piece I write on California.'

He looked out of the window. 'I have to be in London for a while,' he said. 'Give me the number where you'll be.'

She shook her head, 'I do not know it.'

'Then call me.'

She did not answer. She waited with him at the airport. When his flight was announced he reached for her impulsively. He buried his face in her dark hair and for the space of thirty seconds they clung together at the departure

71

gate. His heart sagged with desolation; he did not trust himself to speak. Then he broke from her and walked away, not looking back.

Chapter ten

He landed at Kennedy at 2 p.m.

A porter and VIP stewardess were waiting for him as he came off the plane. The man recovered Adam's suitcase from the conveyor then followed as the girl escorted him through Customs and Immigration with a nod.

His attorney, Warner Harriman, waited on the other side. 'You're on Pan Am for London at 9 p.m.,' the lawyer informed him. 'I've booked your usual suite at the Plaza. I thought you'd like to change and have a meal there while we talk.'

It took an effort on Adam's part to recall what they would talk about. 'You're so sure I want to do that deal in Colombia?' he asked.

Walking by his side across the crowded concourse the other glanced at him in surprise. 'You don't? It looked a good one to me.'

'I suppose so,' Adam answered, realising he had not even thought about it all weekend.

They came out of the terminal to where the limousine waited before the building. The porter set the case down upon the kerb. Warner felt for change. Adam stooped to enter.

'Sir, wait.'

A man came running from the terminal. A young man in a white trench coat and imitation snakeskin shoes, lugging a suitcase as he hurried to catch them up.

'Sir, wait.'

They heard the call again, urgently repeated. Adam straightened up and looked around.

'Sir, wait. You have my case.'

The young Arab hurried up to them. The valise he carried was identical to Adam's own.

The man had halted, panting deeply. He coughed, then harshly laughed.

Adam hesitated. 'You're sure?' he asked, reaching for the remains of his ticket with the claim stub.

'Sure I'm sure. These Customs people opened it. Really lucky they did huh? You went through so fast I couldn't catch you.' While he spoke he had laid the case down and was unfastening it. As he raised the lid Adam recognised everything inside as his.

'I'm very glad you found me,' he said. The chauffeur picked up the suitcase and loaded it into the trunk.

'Sure.' The Arab threw a cool appraising glance over him from head to toe. He took up his recovered case and walked toward the taxi line.

'So who's your flaky friend?' Warner asked, as they settled into their seats. 'What a terrifying looking man. Did you see his *eyes*?'

'His eyes were extraordinary,' said Adam.

The Cadillac swept around the circuit of airport roads to join the freeway. 'OK then,' the lawyer continued, 'How did you leave it in Colombia? Tell me how it went . . . '

Snow white, elaborate and decorative as wedding cake, the Plaza Hotel stands at the very hub of mid-town Manhattan, an elegant anachronism.

The interior of Adam's suite was old fashioned and ornate as the hotel's facade. The hotel was certainly not the city's best. It was pretentious and overpriced, the service was poor and the messege desk functioned not at all without a fifty dollar tip on arrival, yet it pleased Adam to stay here.

There was a sort of improbability about the place, an extravagant romantic quality such as once existed aboard a venerable, first class ocean liner. The living room of the suite with its high moulded ceiling, and marble fireplace, might have been confectioned out of icing. Gauze curtains filtered and diffused the pallid sun of afternoon. The room overflowed with sugary white light.

Adam showered while Warner ordered lunch delivered to the room. He dressed in a clean shirt and suit from his

74

rescued case then sat down for the meal while they worked out the draft of an offer for Jose Vincente's corporation.

The afternoon was passed in this fashion.

At seven they left again for Kennedy, taking the Triborough bridge. The two men spoke little on the drive. When they reached the airport Adam told Warner not to wait. Delayed by fifteen minutes his 747 took off at 21.20 EST. Exhausted though he was, during the flight to England he could not sleep at all.

He landed at London Airport at 9 a.m. local time.

The chauffeur was waiting for him. He drove home to bath and change. He found his house in order and functioning but Vanessa already gone out. A note from her stood propped upon the hall table:

'Darling, super you're back. Hope everything went well. Had to go to breakfast press conference. Think I'm becoming a workaholic too. All love darling. See you at dinner. V.'

After coffee and toast in the dining room where he read the *Financial Times*, Adam went on to the office in the Rolls. He passed the morning with Tony, catching up on what had happened in his absence.

In the afternoon a long telex came through from Warner with a draft of the offer they had worked out the day before.

Adam and Tony went through its text section by section, annotating, editing and amending. Three hours went by in this careful work. It was 7.30 when Adam left for home where Vanessa awaited him.

'Darling, tell me all,' she said as she embraced him. 'Did you have the most *exotic* time in Rio?'

'Not Rio, Bogota. It's not quite the same thing.' He tried to smile for, once, it would have amused him.

'It must have been simply *super*,' she observed. 'You have the most fabulous tan, I'm wildly envious.'

They went in to eat. 'You look very well,' he told her.

It was true, she did. There was a high healthy colour in her cheeks. Her eyes sparkled. She looked five years younger than he remembered.

'You've been busy?' he asked and she answered immediately.

75

'Darling you wouldn't *believe*. It's been a madhouse, my feet haven't touched the ground. Did you see the letter from Prosper? He's been picked for the first eleven and he's bringing a girl down to the Hall for the weekend.'

'That's great,' said Adam.

'Darling,' Vanessa said, 'I know you must be exhausted and won't feel like it but I simply *must* pop into the club this evening. Actually, something rather exciting's happening.'

'Oh yes?' he asked.

'Well, I mean the columns and all that. Princess Margaret's dining there and I absolutely *swore* to Freddy that I'd help him for a drink with Nigel Dempster. I knew you wouldn't mind.'

'That one owes us a favour,' Adam remarked about the columnist. 'No, I won't come but give him my regards.'

Vanessa promised to do so. Immediately after dinner she departed, taking the car and chauffeur.

It was 10 p.m. when Adam went up to bed. He had been awake for more than thirty hours yet still he could not sleep.

He lay upon the twin bed in that familiar room where everything was in place, his mind bubbling with a stew of conflicting images; his brain fevered, his body cold.

Unbidden scenarios like strips of film would unreel rapidly behind his eyes, flashing on, abruptly stopping. The scent of Jutta still lingered on his skin; everything they had done was vivid in his memory; she was printed upon his flesh.

All Adam's recollections of her were warm and sure, without ambivalence, voluptuous and good. Not one nudged him differently as he thought about their time together, and the last few days. Not a single memory raised doubt or query or suspicion. Why should it? How could he have known that as a first class specially escorted VIP passenger he had muled into New York in a lookalike suitcase two kilos of cocaine. In the hot restlessness of his newly awakened sexuality how should he suspect that the girl he had fallen for had used him as a courier, her instrument and a willing fool?

76

Chapter eleven

It was 11.30 p.m. in London when Adam finally fell asleep.

In New York the time was half-past five and the sun had dipped below the buildings which line Fifth Avenue on the west when a man came out of the St Regis Hotel and ran down the steps to enter a waiting cab.

'The Guggenheim,' said Alan Spigelman.

He sat back in his seat, a man thirty-five years old in a white silk suit and black shirt open at the neck. His dark hair was cut short and neatly groomed. His skin was tanned. He was light and agile, quick in his movements. Seeming and looking younger than his age he passed for a well preserved twenty-nine. Owner of an art gallery in Geneva; Swiss by passport, by nationality Alan Spigelman was one of the Beautiful People.

His taxi swung from Fifth toward Madison. At Gucci's window stood a check-trousered visitor from out of town, his eyes bright and covetous as he stared, his mouth tight in an expression which said how expensive it all was.

The taxi turned north and, moving through heavy traffic in the warm evening, Alan drove uptown through a springtime world of Mammon-come-true. The windows of the stores blazed out as brilliant temples of affluence and display raised to the great god Plenty. Inside, shoppers stood in line to pay; the aisles were jammed, the strident air was sprayed with perfume, and all within were charged and vibrant, high tuned and frantic in their urgent haste as though time itself were not enough for all there was to buy.

The Upper East Side through which Alan's taxi passed gleamed bounteous with wealth. He rode through man-made canyons of shining glass, plumb lined from the narrow crack

77

of sky and at every intersection he went by crosstown streets of dulcet tree-lined calm where a half million dollars would scarcely buy a maid's room.

The avenue was dense with traffic. It was jammed with cars, limousines, taxis, trucks, raucous with blaring horns, engine growl and roar, racketing clatter of construction drills, the grunt and bellow of a garbage truck ponderous as a rhino shouldering into the traffic flow . . . the din pierced suddenly by the shrill squealing of a police car. Followed by a howling ambulance, it swerved to where a fire truck and other police vehicles stood double parked and flashing a disco dazzle of coloured whirling beams.

'Light show by Pig,' growled Alan's driver as he gunned by and stopped in front of the museum.

At the entrance to the Guggenheim Alan's invitation was taken from him by a guard then passed to a girl in a Halston dress who checked his name against a printed list. She looked up in smiling welcome, 'Have a nice evening, Mr Spigelman.'

He went into the museum.

It formed a stunning, an overwhelming setting for a party. On coming in, the impression was only of wrap-around airy space, of penetrating the interior of some vast balloon filled with soft and milky radiance. A place without shape or shadow, lacking corners, perspective and horizon, the eye was confounded by such volume of luminous emptiness. It was disorientating as a dream.

Yet the effect of this great stage was to diminish the actors which it contained. Dwarfed by their surroundings, the two hundred guests assembled in the well of the vast building looked puny and insignificant, like an afterthought to the splendid set who had not yet been correctly arranged in place or prominence.

Perhaps they were aware of this, Alan thought as he stepped between them to the bar, but it did not seem so. They did not appear daunted by the scale. Movers and shakers of the In Crowd, their surroundings were unimportant; it was the *people* who were here that mattered. Alan recognised the de la Rentas and others that he knew. A glittering throng, this lot was definitely the A list.

78

He accepted a glass of champagne and looked over the array of food. 'How's Bianca?' he overheard. 'As ill as can be expected?' and then the same voice spoke again beside him at the buffet. '*Excuse me*, that's not *Iranian* caviare?'

The waiter spatted a pulpy grey mound upon a plate and passed it over. 'No sir, no way. From Russia.' He indicated a small sign confirming this, half hidden behind the silver bowl.

As the well of the museum became crowded with new arrivals, the guests drifted from the bar into the galleries which housed the exhibition and reason for the party. Though they carried glasses with them they drank little. In the whole gathering there was no sign of drunkenness. The animation shown by all was due not to liquor but a natural condition of their spirit. Strolling through the sculpture, they demonstrated a lively and vivid interest in all they saw.

The first composition was an ancient enamel bath on legs, stained and chipped and bandaged with elastoplast. In its bottom a congealed dribble of fat lay in what looked like blood. 'A Wound Tied Together With Plaster' was its title.

' ... an autobiographical statement, the fat represents creativity,' a balding man by Alan was explaining to a girl with asymmetric hair, 'Creativity is an anthropological, *human* sense. He believes that chaos may be used to heal you see ... '

The girl was listening to him with deference. At most nineteen, she wore her modish dress in a manner which suggested that she herself believed she was wearing nothing and was, moreover, painfully embarrassed by her nudity. The effect was remarkably erotic, Alan thought.

He attatched himself behind them as they moved on to the next exhibit. As they did so a waiter bearing a tray of canapes came down the ramp toward them. He paused to offer up the platter, both lecturer and girl accepted, and then the waiter passed through the group while others reached for his titbits. The tray was extended toward Alan.

The waiter's glance crossed his own. For an instant Alan stared into the fearsome intensity burning from those eyes. Shocked by what he saw he dropped his look. To cover his confusion he reached out to take a canape. And that tiny

79

moment of indecision and greed cost Alan Spigelman his life.

The waiter continued down and out of sight, carrying his tray. The group strolled on to the next piece, a felt wrapped piano created, a card explained, during a five hour action in Dusseldorf and entitled 'Infiltration Homage for Grand Piano'.

'He believes, you must understand,' the balding man continued, 'That the thalidomide child is the greatest contemporary composer ... '

The party had filled up. Below the gallery, in the well of the museum, a mass of people swirled around the bar and buffet, men in crushed linen baggy suits who were not afraid of looking fashionable, girls in iced mauve and raspberry pink and scarlet crêpe de chine on legs like stalks in high heeled boots and fuck-me shoes, and others silver-haired, distinguished and beautiful in khaki and deep red and yellow ochre and burnt sienna. The sea of colour ebbed and flowed and merged and bled together and all the noise of voices mounted to a shriek ...

Alan lifted his gaze up sharply. He shook his head to clear it. Everything was suddenly very loud, all the colours sharp and bright. He blinked and looked at those around him. And then he saw something very weird begin to happen.

The group stood before an exhibit composed of two tons of honey, two ships' engines, a steel container, plastic tubes and three bronze pots. The balding man was speaking, ostensibly to the girl though now, aware that his discourse was reaching wider, he addressed some remarks directly to this respectful and attentive audience.

' ... chaos recognised as closer to reality than other forms of so called reality ... ' he said.

The speaker was clearly a critic or expert and the girl, whom Alan was watching, till now had paid him close attention, her look expressive of the utmost gravity. It was, therefore, all the more startling when suddenly he noticed that her face was slipping out of shape. Her features blurred, began to soften and to sag. Her gaze grew vacant, her hair dishevelled. Before his eyes she started to disintegrate and collapse. He stared with digust and disbelief as a huge pink tongue flapped from her lolling mouth.

Then, at once, her blank gaze focused into horror. Her eyes flared wide. She spun and stared around her at the crowd and then clawed at her own body, slapping and flailing at it as if on fire. And all the time no sound issued from her mouth but the voice of her companion lectured on, ' ... expressing the principal of the Free International University working in the bloodstream of society flowing in and out of the heart organ through ... '

A voice growing louder, it seemed to Alan. Louder, louder and faster as though everything was gathering pace, speeding up ... Desperately he shook his head to clear it. He felt drunk, then he remembered that he had drunk nothing.

' ... flowing through the main arteries through which the honey is pumped out of the engine room with a pulsing sound through the Free International University area and returning to the heart ... '

The man's voice had grown very loud. He was shouting, Alan realised and his face had oddly changed. The eyes burned fierce and fevered and a rictus snarled back the lips to his bare teeth and he was shouting,' ... Arteries ... Life ... Honey ... Heart ... '

Suddenly ragged sound tore from the girl's mouth, frozen open. She screamed. She screamed - and in the sudden silence another voice screamed out in answer and, at that, a wild mad light struck across the face of the girl in the Guggenheim Museum as if some signal had been exchanged. Leaping forward, arms outstretched and rigid she flung herself upon the exhibit, plunged her hands into the honey and dragged the mass of it onto her breasts.

Alan was thrust aside as another dashed past to join her. All around him was the sound of screaming, a screaming not of terror but of ecstasy, of revelation and of bliss, the crowd jostling past him as others ran to join, pushing and shoving so he too was thrust forward in their frantic midst, with them scrabbling, crawling, fighting to plunge into that warm golden liquid sun which was the source of life. And the screaming was all around him as he clawed and struggled, ringing and deafening in Alan's ears so he knew that it was coming from

81

inside himself as well and that he was united with them and all was ecstasy and joy and he was screaming too.

Within a few days it was determined that the mania which attacked twenty-seven of the guests at the Guggenheim Museum was due to the effect of some toxic substance which they had ingested at some stage during the course of the party.

Acting directly upon the brain, the poison had excited hallucinations and delirium rapidly succeeded by convulsions and by coma. Transported by ambulance to Lennox Hill Hospital, Alan Spigelman and every one of the twenty six other victims of the accident had been dead upon arrival.

An intensive enquiry was put in hand by medical specialists working closely with the FBI to determine the exact nature of this compulsive chemical, how it had come to be present in the food or drink served that evening, whether this had been the result of accident or intent and, if the latter, what might be the motive for this horrible atrocity.

Chapter twelve

Danton Hall, the Lupus' country house, had been built at the height of Victorian prosperity in   England. It had been designed to impress and command respect. The fact that it still did so - and now even more than then - had played no small part in Adam's decision to buy the place in 1974 for half a million pounds.

The appearance of the house suggested an older and more noble architectural period than was in fact the case. The tall white columns of its Corinthian south front, the imposing scale and symmetry of its classical facade, the sheer size and grandeur of the edifice formed a landmark and showpiece of the district. How, people wondered, could anyone afford to keep it up? The place dominated the valley of the Thames. It could be seen for miles.

Occupying the crest of a low hill, the Hall was set back more than a thousand yards from the river. The punts and sailing boats which crowded the water of this warm spring Sunday and the strollers and picknickers on the bank - separated from the house's grounds by a chain-link fence – formed a pastoral, even timeless, panorama for the group of people drinking Pimms upon the lawn. From up here the distant children's shrieks and noise of transistor radios were not audible. Squalid in close-up, at this remove the view was picturesque.

Adam set down his goblet on a stone table and surveyed his guests. 'Well,' he suggested, 'shall we begin?'

Willingly and less so they took up croquet mallets and moved to obey their host.

The players numbered seven: Adam and Vanessa, their son Prosper down from Eton for the weekend with a girlfriend, Freddy Reynolds, Vanessa's business partner, Tony Carvell and Jane, the model who lived with him. These last had only just arrived, sweeping up the drive in the Bentley which Tony had received recently as a corporate gift. He glowed still from the pleasure of the drive. He rejoiced in the car, wearing it as a proud badge of rank.

Having chosen their colours, the various contestants lined up to play. A well-turned figure in white pleated skirt, Vanessa set her feet astride a yellow ball and drove off through the central hoop. The crack of her mallet rang out on the still warm air.

'Good shot,' Freddy called. 'I say, Adam, would you mind if I married her?'

'Shut up and play,' Adam told him.

Freddy grinned and moved into position A large, cheerful, wildly energetic man of forty-some who drank too much, he had been Adam's friend as well since Vanessa had introduced them a decade ago.

In turn Adam took his shot then strolled to join Tony and Jane. He stood with them as they watched Prosper cannoning expertly through the hoops. Adam felt warmed by the sight. Prosper had been a clumsy withdrawn child, regarded by his teachers as lazy and a fool. It was Adam who had first guessed he was dyslexic and devoted three hours a day to being with his son, getting to know him and encouraging him to read.

'Quite an operator,' Tony observed. 'That's the third I've seen him with this year.'

A frown touched Adam's face as he glanced toward Prosper's girlfriend, a plump, rather common, seventeen-year-old entirely unabashed by the company or situation. She wore a tight miniskirt exposing black mesh stockings above absurdly high-heeled shoes. Where *does* he find them? he wondered, then thought the only thing that mattered was that Prosper should be happy.

The Spanish manservant appeared from the house with a fresh jug of Pimms to fill the contestant's glasses. He came down every weekend from the London house to reinforce the Hall's residential staff. Under Vanessa's control the arrangement functioned well; Danton Hall ran smoothly.

It was a pretty scene they made, this carefree group in summer clothes at play upon the lawn. The day was fine, the garden at its best. There was a background of laughter and conversation, the scent of flowers, the song of birds. The Pimms was just beginning to take effect; Adam's guests were cheerful and at ease. Everything was in place, he thought as he looked them over, all was right and fitting and as it should be.

But Adam was not consoled. The prettiness of the scene was lost to him. He was not happy here, or in himself. A cloud lay across the sun. He started, aware that Tony Carvel stood beside him and had said something. 'What's that?' he demanded abruptly.

The other was set aback by the sharpness of his tone. 'I only asked did Warner call.'

'Yes, last night. He's talking with Jose Vincente on Monday.'

'Did he get a reaction?'

'Well, as he puts it, they're nickel and diming over the price but they're keen enough, it seems.'

'And you?' Tony questioned.

'Sure. We've got a lot to lay off this year and you know my views on sterling. Incidentally, Warner mentioned that he's got a local group who are good for five or six million dollars in a participation deal provided it's US based.'

'What are you thinking of?'

'Something that doesn't demand too much management from us. Real estate . . .' Adam tamped down the lawn with his mallet. 'California maybe.'

'California?' Tony sounded startled.

'The dollar's very cheap at the moment. It can only move to our advantage and land values there are going up remarkably. It's an excellent area for second homes; California has to be the last refuge if things start to go seriously wrong in Europe. I was thinking of taking a look at it.'

'You were? When?'

'I don't know,' said Adam vaguely, moving off to take his shot. 'Soon as possible, I suppose.' On Friday, just as he was

85

about to leave the office for his weekend, Jutta had called him.

The French windows were open to the lawn, and diffused by their awnings, a soft haze of sunlight drenched the dining room, reflecting from the linen tablecloth to gleam on cutlery and glass. Slanting, mote-filled beams reached to the paintings which hung upon the further wall and burnished their darkness with a mellow lustre.

The room was airy and high-ceilinged, the table large, the chairs padded and comfortable to sit upon. The glasses set before each guest had been filled and refilled with champagne. Within each the bubbles still rose. The wine sparkled with a dusty glow which seemed to capture in its golden heart the opulent langour of Sunday afternoon and a heavy meal, late begun, now nearly ended.

All - save Adam - were captive to the summer mood. All were in that pleasant condition of appetite and senses sated, several drinks ahead. The servant moved between the guests, serving a chocolate mouse with cream.

'Ran into Duggie the other day . . . ' Freddy was saying to Vanessa as he heaped his plate.

'Who?'

'Duggie Latham, *you* remember. Used to play at Wimbledon. Mind you,' he added, 'he's not what he was. Lost an eye, half his stomach gone, he's an old man now . . .'

From the other side of the table Adam heard Prosper say, '. . . you get these patches of dead air, I mean like *holes*. I was flying over Virginia Water at about 1,500 feet when . . .' He glanced across at his son and the girl who sat beside him, plump, dough-fleshed, white and soft. Gorged on food she rubbed herself against the back of the chair like a cow against a gate, easing fat thighs beneath the table.

'We'll take a drive down there later in Dad's Roller,' he overheard Prosper say. He looked away sharply, stung by an uncomfortable sense of irritation mixed with love.

Freddy had raised his wine glass, addressing the table. 'Now drink to us,' he told them. 'To the club after our first week. Wish us luck.'

'You don't need luck,' said Adam.

Freddy's glass was halfway to his lips. 'You bet we do,' he answered cheerfully.

'Not *luck*.'

'Oh, do we ever,' Freddy corrected him. 'You don't *know* the financing. You're such a tycoon Adam, you don't *know* what this little hostelry represents. Step down, dammit, join the human race, wish us luck.'

'Luck's got nothing to do with it,' Adam insisted.

'But Dad . . . 'Prosper began.

'Luck has got nothing to do with it,' Adam repeated in a voice which brooked no argument. 'Nothing at all.'

'But surely . . . '

'*Nothing*. Luck, there's no such thing. Each man makes his own. It's the will that counts, determination and the will. The 'unlucky' and the poor are only so because they choose it. They do not *want* to change. The will, that's the only thing that matters.'

Freddy blinked. 'It's a bleak theory,' he objected.

'It's the truth. I can't *stand* people whining about their luck. It's their own decision, their own fault - always.'

Prosper began again, 'But Dad, it's a corrupt system. When *you* started to make it . . . '

Adam brushed him aside. 'That wasn't *luck* . . . ' his accent was scornful, his words both forceful and confident as he continued, yet he felt curiously disconnected from his audience, even from his family. What did they know about it? Profiting only, they had not been involved. Ambition was a rat dwelling in his gut; it had given him no peace. His life had been a ruthless and lonely business. He had never been able to confide in them.

He stopped talking as abruptly as he had begun. He resumed his meal, estranged by his ill humour, a wintry presence who chilled the air, discontent seething in his chest.

'There's a call for you, sir. Important.' The servant leaned to speak to him.

Adam thrust back his chair with a screech across the marble floor. 'Excuse me,' he muttered and hurried from the room.

He left behind him silence and polite dismay - but it lasted

87

only for an instant. Vanessa looked brightly around the table and the circle of her guests. 'Well,' she remarked, 'The tycoon's off to make more millions. So who's for coffee?'

Adam walked quickly to his study, closed the door, sank back behind his enormous desk, fumbling for cigarettes. He picked up the telephone.

'Lupus,' he said, and heard the extension go down in the kitchen.

'Adam?'

'Who is this?' he demanded.

His question was answered by a laugh. 'Adam, get loose, it's Sheldon.'

His pulse quickened. 'I thought you were in the States.'

'I was. I'm back. How's things?'

Adam drew on his cigarette. 'It would take too long to tell you. You want to meet for a drink sometime?'

'Well, in fact I'm calling to invite you. To a party.'

'What sort of party?' Adam asked. 'Where?'

'At the Embassy. Health foods,' Sheldon said.

'*Health foods?*'

'Health foods,' Sheldon repeated wearily. 'Wheatgerm, ginseng, natural vitamins. He's into all of that. It's his crusade, you'll have to put up with it.'

Adam was baffled. 'Who? Whose crusade?'

'My ambassador's. He's wiggy about diet. In that area he's totally out to lunch. He wants to meet you, asked me to fix it.'

'Why?'

'Well, I've been talking to him about you and he's seen your press cuttings and knows who you are and he's mightily impressed. Fact is there's something going on that maybe you can help us with. Can you come?'

'When?'

'Wednesday, six o'clock. Formal, put on a tie.'

'I always do,' said Adam.

Sheldon was unperturbed. 'That's right. You know, dark suit, wear socks. Don't be late Adam. It's kind of important.'

Adam replaced the receiver slowly. Beyond the windows the garden slumbered in the lull of Sunday afternoon. He sat at his desk, smoking thoughtfully.

He had been appalling that afternoon. He had been heartless, unfair and cruel to his family and old friend. He did not even believe anymore in what he had said; it had been a reaction of pure ill humour. But he felt so angry and so trapped. He longed to be free, to be alone.

No, that was not so, he told himself as he leaned forward to stub out his cigarette. The truth was different. The truth was he longed to be with Jutta. It was a shitty thing to do to Vanessa, it was deceitful, irresponsible and destructive, but he just longed to be with her. It was all he could think about.

Chapter thirteen

Adam's car delivered him to the Upper Brook Street entrance to the American Embassy where he presented his invitation to a six-foot-six black marine who examined it carefully before allowing him through the doors where it was checked again, this time against a list. He was given a card bearing his name to pin in his lapel.

Up a shallow flight of stairs a large reception room had been converted into a market. Aisles, packed with people, ran between booths and displays of produce, each stall tended by a pair or more of men in suits all in earnest conversation with their customers, pressing upon them paper cups of citrus and apple juice or samples of their speciality balanced upon small triangles of whole-meal bread. 'American Ginseng Company', Adam read of the sign above one booth, 'Cell Life Corporation', 'Earthwonder Inc.'

He found Sheldon tasting millet stew. A waiter held out to Adam a tray of Carob-Cashew Snacks. He shook his head.

'Smart to pass,' Sheldon agreed, 'But when the ambassador comes over, chew on something, please. It's the way to his heart. He made his money on Texan beef but since his appointment he's seen the light.' He was looking intently across the room to where the personage he spoke of stood in conversation at the Ginseng stall.

'I'll wheel him over,' Sheldon said and left Adam to thread his way through the crowd and speak to a redhead girl with a clipboard. He watched as, together, these two approached the ambassador, detatched him from the stall and guided him toward Adam, a journey interrupted by several social halts.

'Mr Lupus,' a strong dry hand gripped his and shook it

vigorously, 'Glad to have you with us, sir.'

The US Ambassador to the Court of St James was a burly, well-groomed figure smelling of after-shave, his face set into an expression of alert benevolence. 'Enjoying yourself?' His Excellency enquired.

'Most interesting,' Adam answered.

'I'm happy you think so. It's taken time, but Europeans now are waking up to the vital role their diet plays in all things. Communication, education, we are what we eat. We have a duty to set an example. I'm happy you could join us, Mr Lupus, I've been reading good things about you.'

'It's a pleasure to meet you, Mr Ambassador,' Adam said.

'For me as well.' The firm, tanned hand rested briefly on his upper arm. 'Glad to have you with us.'

The audience was ended. The redhead was already busy with introductions to the next group. With a bright departing smile of extraordinary friendliness the ambassador had moved on.

'Political appointment,' Sheldon confided. He swirled the content of his paper cup and peered into it distastefully. 'Let's get out of here and get a drink. Like natural health's gotten to be his *cause*. He talks about it non-stop. It's thrown him totally out of whack.'

'Must be a disadvantage in his job,' Adam remarked as they struggled toward the door. 'Doesn't he have to eat for a living?'

'Sure, banquets and stuff. "There have been moments" as you Brits say.'

They reached the lobby. 'Where are we going?' Adam asked.

'I won't take you to the bar here. Real dull people and everyone watching who you're with, me particularly - spot the spook. You have wheels?'

Adam nodded. Leaving the embassy they came down the steps to the pavement. The chauffeur held open the car door. 'The Connaught,' Adam told him.

The two men settled into the Rolls. 'All right Sheldon,' he said, 'What's it about this time?'

The American minutely raised his hand and indicated the

open partition between them and the driver. Adam touched the button; it slid shut noiselessly. 'All right?'

Sheldon sighed. 'You're so *ardent*, Adam. I'm aswill with apple juice. I can't talk without a drink.' He seemed exasperated by his attendance at the party. 'I don't have to *answer* to him,' he broke out suddenly, 'but I got to work with him. My lines go direct to Washington but I'm responsible to tell him what goes on . . . '

By then the car had completed the 200 yard journey to the hotel. 'Fuck him, life's too short,' Sheldon said abruptly. 'Let's get out of these wet clothes and into a pair of dry Martinis.'

He led the way out and through the revolving door. Together they walked across the narrow lobby and past the porters' desk. They entered the bar. 'Martini or what?' Sheldon asked, seating himself in one of the leather armchairs and signalling for attention.

The waiter came over, addressing himself first to Adam. 'Good evening, Mr Lupus, nice to see you. What can I get you gentlemen?'

They ordered. When the man had gone Sheldon observed irritably, 'That's it, you see. You own this feudal relic of a country, you're one of the Establishment. That's why the ambassador wanted to meet you. It intrigues him. You're just not our usual class of operative.'

'You mean "spy"?' Adam asked, quite loudly, and the other winced.

'That's not a word we use.'

'No. And so far,' remarked Adam, 'I must say it hasn't proved a very glamourous occupation.'

'You give me the shudders,' Sheldon told him.

'Oh yes? And how are things with *you*?' he enquired and tasted his drink. 'How's *trade*?'

'Compared to what?' Sheldon answered sourly, then added, 'It may not have been glamourous, my friend, but those construction plans were useful. Our people are working on them now.' He too paused to drink and then went on. 'No, it's not glamorous, it's often not even complex or elaborate or even *interesting*. What profession is, once you're part of it?

92

No, it's a dull business Adam but we'd like you to perform a service for us, if you will.'

'What's that?'

'Well ... to get to know someone maybe.' Suddenly he looked tired.

'Who?'

'Not your sort of people, A-rabs,' Sheldon said wearily. 'There's a war on, or hadn't you noticed? There's a terrorist squad operating in the US right now and it's not the first. They're well-armed and well-trained and they move around with remarkable confidence. They're backed by real money and powerful patronage. We believe we know who's behind them and we may want you to get to know him.'

'Why me?' Adam asked.

'For a start because you're British and so well-dressed. He's a businessman, so are you and your cover's excellent - it happens to be the truth. If you want to get cosy over a business deal who's to suspect you? You pass.'

Adam drew on his cigarette. 'It so happens that I could arrange to be in LA next week, if that fitted,' he said carefully.

'Yes?' Sheldon threw him a quick sharp glance. For a moment he appeared about to ask something else. 'Yes? That could fit very well. Where will you stay?'

'The Beverly Hills or the Bel Air, I suppose.'

'That's fine,' Sheldon said. Then grinned. 'On the other hand, if it's luxury you're after combined with privacy and discretion there's a place I'd recommend to you, The Sunset Marquis, just off Sunset Boulevard.'

'Comfortable?'

'Very. Very laid-back, very California.'

Adam extinguished his cigarette and glanced at his watch. He felt suddenly in the best of humours. 'Would you like to dine with me somewhere?' he proposed.

'I can't.' Irritation flooded back to Sheldon's face. 'No, I'd like to but I've got a report to write then I must get to Washington.'

'Tomorrow?'

'Yes. When I contact you it'll be from there. Sorry about

dinner.' He saw Adam reaching for his pocket and stopped him. 'No, this one's on me.'

He spilled pound notes onto the table, carefully folding the bill and putting it in his wallet.

They rose to leave, walking out through the quiet lobby now tenanted only by the porters and a broad-shouldered, white-haired man lecturing another, younger and smaller who beamed and swayed beside him. ' . . . not being silly about this, I'll take a breakfast with the Jesuit Fathers here tomorrow . . .' Adam heard him saying and wondered for a second what it meant as they came out onto the street.

'Can I drop you?' he asked.

'Thanks no. I'm going back to the Embassy. I can use a walk.'

Then, as the car was about to drive off, he leaned in to the open window. 'OK?' he asked. 'You're on?'

Adam nodded.

'Right,' said Sheldon. 'Soon as I know something I'll call you.'

He straightened up. As the car drew away Adam looked back and saw his friend walking toward Grosvenor Square. He went fast and purposefully, a man preoccupied with a matter which weighed upon his mind.

Then the Rolls turned the corner and Sheldon was lost from Adam's sight.

Chapter fourteen

The plan was firm. Though it was discussed no further, the arrangement remained fixed and definite. Adam's heart lifted at the prospect.

Next day his secretary reserved a suite at The Sunset Marquis and booked him a flight to Los Angeles for Sunday night. He called Jutta with the time of his arrival.

The weekend he passed at Danton Hall. Freddy Reynolds was down to stay together with another couple, friends of Vanessa's. After tea on Sunday, Adam excused himself from this group and went upstairs to lay out the clothes for his trip which the servant would pack for him. It was 5 p.m.

In New York it was eleven in the morning and the bright sun was still climbing to the meridian; its rays lanced down the whole length of Park Avenue, reflecting and dazzling, as upon a canyon whose walls were built of shining ice.

Outside St Bartholemew's Church at the corner of 51st Street all kerb space was already filled. The black limousines now stopped there only long enough to discharge passengers before their chauffeurs drove into the crosstown street, parked, then returned to join the fifteen or twenty uniformed drivers who stood together on the church steps, smoking and chatting while they watched the congregation arriving for the Sunday service.

The Murray Bruces came on foot. The morning was bright but unseasonably cold. It was not a long walk from the Waldorf Towers where they lived but Murray, clean-cut, blond and thirty-eight, was dressed in a top coat; Gail, his second wife, wore mink.

Both were regular worshippers here. Murray was a

member of the vestry council. In the nearby ad agency which he ran he had dedicated a Wednesday room for a Christian prayer group where employees might receive counselling. A brief service was held there, rather well attended, for any who wished to join in as he did.

The Murray Bruces entered St Bartholemew's and took their usual places in the front. By eleven o'clock every seat was occupied. This was no special festival but a normal Sunday, yet 2,500 local Christians filled the pews of the lofty nave whose doors depict the prophets in company with the sybils, the owl of Desolation, the serpent of Sin and the curled dragon who represents the Devil.

This was a solid, wealthy church in a wealthy mid-town parish, the most wealthy in all New York; the congregation were dressed as befitted the occasion and their standing in the community. It was incumbant upon them to set example to the world, and, like Gail, they sat straight-backed in silence waiting for the service to begin or, like Murray, engaged in subdued conversation with a neighbour - an exchange instantly abandoned when a rustle touched the crowd, a stir of those at the back rising to their feet and the motion sweeping forward through the assembly like a wave. The procession was entering. The organ blared out in lively hymn and a roar of voices sang out the words above the tramp of feet:

'Oh God our help in Ages past
Our hope for years to come . . . '

A young man marched at the army's head with uplifted glassy gaze and the eyes of a statue focused on infinity. White-knuckled, his hands held high the ten foot cross.

Behind him the procession was endless, a twin column marching as they sang, led by the women of the choir in college hats and blue-tipped robes. After them, came men in surplices, then the assisting priests. At the rear strode the rector, serene, composed and Godsure, moving to assume his place beside the altar and begin the service.

This was Parish communion, central ceremony of the Christian week. The pattern of it was well known to the Murray Bruces and all others there. The organ pealed.

Unbidden they rose to sing, sat for the lesson and kneeled to pray.

The ritual followed its prescribed time-honoured course up to and beyond the consecration of bread and wine when the rector lifted up the host into the sight of the congregation. 'Behold the Lamb of God who taketh away the sins of the world.'

The wafer snapped between his fingers with the amplified sound of a pistol shot.

The choir filed from their stalls to kneel at the altar rail. The rector moved along the line administering the communion cup, giving comfort and forgiveness to all who took of it, as he had himself.

'The Blood of our Lord Jesus Christ keep you in everlasting life . . . '

The Murray Bruces returned to their seats. Those in the next block of pews filed toward the altar. Endorsed and sanctified by 2,000 years of use, the sacred rite continued, solemn, unvaried and immutable. Then something changed.

'The Blood of our Lord . . . ', and there, mid sentence, the rector choked. He halted, turned to stone. Murray, watching from the nave, saw him freeze then suddenly convulse, his body rose to jerk and shudder as though it had been caught up and shaken violently in the jaws of the hound of Heaven.

Murray stared in disbelief as the rector was set down to earth to stand again unmoving, not rigid now but unnaturally composed, then raise toward the congregation a face become unrecognisable and gaunt, aged immeasurably yet beautiful. It was the ecstatic countenance of a visionary lit by an inner fire which scorched from his eyes as he fixed them on his audience and spoke.

'You are damned,' he called to them and his words boomed and rang around the church. 'Damned, each one of you, warm, well-fed, decent, law-abiding, rich and damned. The sun, the warmth of life and fellowship will be cut off. You will perish in outer darkness, in the arctic tracts of desolation and despair.

You are taking in your mouths his liquid blood,' he cried, 'eating of his living flesh. And you are worshipping a *loser*!'

Quiet obtained always within St Bartholomew's - but not a quiet as now. There was no movement, rustle, shift of shoe or clothing or of hymnbook, no whisper, no sound. The dim and lofty nave was filled by the silence of horrified dismay.

'He *failed*,' the rector shouted. 'He failed. He went too far. He lost his following and was put to death. Do you *trust* such a man?' he demanded. 'Would you give him a second chance? Lacking in judgement, in political and diplomatic skills, unreasonable, possibly insane, would you want him to run your corporation? Would you wish him as chief executive or elect him as president of your country?'

It was the silence of horror which prevailed, that blank horror which results when the ordered world breaks down. The rector had gone mad. No one moved, nor knew what to do.

'Trust him? You would?' he questioned loudly. 'Do you know the price, the rules of membership? If you are mugged, yield up your face to your assailant. If you are robbed, seek out the burglar and offer him your savings. Give away freely all you own, love the lobby who oust you from the board and pray for those who jeer at you for preaching the word of God.

'Do not deceive yourself,' the rector cried. 'The price is not less than everything, the sacrifice of all you are. That is the price, but the reward is certainty and joy, a holy force that will sweep you in all wisdom through the world and carry you to heaven where you will exist forever in the smile of God.'

'Hallelujah!' cried a voice suddenly from the choir and, after a moment, others beside it took up that cry with faces raised and that same exalted light burning in their eyes.

'Hallelujah! Hallelujah!' called out the choir. But in the congregation silence reigned, embarrassment and total quiet.

'Blessed are the poor,' cried the rector loudly. 'Blessed are the meek. Theirs shall be the kingdom of Heaven and ownership of this planet Earth. Give up your money! Liquidate your assets! Cancel your charge accounts! Abandon your retirement plans, order neither food nor drink, think not what to wear. Take no thought, no thought beyond this moment. Embrace the Kingdom of God! Follow him in humility and poverty and preach his laws! Give!'

Inside himself Murray Bruce felt something extraordinary begin to happen. It was as if a bud of light were unfolding in his chest, a glow of flame growing, swelling, expanding to incandescence. From the dark and innermost recesses of his being a rush of glory exploded into splendour. Give! At last the way was lit and clear. 'Hallelujah!' shouted Murray Bruce. The cry burst from him.

'Hallelujah!' he heard Gail shout beside him as he rose to his feet and started toward the altar rail, already unsnapping the bracelet of his Cartier watch.

His wife was beside him as he ran, and others too. He was at one with her and with those others, joined with them in the bright clear light of unity and love, of purpose and of joy, as they tore off their watches, their furs, their jewellery, emptied their pockets and flung their handbags down in a heap of gold and mink and precious stones, billfolds and rings, broaches, clips and wallets in a mound before the altar cross . . .

The happening at St. Bartholomew's was reported very fully by the media. Radio and television relayed it to the nation. Newspapers throughout the world next day carried tale of the extraordinary event.

It involved many whose names were household words, the presidents and officers of corporations, politicians, brokers, bankers, lawyers and accountants, men and women of substance and position. All had been affected in the same way, caught up into the same frenzy which had swept through the church and caused them to act together.

But not everyone in St Bartholomew's had been so transported. The revelation, frenzy, ecstasy, delirium - the words of description varied - had attacked rector, priests, choir and the occupants of the first nine pews. Those seated further back, who had not received the sacrament, were unaffected.

On the Monday it was announced that the hysteria which had attatcked 300 of those in church was due to a chemical substance in the communion wine whose nature had not as yet been precisely determined by analysis but which resembled in its effect the drugs LSD and psilocybin.

99

In one respect, however, it differed markedly from these drugs. The effects showed no evidence of remission. Those who had ingested it remained displaced in the same abnormal state.

The victims of the event received, every one of them, the best medical treatment available. They were kept in hospital under intensive psychiatric care. For their own good they were denied all visitors except for immediate family and prevented from communication with the outside world.

The patients protested lucidly and, in some cases, so violently against these conditions that they had to be restrained. In order that diagnosis might continue and a cure determined, it was considered best to keep the invalids heavily sedated.

Despite treatment by a variety of drugs the anti-toxin to their disease was not discovered. Only after a period of several weeks and consultation with second and third medical opinion was it decided to employ electro-convulsive therapy in their cure.

Terminals were applied to the subjects' skulls and a charge of electricity passed through their frontal lobes until the events of the recent past were burned away. Short-term memory was destroyed, as were the offending brain cells. Their delusions left them, along with the capacity for speech and rational thought. The end result was benign and calm, and permanent. A few were released into the protective custody of their families whilst others remained indefinitely in hospital supported by the best of care.

By the group of three who also attended the service in St Bartholomew's - three men darker than most of the congregation, led by the one who kept his gaze trained down for he knew his eyes were always remembered – by these three the result of the experiment was judged satisfactory. This time the dosage was correct.

Rehearsals were completed. The terrorists waited only for the moment now, for the main event, a meeting of the leaders of the world. From now on their action would depend on that opportunity, on timing – and on finance.

100

Chapter fifteen

The 747 lost height over the San Bernardino Valley and came down twenty minutes late into Los Angeles International Airport. It was half-past midnight, Pacific time.

Adam saw Jutta waiting for him as he entered the baggage claim area. She stood there tanned and dark-haired, a tall, slim figure in narrow jeans and shirt, her feet slightly apart and stance taut as she scanned the crowd of passengers.

He caught her to him and held her. His heart went out, for a second his body melted.

He straightened up, his arm draped around her shoulders, his other hand gripping the suitcase. 'Let's go somewhere less crowded,' he said.

She nodded. 'Yes. I have a hire car,'

They drove out of the airport and into the city which Adam had viewed from the darkness at 5,000 feet as a sparkling metropolis of light scattered over 2,000 square miles of uneven, rolling country, They hardly spoke. Tension wound tight in both of them.

They drove for forty minutes through the city to where the grid of roads slanted sharply upwards into the Beverly Hills. A detached three-storey building, The Sunset Marquis stood in a floodlit garden of trees and shrubs set back from Alta Loma road.

They checked in, were shown across a courtyard with a swimming pool to the suite Adam's secretary had reserved. Deep-carpeted in white, marble bathroom with bidet and twin basins, with king-sized bed and wall-sized picture window, it overlooked orange trees and the scented dark.

The porter set down their cases, Adam waited patiently while he explained the working of the TV set then slipped five dollars into his ready hand. The door clicked shut behind him.

Adam pulled her roughly to him. Desire ran like a hot wire through his nerves. There was a fierce hunger in him to possess. He was impatient, clumsy in his haste. She freed herself from him to undo his shirt, zip down her jeans and toss them on a chair. He was struck dumb by the beauty of her.

He put his hands upon her shoulders and pushed her to the bed. For a moment she resisted him, then slackened. She rolled away from him and smiled; raising her arms, she stretched her body, warm and langorous as a purring cat.

He came after her deliberately and slowly, gripped her wrists and pressed her down. He bent his knee to nudge apart her thighs.

She was wet for him. She twitched as he went into her.

He took her hard, taking her up there fast, knowing how she was and exactly what to do to make her gasp. He compelled her right up to it, forcing her on, then slowed and held her on the brink for timeless seconds before he drove in again, deep and wanton, taking both their pleasure to the limit and coming hard, holding nothing back.

He rolled away, reaching for the cigarettes. He was not yet spent. With her he was young again, another man.

Chapter sixteen

Displacement. Time out of time. Three days later in Los Angeles that was how it felt to Adam, and here even more so than in South America. Not that he minded. The sense of dislocation and of nowhere, engendered by this place, suited him just fine.

The two calls which had reached him from the office had not even dented his detachment. In both cases he had been drunk when he received them. His conversation had been brief; it mattered little to him what decisions he made so long as he made them quickly. Vanessa, busy with her nightclub, had not even attempted to contact him. From Sheldon there had been no word.

In such a state of disconnection this was the perfect spot to be. The wide roads dense with cars, the empty pavements, the low featureless buildings, the endless suburban landscape lined with hoardings, handpainted billboards which were works of art, incomprehensible to those unprogrammed to the culture and the place. 'Spanish Fly', 'Dong Gong Rompers', 'Slunt'. What were they? Adam wondered. Pop Groups? Films? Products? He had no idea.

Who were these people anyway, he wondered, the inhabitants of this vast suburb without a city who floated by, sealed into their air-conditioned cars, one hand on the steering wheel, another holding a telephone to their mouths? Where were they coming from or going to? Was this their life?

The traffic flowed along the city arteries, organic and friction-free as blood. Flowed and flowed. No one drove fast. No one drove dangerously. No one ever wound down their windows to yell in fury for no one ever lost their temper or their tan.

Their smiles were bland, their teeth were gleaming white. 'Have a nice day,' they murmured when they brushed against him then drifted on with the indifference of figures in a dream. Insubstantial, random, desultory, Los Angeles did not feel like a real place at all.

'An air-conditioned nightmare,' Adam said to Jutta. 'That's what Henry Miller called it.'

He was seated with her in the green gloom of the Polo Lounge beneath a ceiling of olive midnight set with spotlights. Its windows opened on an atrium of ferns, of hanging and climbing plants. It was like being under water in a softly carpeted aquarium.

'Did you receive the paintings from Columbia?' she asked.

'Not yet. The South American postal system is even worse than the English.'

'Where will you put them?'

'I'll hang them in my office,' he told her. 'When I look at them I'll think of you. I'm mad about you,' he said.

She reached out to touch him.

Jutta had been fifteen when she had taken her first lover, precociously advanced by the spirit of the times, revolting against the way that she was raised.

Christo had been twenty-three, a student still and militant, inspired by the passionate conviction shared by most who happened to be young, over-educated and over-endowed, in West Germany in 1969.

Christo woke her and brought her out. She was his creature; she worshipped him, though she considered him an old man. Adult males were visitors from another planet, mysterious and glamorous, dangerous and exciting aliens.

Christo's power over her had been enormous. Within that rounded puppy flesh he found an impure adolescent nerve, directed it and formed her tastes.

There was nothing she would not do for him. Squeamishness was no hindrance, disgust did not deter her. She became his prodigy, his plaything, his lewd and wanton slave in his political activities and the other perverse and special world she shared with him.

And after he had been struck down she was bereft. After such knowledge, what forgiveness? There was no one else she had found who had those delicate specific skills. No one had ever ignited her blood in the same fashion - till now, till Adam. That accident of sexuality confused her strangely in what she had to do.

They rose late, those mornings in Los Angeles. Their days they passed mostly by the pool, sedated by that slothful ease which comes from sex.

Their second night they dined in a restaurant on Sunset and Vine, in a room whose walls were one enormous frieze. Bucolic America surrounded them, giant figures in a lifescape of pastoral pursuits; hunting, golf and logging in autumnal tints.

'The last time I was here,' Adam said, 'I came back to the hotel at 4 a.m. and pressed the button for the elevator. It came, the doors opened and it was *full*. Packed tight with people. It's surreal. This city is more foreign than the surface of the moon.'

'It's hard to write about,' she complained. 'It's the things which are *not* here which makes the atmosphere so strange. Yet in consumption fascism and the illusion of contentment it is more than Germany. I buy, therefore I am.'

'"Consumption fascism",' Adam laughed at the phrase. 'Yes, if you're doing an article you can write about Rodeo Drive,' he said.

They had gone there that afternoon to find Jutta a pair of shoes. At first sight it looked a small-town street of ample pavements shaded by leafy trees. The one-level buildings conveyed a simple and homespun air yet all the stores had valet parking. The narrow facades which housed their wondrous windows were delusory for, inside, the shops stretched a block deep in corridors of prosperity on display. Gucci, Courreges, St Laurent, Bottega Veneta, Wally Findlay and Ted Lapidus . . . all were here with excessive floor space in the most expensive real estate on earth.

'What kind of stuff do you write anyway?' Adam asked.

She frowned. 'Critical, and I have not done so many. It is

no more a fashionable point of view among the *schili.*'

'The *schili?*'

'The smart rich lefties who indulge their guilt. They're out of drugs and protest now and into making money.'

'If I accquire a newspaper,' Adam said, 'There will be no question of you working for it.'

'No?'

'No,' he told her. 'Of course not. I'm not sure you shouldn't be locked up. You are a dangerous revolutionary.'

'But why?' he demanded of her the next day. 'Why? You've no right to be disaffected. You're beautiful and bright. You're educated. You were given all you wanted as a child, you were not *deprived.*'

They were driving up Stone Canyon after lunch. Alcohol had fuelled them with energy to continue.

'How do you know *what* I am?'

'Of course I know. You told me.'

'Hah!' She turned on him fiercely, her face alight. 'Yes, that I was raised as a Nazi princess? Germany is not like England,' she told him passionately. 'The youth in your country is not political, but I was at university in Berlin when there was still war in Vietnam. We knew that everybody in power was crazy and was cruel and was wrong. Students were shot by the police. We attacked the US Embassy and they broke my lover's back. They made him paralysed, in a wheelchair.'

'You were part of that?' he asked.

'Of course, I believed in all of it. By burning department stores we would change the world.'

He pulled wide to pass a tracksuited figure jogging up the canyon. 'It didn't,' he said.

She glared at him, her eyes flashing fire. 'We . . . '

'What?' he asked, for she had caught back her words, 'Well what?'

'Nothing.' Her voice had gone flat. 'You're right.' She shrugged and smiled. 'It changed nothing, but they were such exciting times and I was young.'

He laid his hand upon her thigh. 'You still are,' he said.

106

Set in low gear, the car laboured up into the hills. The valley was dry and brown but he glimpsed fine houses half hidden by the foliage and the glint of sprinklers on emerald lawns behind the trees.

He parked outside the Hotel Bel Air whose pink cabanas were sculpted into the hillside, veiled by shrubs and cacti.

They ordered drinks in an empty bar, dark and timeless as a well-upholstered womb.

'We were all so *angry* then,' she said. 'It was then I decided that I must write. With my words I would rip away all the complacency and hypocrisy . . . ' She waved her glass at him, spilling some.

'You are enchanting,' he said.

'Bah!' She glared at him. 'I tell you about the injustice of the world and you say I am 'enchanting'. You are smug, English and impossible.'

'I am a consequence of my time,' he said. 'Like you.'

She was no more qualified to understand him than he her. She had grown up with her contemporaries in the realisation that all the institutions of their country were based upon a lie. Justice, Education, Church and State were balanced upon the denial that the Nazi Reich ever had existed. Her parents and the society that surrounded her were part of an old order, believing in the past yet living its repudiation.

And along with that, resulting from that, was such material prosperity, such wealth and ease and complacency that the young were fired by a mission to havoc. They despised and loathed the old order that had born them, the tiled bathrooms and Mercedes of the economic miracle. They longed to loose a storm of chaos and blast it into shreds.

'Do you want another drink?' he asked.

'Are you crazy?' She grinned catlike at him.

'Why?'

'I'm so *drunk*,' she said. 'Don't make me argue. I don't *want* to have to hate you. All I want is to take you home and kiss you everywhere.'

He nodded and signalled for the check. It was what he, too, most wanted to do to her.

And now it was night and they sat in another place. A restaurant on Sunset Boulevard not a hundred yards from their hotel, Adam had noticed it in passing. 'Open Midnight to 7 a.m.', the sign on its closed door, 'Supper, Breakfast, Drinks.'

The light within was non-existent. Comfortable banquettes enclosed secluded tables, partitioned for privacy. It was a place of assignation and intimate rendezvous, betrayals, conspiracy and shady deals. It was perfect for their mood.

The banquettes and tables were arranged in rising tiers, looking over those below at a panoramic glass wall. The restaurant was sited high and its view was over all the night-time city of Los Angeles glittering to the horizon. The sweep of night above was vast, wrap-around and black, containing never less than half a dozen distant aircraft trailing coloured stubs of light in their path across the sky.

Music was playing, low but insistent. It was the same number repeated again and again by someone who had fed the jukebox with a million quarters.

When Adam and Jutta danced they spotted the couple responsible for the song's trancelike repetition, identified them as the only other figures on the tiny floor entwined indistinguishably together with faces hidden by the darkness and her tumbled ashblond hair which covered both.

' . . . *Help me make it through the night*,' pleaded the singer in a throbbing wail.

The organic pulse and tremor of the music shivered in her gut. This is crazy, Jutta thought, not for the first time. It was not what it was supposed to be, not at all how she had intended it, yet what it had become was thrilling; fear produced in her an excitement that was almost sexual. She craved for ecstasy and terror.

She clung to him in the music's throb, hardly moving to the pulse of sound with breast and thigh and belly pasted close. The scented air enfolded them, warm and dark. She looked up at him and her lovely face filled all his sight.

'I wish you'd known it,' she whispered. 'For it was how life was *meant* to be, how Christ and all the great philosophers described it, the great impossible dream of justice and of love

108

. . . and it was coming true. That is what we fought for . . . '

Her body smelled of musk in the summer night. Her silken skin felt warm and vibrant against his own as they drifted in erotic langour through the dark.

'You can't imagine it,' she breathed. 'The incredible excitement. Oh Adam, I wish you could, that incredible excitement of outside the law in something that you *knew* was right . . . Oh, I wish it more than I can say that you should know the thrill - and not alone, but *shared* . . . a closeness in all you do, the plans, the act . . . It was extraordinary, like sex, like the very best. Oh, I wish that you could know . . . '

'I don't care who's right or wrong
I will try to understand . . .'

Again and again the song played over, again and again. He would never forget it, Adam thought.

'Come lay down by my side
Till the early morning light,
I don't want to be alone,
Help me make it through the night . . .'

sang the words in the warm embracing dark. Strong and powerless he sank deep and drowning in her eyes. He was wild for her. He had two more days and Sheldon had still not called . . . and nor did he care. All he wanted was in his arms.

Chapter seventeen

When Adam prepared to leave The Sunset Marquis and return to London he was alone.

Jutta was here in Los Angles to work, she had explained. For her too this was stolen time, these days they had passed together. She was in California to prepare a magazine article. She had a number of interviews set up and from time to time whilst here had left him to conduct them. So she had said.

He had not protested at her absences. For him it was a luxury to keep company with a woman who led an independent life. There was a side to her he did not understand or dominate, nor wanted to. The fact of its existence was oddly stimulating.

In truth, the preparations for departure which Adam was now engaged in were minimal. With perception that he had not packed a suitcase for over a decade, Jutta had done it for him. All that remained was for Adam to collect his razor and other things into his shaving box and add this to the case. It took him no longer than a couple of minutes.

He stood at the window looking out over the garden and the pool, empty of people now at the end of the afternoon. In half an hour Jutta would return to drive him to the airport.

It had been a magic time he had spent here with her; everything had conspired to make it perfect. The meeting with the Arab which Sheldon was supposed to arrange had not come off. His days had belonged entirely to himself; for the first time in years he had done exactly as he pleased.

The story of a development deal in the US had explained his absence to his family and associates in London - yet departure for home after an illicit holiday is the cue of conscience. Adam realised that he had come here on the excuse of work yet for five days had stayed totally out of touch. Except for two telephone calls on arrival he had had no contact with his office; he had no knowledge of what had developed in his absence nor of the problems that awaited him upon return.

Guilt nudged him. He glanced at his watch, then picked up the telephone and asked for the number in London.

Smoking nervously, he waited for the call to come through. The thought of going back was unsettling. Nothing there attracted him one bit.

The number connected. 'Good morning Lupus Group.'

He recognised the operator's voice. 'Mr Carvel,' he said.

'Putting you through now, Mr Lupus.'

Bypassing the secretary, he heard his assistant on the line.

'Tony, it's Adam.'

'Thank God. Where are you?'

The question came over urgent and his heart bumped. 'In California of course, I'm just leaving. How are things?'

'I'm very glad you called.'

There was something distinctly odd about Tony's voice. It did not seem like his normal tone at all. 'Any problems?' Adam asked.

'Well . . . now you ask, yes. When are you back?'

'Tomorrow. Ask my chauffeur to meet me at the airport, will you?'

'Yes. When though? Adam . . . ' Then silence from London. For a moment he thought he had been disconnected. He was reaching out to tap the receiver rest and recall the operator when he heard another voice demand his name, 'Mr Lupus?'

'Yes, who is this?'

'Where are you Mr Lupus?' the voice enquired.

'In Los Angeles. Why? I was talking to Mr Carvel. Who is this?'

'Police Inspector Nicholas,' the unknown speaker identified himself.

'Who?' This was ridiculous.

'Will you please tell me what flight you're returning on, Mr Lupus.'

111

'No, I bloody well will not,' Adam snapped. 'Who the hell are you?'

'I informed you, sir. We are with Mr Carvel and would like your assistance Mr Lupus. If you tell me your flight I will meet you at the airport.'

'You will do no such thing,' Adam said sharply. 'Give me Mr Carvel.'

'Yes sir, and then I would like to speak to you again.'

'What the hell is this?' he demanded when he heard his assistant's voice. 'What on *earth's* going on there?'

'I'm sorry. There was nothing I could do about it. The whole pack of them came barging into the office half an hour ago.'

'Why? Whatever for? The police?'

'With a search warrant,' Tony informed him unhappily. 'They're taking the place apart.'

'A *search* warrant?' Adam was dumbfounded. This was incomprehensible. 'A warrant? What in hell do they think they're up to?'

'Well . . . '

'Yes?' he prompted sharply.

'Well, it seems they've intercepted some sort of parcel addressed to you and examined it,'

'Intercepted? Examined?' Adam felt totally at a loss. 'Who? Who have?'

There was a pause. 'Scotland Yard, the Drugs Squad,' Tony told him. Adam struggled to comprehend, then Inspector Nicholas again was on the wire. 'I understand you've recently visited Columbia, Mr Lupus. Can you confirm that?'

A switch went over in Adam's brain. 'Certainly.' He was coldly in control. 'What is this about?'

'A parcel addressed to you at this office was detected by the Post Office spectrascope and we would like to ask you a few questions re the matter as soon as possible. Now will you please inform me of your flight back, sir.'

Adam breathed in slowly. 'Inspector, I suggest you get your men out of my office at once or you will be in very serious trouble. There are laws to prevent this kind of thing.

112

Do you realise these are very serious allegations?'

'Yes sir, I do.' The tone was dry. 'Will you give me the number you're telephoning from, Mr Lupus,'

Fury backed up in Adam's throat. Tense with anger he opened his mouth to reply. He would cost this joker his job; he would have his balls . . .

And then he thought, a parcel . . . the pictures . . . Colombia . . . spectrascope . . . drugs. The words laid a quick chill touch on him, turning his limbs to ice. The world swayed then levelled as his mind clicked forward remorselessly into the connection: Jutta!

His hand swept the telephone down upon its cradle, cutting off the call. He sat immobile, frozen. That parcel. Jutta. It was not possible. Had he been set up? His brain reeled away from the thought.

Suddenly he glanced at his watch. He rose and paced the room, obsessed by what was taking place in London. Police . . . search warrant . . . *search* warrant?

Why? For what? What could have been in that parcel. Drugs? If so, then they must have been added subsequently. It was inconceivable that Jutta should be responsible.

His glance fell upon the suitcase packed and ready on the bed.

No, he told himself, it was not possible. This was the girl whom he adored. And she? She had experienced all and more than he had felt. He had known it in her response and her body. He was certain of her, and about her.

But yet?

He stared at the suitcase and fought to put the terrifying suspicion from his mind. Jutta? Was there something for London in there as well?

He ground out his cigarette and stepped to the case. He snapped it open and threw back the lid.

His suits, his shirts, all lay there neatly folded. He thrust in his hand and felt beside them. His shoes . . . his socks . . . two books. Books? He drew them out, a package wrapped in brown paper and sealed with scotch tape. By the feel and weight of it undoubtedly two books - but unrecognisable. Not his.

113

He dug his nails below the tape and ripped it back. He peeled off the wrapping. Books indeed - two hardback novels, but glued together. He weighed the package in his hand. He studied it with a dread certainty gathering to his mind.

He set his fingers to the cardboard binding of the topmost and tore it open. Firm sealed, the cover yielded slowly then ripped away. He picked out the tissue wadding.

In the hollowed cavity inside lay a tight arrangement of polythene envelopes, each containing a dense white powder.

Staring at them, he was poleaxed by dismay. The truth, already in his veins, solidified to ice.

Fool, he was. He had been set up. A dupe, a John, he had been set up. And *well*, he realised bitterly, as the truth flooded his mind. Entirely successfully. A consignment in his name, addressed to him, had already arrived in London - accompanied by the police. Blithely and unwittingly he was about to mule another shipment.

The police! he thought. They occupied his offices in London. The inspector had been on to him, showing intense interest in his return, asking for his number. And what were they engaged in now? Locating him? Wasn't this hotel he stood in booked by his secretary? They had only to ask her where he was. Then what . . . a call at *his* expense to the Los Angeles Police Department asking them to pick him up?

He stiffened, listening for the wail of sirens. For God's sake, he wasn't ready for that yet! He was totally unprepared. He would sort it out, but he needed time to think.

He still gripped that lethal package in his hands. He looked wildly around the room for a place to hide it. Impossible, and he couldn't get rid of it down the lavatory. Whatever it was he would need it to prove his unlikely tale.

His eye fell upon his briefcase. He snatched it up, crammed the package inside. He snapped it shut and locked it.

He picked it up and left the room. Avoiding the elevator, he went fast down the single flight of stairs, slowing only as he stepped out into the garden.

He went by the deserted swimming pool and through the garden overhung with palms. He reached Alta Loma road without passing through the Reception. He walked fifty yards up the hill and turned right into Sunset Boulevard.

The brightly coloured cars streamed past in a steady flow. Adam was the only pedestrian in sight. Carrying the briefcase he felt horribly conspicuous.

He forced himself to walk slowly, not to stroll but step out with intent. He was a man returning from a business meeting to his car, parked nearby. He relaxed his face.

He passed by the restaurant where he had dined with Jutta. Locked up tight.

He went on. A hundred and fifty yards further he found stairs leading down the hillside beneath a sign: Glory's Rendezvous. He turned off the street and descended the wooden steps to an open courtyard, arranged with tables, beyond was a bar. He went through, chose a stool and set the briefcase by his feet.

'What's your drinking pleasure sir?'

'A vodka,' he ordered 'On the rocks.'

'Straight up? Lemon twist?'

He nodded. The adrenalin of fear had driven him through that brisk hot walk. Now he was sweating profusely. He raised his handkerchief to wipe his face.

The loose-limbed young barman drifted back and set the drink before him. 'You new here?' he asked.

Adam stared at him, his heart beating so fast he thought that it would burst. All at once he became gripped by unbearable tension. His body seized rigid with terror. His movement as he raised his glass was stiff and clumsy. Though he heard the words he did not know how to respond correctly or adjust his expression.

He read in the young man's eyes that whatever he was doing was inappropriate. He spoke again, asking something else, but now Adam saw only the flapping of his mouth. There was no sense, no sound beyond the cataract of blood roaring in his ears.

The barman lingered, looking at him strangely.

The tension drew itself tighter and tighter around him. Every muscle locked, Adam was wound so tight he thought he would snap.

'Yeah, have a nice day,' said the man and wandered

115

toward another customer.

Adam grabbed his glass and drank long and deep. Forcibly he subdued himself, choking back the wave of hysteria which was rising to engulf him.

He took another pull of vodka and felt for his cigarettes. Very deliberately he curbed the panic squirming in his mind.

He lit a cigarette, raising his glance above the bar to the wrap-around picture window and the evening view which stretched beyond. It was the same scene he had overlooked with Jutta over dinner two days before at the nearby restaurant. How differently he felt now as he gazed upon it.

Jutta! At the thought of her he sagged in disappointment and in loss. He had adored her and she had used him for a fool. How many other men had she used in exactly this same way?

It was a gross betrayal, a cynical, skilful manipulation of his absurd attachment. Now he must return to London and explain away this sorry tale, embarrassing and foolish as it was and tinged with a harebrained criminality. Ludicrous!

He cringed from the thought of telling it. To the police? To Tony? To Vanessa? He could hear them snigger afterward at this fatuous saga of a middle-aged ninny besotted by a girl.

To hell with that, he thought savagely. He refused to be put in that position. The police — so what? *That* could be arranged. Power and connection were tools he still knew how to use.

He rapped upon the counter. 'Give me change,' he ordered. 'Quarters.'

He carried a handful with him, to the telphone. He took out his address book.

'A call to London, England,' he told the long distance operator. He fed in three dollars and waited for the connection.

He was telephoning Sheldon's home number. Sheldon would know how to handle this, could fix it and save him from his folly. He would ask Sheldon to take care of it, to use diplomatic muscle, to speak where it mattered, silence the Press with a D notice and straighten it away. The CIA would do it, they owed him something after all.

116

He heard the number ringing. He prepared his words. But the telephone rang on unanswered . . .

The operator came back on the line, 'Do you have an alternative number?'

'Yes.' It was written just below. '499 9000.'

He was through at once. 'United States Embassy.'

He asked for Drury Sheldon and waited, smoking.

'Who is this you are calling?'

'Mr Drury Sheldon,' he repeated firmly.

'Of what section?'

'Foreign Affairs. He's an attaché.'

A further wait, then a man's voice on the line. 'Yes, can I help you?'

'Mr Drury Sheldon,' he asked again. 'This is Adam Lupus, if he's not there will you tell me where I can reach him urgently.'

'Who?'

'Mr Drury Sheldon.'

The response was swift this time, horrendously so. 'No, Mr Lupus, there's no one of that name working here, not at the US Embassy. Is there anyone else who could help you?'

A fat blue fly alighted on Adam's wrist. He glared at it, then the truth smacked him in the face like an open hand, hard and blinding; Sheldon was part of it. Sheldon and the girl. They were together in this and he, Adam, was their dupe. He was a complete utter bloody fool.

He set the receiver down very, very slowly . . .

Chapter eighteen

Jutta Metz returned to the Sunset Marquis to find Adam no longer in their room.

His case stood beside the door. He would be in the bar, she thought. There were still several minutes before they need leave for the airport.

Awaiting his return, she started taking her clothes from the wardrobe and to pack her own suitcase. When Adam took off for London her mission here was done.

She glanced at her watch. He would be back any minute now, she thought.

Two hundred yards away Adam sat in the bar of Glory's Rendezvous, his third drink before him, and looked out at the brilliant nightscape of Los Angles with sightless eyes.

He could scarcely think straight, so acute was his dismay.

How could she have done this to him? He felt weak from disappointment. How could he have been so wrong about her? He wilted from the hurt, he was sickened by his own stupidity.

He was tormented by the memory of moments of passion and closeness they had shared. Had she *acted* every one? It was unbelievable, yet the answer obviously was yes, and Sheldon was her director.

At once sheer loathing drowned out all other thoughts. Sheldon! The very name of the man he had liked and trusted filled him with hatred and revulsion.

He had been humiliated and used. First his good nature, then his emotions had been cynically exploited. And he had gambolled to their tune. He had performed as dutifully for them as a puppet or a dancing bear, performed impeccably. It was no longer even private that humiliation.

Deceived, exploited, betrayed, now the police had flooded into his London office armed with search warrants. The acid of fury scalded through Adam's veins; he was incensed by their intrusion. They had come barrelling into *his*, the best, most profitable, esteemed and straight-run company in England. And all because he had allowed himself to be used, to be suckered. By those two!

Caustic loathing stung and percolated in his veins. No one had ever played him for a fool before. How dare they!

He sipped his vodka. It tasted like water; the alcohol had no effect.

Their effrontery was insufferable. *He would not have it.* They would not get away with this, either of them. No doubt they thought they were very clever. They despised him probably, but he would fix them. Scheming was *his* craft. The manipulation of individuals and events, that was the skill which had served him well and brought him to the top. They had underrated him, grossly.

He downed his drink. 'The check,' he called out sharply to the barman.

He paid, then added a ten dollar note to his tip. 'Look after this for me,' he said and handed over the locked briefcase.

He stood and walked rapidly across the courtyard to the flight of steps which led back into Sunset Boulevard.

Jutta had finished packing. Prepared for depature, her suitcase stood beside Adam's by the door ready to be taken down.

She glanced again nervously at her watch. He was late. They would need to hurry to make his plane. At that instant she heard Adam's key turning in the lock.

He came in. 'We have to go now,' she said at once.

Adam did not answer. He moved slowly across the room and threw himself upon the bed.

'We had better carry down our own cases,' she said. 'There's not much time.'

Still he did not answer. He was not looking at her, she realised. His unfocused eyes were fixed upon the ceiling. She wondered what was wrong with him.

'Adam . . . ' She began again, 'Adam . . . '

'I'm not going,' he said.

'What?'

He did not answer. 'What do you mean?' she demanded, her voice quickening. 'What has happened? What do you mean?'

He repeated 'I'm not going.'

She stood electrified. 'To London? But yes, you have to go.'

A burst of music reached her from the open window, a radio next door instantly turned down.

'You must go,' she told him passionately. 'You said so. Your work . . . '

'I'm fed up to the teeth with all of it,' he said. 'I'm disgusted. I'm through.'

'What has happened? Where have you been?'

'In a bar drinking. I had a lot to think about.'

She glanced toward his case. Her voice came high and strained. 'What do you mean?'

'I was drinking,' he repeated. 'I had - what's it called - an illumination, a moment of truth.'

'Truth? About what?'

'Me. My life. Going back. I can't.'

She refused to accept what he was telling her. 'But yes, you must go home.'

He shook his head, 'No.'

His meaning struck her with consternation and dismay. She had to turn away to conceal her agitation.

'Why *should* I?' he demanded of her.

She stood at the window, her back to him. 'You can't do this,' she whispered and he could barely hear her.

'No? Why shouldn't I? I'm fed up with all of it, my home, my marriage, my job. Do you know what it is, my life? It looks grand, I know, but have you any idea what it's really like. I'm forty years old and there's no pleasure left in any of it. I had no youth and spent every moment getting there and now that I have it's garbage. It isn't worth a damn.'

She wheeled on him tensely. 'Your family . . . your business . . . '

'My *business*.' His tone was harsh and scornful now. 'The

120

success I've made of it, yes I thought *that* would bring happiness. It was what I wanted after all . . . '

She glanced again at her watch, frantic at this irrelevance.

'Success is worth nothing,' he said, sitting up abruptly and reaching for his cigarettes. 'It cures nothing, changes nothing. I've never been free to do as *I* wanted . . . '

He swung his legs from the bed and jumped up, suddenly unable to stay still. He paced the room, his voice loud, contemptuous, his gestures savage with impacted rage.

'I *lie*,' he shouted at her. 'Don't you understand. I deceive, I bluff, and exist in dread that others will find me out. I take pills every night to sleep. I have no drive, no curiosity and no hope. It's two years since my wife and I made love. My marriage is a nonsense. I'm bored. I'm trapped and fearful and *bored* . . . '

Jutta crossed to the bed, picked up Adam's cigarettes and took one. Her fingers were stiff, her movements jerky. It was the first time she had smoked in two years. She had no idea at all what she must do.

'But I *accommodate* . . .' she heard him say wearily. 'I function, but if I fool others I do not fool me. I cheat, I embezzle and I over-eat and I've *had* it. Had it to *here*!' His fingers sliced brutally across his throat.

She stared at him blankly. The power to think had left her.

'And then *you* happened,' said Adam. About to stride by, he wheeled on her. 'You happened,' he repeated softly, calmer now. 'You've changed my whole life and I want to be with you.'

Jutta sucked smoke deep into her lungs and a cloud of black spots swarmed before her eyes. The room rocked. It was worse, far worse than she imagined. Catastrophic. Appalling.

'Come on, *move*,' Adam said abruptly. 'Let's get out of here.'

'But the bill . . . ' she protested weakly.

'I've paid it,' he told her. 'We're going somewhere else, and fast. The moment they discover I'm not on that plane when it lands in London all hell is going to break loose. I want to be somewhere that no one can trace us. Quickly move!'

He snatched up both their cases and opened the door. Numbly, unable to reason clearly, she found herself following down the stairs, across the lawn, out to the car.

He took the keys from her unresisting hand. 'But where are we *going*?' she asked him desperately.

'Anywhere,' he answered as they got into the car. 'Anywhere they can't find us.'

He jerked off the handbrake and smacked the lever into drive.

Chapter nineteen

It was 2 a.m. in California but in London the clock on the reproduction dressing table in Sheldon's bedroom at Flat Four, 27 Park Street read 11 a.m.

The apartment consisted of two rooms, plus bathroom and kitchen. Though small it was furnished with a threadbare pretension. Some years had passed since it had last been painted. It rented for £200 per week and no one stayed here long, or cared.

Sheldon had just stepped from his bath when he heard the telephone. He wrapped a towel around his dripping body and went to answer it.

'Yes?'

He recognised Jutta's voice and instantly keyed tense. 'Where are you?' he demanded.

'L.A. Take this number. Call me back.'

'Tell me what . . .' he started, but the line had clicked dead.

Quickly, nervously, he dialled the international code followed by the figures she had given him. He heard the receiver taken up.

'I've been waiting all night. Why didn't you call?' he demanded.

'I couldn't, he was with me. He's not on the plane,' she said.

'Why not?' His voice shot up. 'What's happened? Why?'

Her breath left her in a sigh. She was smoking, he realised. She must have started again.

'You're not going to believe this,' she said

'Why? What happened?'

'Well, . . . he's not going back.'

He did not take it in at once. 'Not going back?' he repeated blankly. What the hell does that mean?'

123

'He's dropped out. Quit. He is not going back to England.'

'It's not possible.' Sheldon said.

'Yes. It is so.'

'Where is the stuff?' he asked.

'In his case.'

'His case? Where's Lupus now?'

'Asleep. I am talking from a callbox outside the motel.'

'Where?'

'Some drecky place called Venice,' she said. 'What do you want me to do now?'

'*Do*? Are you mad? Get it out of that fucking case,' he told her harshly. 'Do you realise what it's worth and what'll happen if he finds it. Get the stuff out and check it into a baggage locker. You understand? Call me back the moment you've done it.'

'It is not easy to telephone,' she complained but he was pitiless.

'You do it.'

'I am not sure I can get away.'

'Don't be a fool,' he snapped. 'You think this some kind of social engagement?'

'No,' she said, 'but what I have told you is not all.'

He said sharply, 'What then?'

'It is true. He is dropped out, but there is worse.'

'Worse? What are you telling me?'

'I cannot get away. He wants to be with me, to live together. For ever. It is why he is dropping out. Lupus has fallen in love with me.'

A dollar's worth of silence followed on the line.

'Oh shit.' Sheldon then said softly. 'Go take the stuff out and call me back. I'll think of something.'

It was less than twenty minutes later when his telephone rang again.

'It's not there,' she said.

'*What*?'

'He does not have it.'

'Why not?' His voice grew sharp and hard. 'Where is it?'

'I have looked. It is not in his case.' She sounded exhausted. '*I* am not cheating you Sheldon. He must have

124

found it and left it somewhere.'

'"Left it somewhere".' He mimicked her viciously. 'You should not have left him for a moment, a second. What the fuck have you been up to?'

'But what . . . ?'

'Be quiet. Let me think. Oh *shit* . . . ' he repeated quietly but with keen emotion. 'Oh shit, you've fucked me up.'

'But what am I to do?'

'Do? Get it back,' he snapped. 'Just get it back.'

'But Lupus . . . ?'

'Just get it back, and call me right away,' he ordered.

Chapter twenty

Even while Sheldon and Jutta spoke long distance over the telephone the news was already on the streets of London.

'POLICE RAID PUBLIC COMPANY' . . .

'MILLION POUND DRUG HAUL' . . .

'LUPUS GROUP SENSATION' . . .

The headlines spread across the front page of every paper. The story spilled over to the inside pages and each carried a photograph of Adam Lupus, Chairman of the Group, believed at this very moment returning on an airplane from California to be met by the police.

The headlines sprang at Sheldon from the billboards the moment he stepped out into the street. He went no further than the first news stall but bought a copy of every paper and returned to his apartment.

The news was a ghastly shock, the second reverse he had received within the hour, severe enough to wipe him out, to destroy him.

The entire operation had gone wrong. It had fouled up totally for the first time.

Since he had volunteered for the US army at the age of nineteen, Sheldon had led a life of criminality.

Drugs had lately been a part of it, but peripherally. The smuggling and wholesale disposal of cocaine had been no more than preliminary and logistical events, the means to fund his larger projects. These started in the army with the theft of weaponry from US bases and its sale. Ambition carried him further; he became involved in his clients' schemes. And swiftly he had comprehended that he was more skilled in these than they. He was international, educated, ingenious and a natural actor. He had exactly what it took to reach the top.

Sheldon now was unique in his position. He knew this to be the case. He was a star, the Robin Hood of international terrorism. His skills had sharpened in the CIA in which he had served when he left the army. Though he had not survived there long, it was long enough. He had determined his vocation.

He was a director of events, other people's political events. It was arms his clients wanted first. He bought in with expertise and came to be accepted for his contacts, know-how and tactical contribution. He had three hijackings to his credit, the provision of the RPG7 Rocket Launcher in Northern Ireland, the takeover of the Iranian Embassy in London.

Without him these operations would not have been successful. He knew this and so did their perpetrators. Yet he had not originated them, they were not wholly *his*.

He yearned for more. For years he had known a joker lay within the deck of cards he played with. His father. The cost in spirit, blood and money that this relationship demanded were worthwhile for, one day, the joker might be dealt into his hand. Now that day had come. He had the card.

Sheldon's father had headed the research team which, in 1952, succeeded in synthesising psilocybin, a hallucinogenic Mexican mushroom, into the drug they named LSD.

The chemical altered a subject's consciousness of himself and the world around him. That was the clinical way of describing a disordered state of mind in which the user could believe he was made of cream cheese or had melted or could fly. It scrambled his brains totally yet all the while that same user believed he had found Truth, that he was sane, sublime and *right*.

LSD was unstable and unpredictable in its results. Infinite in possibility, disastrous in experience. As Chief Chemist, further refinement of the drug was Sheldon's father's career. A second generation immigrant Jew, in 1953 he was named in the McCarthy Hearings, summoned to testify, pleaded the Fifth Amendment, and lost his job.

Sheldon was then aged three. Only as an infant had he

127

experienced the good times. He had no memory of them nor of his WASP mother who had departed when those good times were ended. His childhood memories were poverty, bitterness, disillusion. He had been raised by his father in the discipline of lacerating self-punishment and Jewish acceptance of the role of victim. It disgusted him. To volunteer to join the army, to leave home forever, had been escape.

Yet, with that escape, Sheldon had not broken with the father whom he hated, loved, despised and pitied. He had supported the old man. The money he sent home had funded a private programme of continuing research carried out in the most primitive and makeshift conditions, first in New Jersey then the Everglades.

The programme finally had paid off. After years of setback and disappointments Sheldon senior had synthesised a further stage in the development of LSD.———————

Only in some ways did this new synthetic resemble the hallucinogenic it derived from. Tested upon rats, it caused compulsively imitative behaviour. They went on doing what they were shown to do until they died. The drug appeared chemically to wash-blank the brain, upon whose virgin state any idea, any intention could then be planted. The subject could be programmed to do anything suggested.

The instant this joker came into his hand Sheldon knew how he would play it. To stage the scenario he had in mind would require major finance and the most sedulous preparation. But it was wholly possible. His intent was no less than to subvert the order of the West. When its leaders next met together, when they celebrated their entente, his poison would lie within the cup.

And then before a stunned audience Sheldon would present a theatrical spectacular larger and grander than any ever witnessed in the world. He would alter and direct the course of history.

Sheldon was so close now. He had come so long a way toward realising his heady dream. He had possession of the product, had recruited his crack team of three and successfully brought them to the US. In two sensational

128

happenings in New York the product had been tested upon humans and the dosage determined. His group was poised and ready. Now he waited only to learn the date of the next international conference and they would move. The finance, the money to mount the operation would come from the sale of two and a half kilos of cocaine . . .

Set up by Jutta, this cocaine, ninety-eight per cent pure had been shipped out of Columbia in two consignments.

A half kilo had been packed into the frames of the naif paintings mailed from Cartagena to Adam's office in London. Two kilos had been muled into New York by that same upright and unwitting courier, where some had remained; the surplus had travelled to California and been hidden in Adam's suitcase for onward shipment into Europe.

But now, this morning, Sheldon had learned that both these consignments had gone awry. The half kilo had been lost into the custody of the London police, the other was no longer in Adam's suitcase in Los Angeles.

At the street price of $100 a gram, a value of $50,000 was impounded and a further $150,000 had gone missing.

To invest in that quantity of ninety-eight per cent pure had cost Sheldon his working capital. Not to recover the consignment would critically prejudice his larger plan. Without money the operation would become impossible.

Architect of the plot, the play was in his hands now. There was nothing he could do to influence the course of events. The action lay 6,000 miles away with Jutta and Adam Lupus in California.

Restless and apprehensive, Sheldon remained in his apartment, waiting for Jutta's call to tell him what was happening. He dared not go out for fear that it would come.

He passed the entire day fretting over the problem in California, the loss of his capital, the missing drugs, and the ridiculous circumstances of Adam who had dropped out with no knowledge - Sheldon believed- that his office in London had been raided and he was wanted by the police for questioning. Dropped out for love of Jutta. Shit, he thought, it was disastrous and at the same time absurd.

For Sheldon the hours proved a long and agonising wait.

It was night before Jutta called back.

'You've got it?' he demanded.

She sighed. 'Yes Sheldon. It was in a bar.'

'A bar! How did you find it?'

'It had to be near the hotel. He was on foot.'

'You're *in* the bar?' he questioned.

'Yes.'

'Then take it with you and get out at once.'

'What about Lupus?'

'Fuck Lupus,' he said.

'But what do I do with him?'

'Nothing. Cut him loose.'

'Let him go? But he can describe me, recognise me.'

'Then whack him out.'

'You mean kill him?' she asked incredulous.

'Do it now, then fly to New York. It's best.'

In the silence down the wire he heard the rasp of a match as she lit a cigarette. 'I don't think so,' she answered slowly.

'He's no more use. He's trouble.'

'No, he *is* of use,' she said.

'Don't be a fool . . . ' He was impatient now. 'Just because you've fucked him and he's gotten to you . . . '

'Sheldon!' She interrupted, 'I've had a long frightening day up at the sharp end. I've got back your coke for you and I'm very tired. So, just for a change, will you listen and not shout.'

He picked up his own cigarettes. 'So, interest me,' he said more calmly.

'Lupus. He's bigger than you think, bigger than we've ever used before. He's a fat fish, rich and powerful and very well connected . . . '

He broke in, 'If you think . . . '

'Quiet Sheldon! Listen, I mean *very* well connected. He's been invited to attend a meeting with the Western Heads of State *and* the Russians.'

He could not believe what she was telling him. 'Heads of State? Russians?'

Yes, a sort of informal Summit.'

'When?'

'He doesn't know, but soon.'

'You think it's true?'

'I'm sure it's true. He wasn't boasting. He doesn't even want to go.'

'Shit!' he said expressively.

'Yes Sheldon,' she agreed, and her voice was acid with sarcasm. 'Just as you say, but what do we do now?'

He drew deeply on his cigarette, the significance of what he had heard sparking in his brain.

'I'll tell you *exactly* what we do,' he said. 'Listen . . .'

Chapter twenty-one

The news of the raid upon the Lupus Group had featured prominently in the evening papers that day, expanded by a statement from Scotland Yard which announced that cocaine worth £25,000 had been seized upon the company's Knightsbridge premises.

The BBC, ITV and radio stations ran the report as the main national story throughout the evening but only their last transmissions of the day, at midnight, advertised a new and startling development to the case: Adam Lupus himself had not returned as expected aboard Pan Am 127 from Los Angeles. Booked on that flight, he had not taken it. He had quit his hotel without even settling the bill. He had, it seemed, disappeared and was now actively being sought by the police.

Adam woke that morning in Venice.

Venice, LA, not Venice, Italy, but here as in that other city was the same impression of mouldering decay. The sun crept up behind the haze, exposing a district of low wooden houses, patched and shabby, sand powdering the streets they stood in; those desolate streets expiring in parking lots upon a beach where figures wandered like ghosts in the sombre murk at the edge of a stale expanse of ocean disappearing into smog. The flat white glare of the sky beat on a blurred, shadowless and insubstantial world.

A rundown area, shoddy and decrepit. This was where Adam and Jutta found themselves the night before and checked into a motel, this like all else in sight cheaply made, prefabricated and drab. Every building had the same air of the transient, the impermanence of shanty dwellings on the fault line waiting for the moment when the ground would

132

rumble and heave, the earth's surface tip and all that was here slide like matchwood into the sea.

But not yet. In Venice that morning there was no sign of the earthquake and to Adam, standing alone upon the beach in the early morning, that seemed a pity. The cataclysm would at least solve things, he thought.

Jutta had not been beside him when he woke. Undoubtedly she would be back, he realised. Her clothes were scattered about the room, her case stood beside the closet, she had to return.

He had mastered his regret and considered her only as an enemy now, as he knew he must, an enemy whom he must contend with. At this very moment she was out there somewhere in the city and plotting actively against him.

He stood upon the empty beach and prepared himself for what might happen.

His resources were pitiful yet, so far, his drop-out act had gone well. He nad got away with it, he thought. It was vital that he stay ahead and keep at least the tactic of surprise. The advantage lay with Jutta and Sheldon; theirs was the power. The best that he could hope to do was to try to figure an angle and bluff his course.

He was in trouble, he thought, no doubt about that. Farcical though it sounded, he was wanted by the police on suspicion of drug smuggling.

Yesterday they had swarmed over his offices with a search warrant and undoubtedly today the story had found its way into the newspapers. Of course it had - and prominently; it was just too rich an item not to have been leaked. Also, he had disappeared. Flight Pan Am 127 had landed at London Airport without him and that, quite certainly, had opened the gates to havoc. There must be all hell going on in London at this moment. The telephone wires at Lupus House, at his home, must be positively red hot with use. Even at Eton, to Prosper. He winced at the thought.

He was still furious at that invasion of police into his head-quarters and his life but, he realised, their warrant had proved justified. They had excellent reason for acting as they did. The fact: his own soft-brained idiocy. They had every right.

133

Adam hunched his shoulders and strode swiftly across the dismal swathe of sand harrowed by fury and contempt. How could he have been such a fool. Sheldon and Jutta! He recoiled from their complicity. He *refused* to be their patsy. He would *not* limp home to London with his pathetic tale, seeking to be excused. The embarrasment was too much, the ignominy of the role they had cast him in utterly unacceptable.

No! He would not take it, and he would make them smart for trying to impose it on him. He would maintain the act he had put on for Jutta and he would stick to her till he found Sheldon and then he would bust them both. He would show them who cracked the whip. He was not available as a victim. They had him wrong.

He nurtured his anger, for it kept him from despair. While he could hate her he was cured of love and the debilitating sadness of regret. Fury had driven him but now it had to be subdued. He could not afford the indulgence of emotion, he realised as he tramped the beach; from now on he had to remain coldly wide awake, alert, prepared. For a start he must get back that briefcase . . .

The realisation brought him up short. Of course, he must get the case, take out what was inside and stash it somewhere safer. While he had the cocaine they could not afford to lose him; she was obliged to stay close. He held the goods.

He turned then and headed for where he could call a cab.

The taxi set Adam down in Sunset Boulevard, opposite Glory's Rendezvous.

The place was almost empty. Only four of the twenty stools were occupied. The barman slouched across the counter, dabbing at the keys of an illuminated plastic box which stood before him blinking coloured lights.

'A vodka,' Adam ordered as he stepped up to the bar, but the young man waved him off with a lazy hand, his attention concentrated upon the game.

'Wait man. I'm whipping it.'

With each tap upon its buttons the toy gave out a small excited electronic bleep. Adam hovered while the man's fingers dialled out a sequence. Swiftly the robot countered in response. The barman moved again . . .

'Excuse me,' Adam said sharply. 'A vodka.'

The man looked up, startled by so peremptory a command. At once, with an effervescent run of light, the machine triumphantly blipped out its victory.

'Look man, you made me blow it.' He moved resentfully to serve the drink. 'On the rocks?'

'Yes.'

'Lemon twist?'

'Yes.' Adam spoke fast. 'That case I left with you. I'll take it now.'

The barman carved off a slice of peel. 'Yeah, like that's your hassle.'

'If you'll be so good as to give it to me,' Adam said, leaning over to peer behind the bar.

'"So good as to give it me", you know you slay me,' the barman said. 'I'd really like to help you, but your relationships are your relationships, know what I mean.'

'No,' said Adam. 'Now could I have the briefcase?'

'Where's the percentage in fucking with either of you?' the barman asked.

Down the bar the robot emitted a plaintive electronic mew. Ignored too long it was inviting its human friend to another contest, calling him out to play.

'What do you mean?'

'She was here to fetch it, man.'

'Who was?'

'Your chick man, the German chick. Said you'd sent her.'

Adam set back his drink in one swift movement. 'You had no business to give it to her,' he said furiously.

But the barman was not susceptible to his customer's emotion. Of his time and place, California Now, surface goodwill concealed a much deeper indifference.

'Hey, stay loose,' he murmured. 'Wait, that's two dollars fifty,' he added for Adam was already on his feet and moving.

The white smog of day was bleeding into neon dark as Adam arrived back at the motel to confront Jutta. The empty beach beyond evaporated into seeping dusk.

He walked along the deserted corridor, set his key into the lock and entered.

The room was in darkness, the bathroom lit, its door ajar. Jutta stepped out naked from the shower.

'We're going to talk,' said Adam grimly and moved one pace to grasp her . . . He got not further. A limp, weighted cosh descended soundlessly upon his head. The impact of a pound of soft lead wrapped around his skull.

Agony exploded in his head. The mirror shattered. Blackness wiped him out. The crash of hurt was followed instantly by night. A trapdoor opened somewhere in his brain and he pitched through into the dark which lay beyond.

Chapter twenty-two

'Kidnapped?' said Vanessa Lupus. 'My dear Tony, don't be utterly absurd. What a ludicrous idea. Of *course* Adam hasn't been kidnapped.'

She was lunching with Tony Carvel at Langan's. A week had gone by since the police raid on Adam's office, his dramatic non-return to London and his disappearance. A week of silence.

There had been no word of Adam in that period. Neither from him, nor of him. Interpol and the Los Angeles police were still searching for him without success.

Though nothing fresh could be added to the fact of his disappearance the item remained front page news in England.

The Press had been both active and conspicuous throughout that week. The scent of a sensational story high in their nostrils, they had installed themselves in the marble lobby of Lupus Group headquarters and pitched camp outside Vanessa's house. They attempted to interview everyone who entered or left the two establishments, refusing to believe that no one had received word from Adam or knew where he was. They demonstrated a special interest in both Tony and Vanessa. It had required subterfuge for the two to meet here for lunch.

'Kidnapped?' repeated Vanessa. 'That's a ludicrous explanation. Whatever makes you think so?'

'He wouldn't simply have disappeared like that,' Tony maintained. 'Not without a letter or a call.'

'No? I find it all too hideously obvious and corny. And cowardly. Of course he'd do it like that - the bastard. Who's the girl he's with anyway, did you discover?'

'German,' Tony told her. 'She registered at the hotel in the name of Ilse Bulow. I've got our people in Frankfurt trying to find out more about her. So are the police.'

'Kidnapped? What bloody nonsense.' Vanessa's voice was loud and forceful. 'It's the male menopause, the midlife syndrome. He was afraid he couldn't get it up any more, he fell in with this Kraut tart and now he's run off with her.'

She used her fork to scrape aside the heavy sauce on her lobster mornay and speared a morsel. 'By the way,' she added. 'I've been meaning to ask you, what *is* cocaine?'

'A stimulant drug,' Tony told her.

'Have you ever tried it?'

'Of course not.'

'But what does it *do*?' she asked.

He sipped his wine. 'Stimulate, I understand.'

'Stimulate?' she sounded astonished. 'But was Adam taking it?'

'I saw no evidence of that but who knows? That was a vast quantity sent to him at the office. If it's nothing to do with him why doesn't he come forward and say so?'

'It all seems most extraordinary,' said Vanessa. 'Really awfully odd. Was he taking it, selling it? Why? I've been married to Adam for eighteen years but it makes me think I simply did not know him *at all*.'

'Well yes,' Tony agreed. 'I feel rather the same.'

For a while Vanessa ate thoughtfully and in silence. 'But how are things managing there anyway?' she asked at last. 'At the office, I mean.'

'All right,' he answered shortly.

'But doesn't someone have to . . . I don't know, make the decisions and things. I mean Adam always seemed so *busy*. He never got home till seven or eight o'clock.'

Tony Carvel reached for the bottle of Chablis and poured the last of it into both their glasses. 'Well it's a pretty big operation. It has management. It sort of goes on, you know.'

'I saw that the share price is back up again today.'

'Yes, we seem to have weathered the storm. There was a bit of panic at first as you know but our assets are very sound. Quite honestly I think it's the publicity we've been receiving which has brought the price back up. There can't be anyone in England who hasn't heard of the Lupus Group now.'

'You mean any publicity is good publicity?'

'Odd, isn't it?' said Tony. He turned and called for coffee. It was not true that Adam's disappearance had made no difference to the running of the corporation. It took up every moment of Tony's time and demanded all of his attention. He had not only to administer the company but fight off various attempts of the other directors to seize the reins.

When coffee came he drank it quickly. 'I'm sorry,' he explained. 'But I really out to get back.'

Vanessa understood entirely. From the restaurant the chauffeur drove her to Harrods where it took her twenty minutes to choose and order a new set of garden furniture for the London house. She passed a further twenty minutes at Way In. She had to occupy her mind somehow.

It was past four when she got home. She found an urgent message to telephone Tony Carvel.

She did so at once. Her call went rapidly through the switchboard and his secretary. 'You wanted to talk to me?' she asked.

'Yes.' He sounded breathless. 'We've had news.'

'From Adam?'

'Not exactly but I was right. He *has* been kidnapped.'

'I don't believe it. Who by?'

'The letter was posted in London. It claims that Adam is being held by the Black June Commando.'

'By the *what*?'

'That's what it says,' he told her.

'Go on. What do they want?'

'It doesn't say. We are to wait for their next communiqué'.

'When?'

'That's all it says. To wait. We will be told.'

She asked, 'Have you notified the police?'

'Not yet. I thought I should speak to you first.'

'Yes, we'd better meet ... but where? This place is picketed by the Press. There must be about fifty of them outside.'

'The office?' he suggested.

'Very well. Send a car for me, I told Henry he could go out.'

'What about the police?'

'Call them. They can join us there. Kidnapped?' she repeated. 'I wonder if it's true?'

Chapter twenty-three

Turning and turning in ever-widening circles on the dry desert air the bird of prey spiralled upward toward the pitiless white sun, his gaze bent down upon the world. Infinitely more precise than any wide angle lens, his eyes from that height encompassed a spread of rock, mesquite and sand where nothing moved.

This was a terrifying place, boundless, implacable. Not just a place, a void. A void of light and heat. A desert stunned by the sun and eroded by the wind. Without shadow, it was a world of nothing, of anti-matter. Only the bird of prey drew substance from this cruel land, but, at this hour, no trace of life was visible; even the rattlesnakes lay hidden within their holes. Nothing moved.

The hawk turned and turned, soaring ever upward. Then at the extreme limit of his panorama a minute shift caused his eyes to swivel and focus in. At the very rim of that vast circle of bleached out desert which formed his view a speck of movement edged over the shimmering horizon and trembled into sight.

Movement was life; life was prey. The hawk angled his spread of wings and soared toward it across the slopes of air.

Unblinking, the bird watched as the mechanical insect crawled across the empty landscape. At 2,000 feet the hawk hovered far above. Life existed within that sealed silver capsule, no doubt, but of a form inaccessible to the bird of prey. Except for the very young and very helpless, he had no interest in human kind.

Still, there was no knowing what this unwieldy vehicle contained. From his station high upon the upper air the hawk continued to observe.

The man crouched within the closet, bound and helpless.

He was blindfolded. His hands and feet were tied. He was hunched in the foetal position, his knees drawn up to touch his chin. He had been here for ever.

How long, how many years, how many days had passed while he had squatted here he had no idea. The cut of the cords and the agony of cramp had blurred into numbness. Feeling, sense and reason, even terror, had decomposed into a dull and timeless fog of pain.

War, a fight, he could have dealt with. Challenge was what he was used to, after all, the pitting of one personality against another and the harsh conflict of human wills. On a human battlefield he could have handled himself. This was something else.

Here was no sight, no touch. Sound there was - a muffled vibrating drone which passed for silence. At times his prison lurched and shook. He guessed it was in movement. But how? Where? By whom was he held, and for what reason? His mind shied from such imagining.

Smell there was, his own. Trapped within this narrow space, its stench rose to choke him.

Food there was — of a sort and intermittent. At random intervals a door clicked open, a teat was shoved between his lips. He sucked on it greedily and tasted the sickly milk of life, cut off too soon.

His belly was empty, yet solace it gave him, liquid and sugar and something worse. In his brief moments of lucidity he knew that chemicals were being added to his feed and strove for something to sustain him. Prisoners have endured such isolation and kept sane. Reaching into themselves from all the feat and horror they have found a core of strengh. Faith may give it, the repetition of prayer. Love can provide it, for love, the cure of self, is a prop which shores up the sagging edifice of interior collapse.

These options were denied him. He had no faith, and there was no one in the whole world whom Adam Lupus loved.

He was a special man, intelligent and gifted. He was capable of affection; to his family and those who were loyal to him he could be generous and kind. He was strong in his convictions, single-minded, dedicated and ambitious. He

142

believed passionately in what he did; he was proud of all he had achieved in life.

Or had been. At the moment of Adam's capture the blight was already in the flower. Uncertainty had wormed in. He was afraid at the edge of things. The pathology of doubt had been at work within his soul.

Now, suddenly, in the space of a few hours the harmonious life he had constructed had come apart. His position, his job, his family, his reputation, all had been snatched away. A cosh had wrapped around his skull, destroying in one instant the world as a coherent place.

By violence he had been thrust into the dark. And, since then, nothing. He existed in limbo, in a place without sight or speech or the consoling touch of human hand, or time.

Sucking on drugged milk in a cramped womb of darkness, the mind of Adam Lupus started to erode as the days passed and the motor home crawled without cease around the Nevada desert and the bird of prey hovered and observed.

Chapter twenty-four

'If he *has* been kidnapped,' Vanessa said, 'Then why don't the kidnappers get in touch and tell us what they want?'

'They're softening us up,' Tony Carvel answered. 'The police say it's sometimes done this way.'

'The police!' She snorted. 'Fat lot of use they are.'

It was 11 p.m. They were meeting in the private office of the club. The room was small and functional, their drinks stood among a spread of papers which covered the metal desk.

'The police!' Vanessa repeated scathingly. 'In Los Angeles they're supposed to be so brilliant people make *films* about them. But what have they *done*, actually *done*?' She reached impatiently for her cigarettes. 'Nothing. Absolutely bugger all.'

'They're searching,' Tony told her. 'They've discovered they stayed in a motel in Venice but since then they seem to have disappeared into thin air. They believe they're still somewhere in the city.'

'Both of them?'

He shrugged, avoiding her eye. 'I don't think they know.'

'*Why* not?'

Tonight she wore a full black dress which flattered her figure and hid by its folds her tendency to stoutness. Her fury however was unconcealed. Her face, neck and wrists were pink.

'Why?' she demanded.

'Why? Why indeed?' asked Tony. 'Why us, the Lupus Group? Our history of labour relations is among the best. It seems grossly unfair for a dissident group to pick on us.'

'They didn't pick on us, they picked on Adam.' She

144

crushed out her cigarette though she had only smoked two puffs. 'I feel desperately sorry for him but he's brought it on himself.'

Tony protested. 'Just because he took a holiday with a girl . . .'

'No,' she cut him short. 'It's not just that. He *wanted* something like this to happen.'

'Come now . . .'

'He courted it. Something in him reached out to attract the lightning.The bloody fool,' Vanessa said. 'He can't expect us to handle this alone. How can we? The police have got to deal with it.'

The sound of music and conversation reached them from outside as the door opened a few inches and Freddy Reynold's face appeared around it, suitably composed to what he took to be the mood within.

'Frightfully sorry to interrupt,' he told them. 'But *she's* here with a party and wants you to join her table.'

'Who?' Vanessa asked.

'PM,' Freddy answered, lowering his voice. 'Why don't you both come. She's simply dying to hear the latest on what's happening. Absolutely insists you join her. Come, it sounds to me like a Royal command.'

Chapter twenty-five

Under the harsh sun the desert bleached out into empty light bisected by a straight black line, the highway.

The vast panorama sprawled still and silent in the deadly heat. Along the hairline which was the road crawled a single distant vehicle, the motor home.

The land yacht was a mobile prison containing a single cell, the air within foetid as poison gas.

The closet had the dimensions of a coffin set on end. The bound prisoner squatting in his own waste was a male of forty years, once handsome, rich and powerful. He had been successful and held in high esteem, a man who had had everything.

Enclosed within that stinking tomb his disordered mind had lost grasp on how long he had been held here. In the spacing of his meals his jailers deliberately played accordian with the hours. Sometimes an interval of a whole day seperated those drugged feeds, sometimes only fifteen minutes. The prisoner had lost all sense of the dimension of Time. He had no idea of where he was.

The cords bit; the endless night swayed in and out of pain. He floated half conscious within a blurred and reeking nightmare.

He awakened from it to pure horror.

The closet door was wrenched open. The bandage ripped from his face. Fierce light seared his eyeballs; he screamed with agony as it lanced into his brain. Hands freed, he clamped them to his face, rolling on the floor and howling from the hurt.

He kicked out, straightening his legs, and such a bolt of fire shot into his locked kneecaps he gasped and drew them back,

146

hunching up in spasm. Loosed from the cords his hands burned and stung with blood as if aflame.

The fierce light extinguished. The lance was withdrawn. Pain seeped away to silence. He dared to part his fingers and peer out.

He lay on the floor of a dim white place. The plastic walls pressed close, the ceiling low. Beside him was a table bolted to the floor and fitted with banquettes. Four still figures sat above him, scarcely human, robed in sheets, hooded and masked in conical white hats with black slits for eyes, a hole for a mouth.

'Prisoner!,' The voice of the nearest came harsh and gutteral. 'Prisoner! You will stand to hear your indictment before The People's Court.'

He ceased to writhe. Ashen faced, he gazed up at his prosecutors, his body jangling with nervous shock.

'The prisoner is charged with the crime of International Capitalistic Imperialism. He is guilty of repression, plunder, and exploitation . . . '

Somewhere deep in his brain that harsh accusing voice found an echo. He had heard it before. Where? He struggled to recall as the impeachement was read out. ' . . . Neo-colonialism . . . military-industrialist dictatorship . . . Sionist conspiracy of international capitalism . . . ' The denunciation continued without pause.

And then he remembered where he had heard that voice - the Arab in New York whose suitcase he had taken through Customs at the airport. Of course! With a bored thud of comprehension it all slotted into place. The completeness of it, the wholeness for a moment quite killed the pain. How neatly, how well they all had set him up.

'Prisoner! Before this Court pronounces sentence have you anything to say?'

He stared up at four shrouded figures, all still and all alike. His look flicked between them, seeking to identify if one were Jutta. It was impossible to determine.

The eyes of his judge glittered back at him from their shadowed holes. The silence crackled with aggression.

'Answer prisoner!'

147

Blood hammered in his temples. His parched mouth was full of dust.

'Stay silent then.' The eyes behind overflowed with contempt. The white robe twitched in a savage gesture. 'Put him back!'

Two of the masked figures rose and came at him. His hands, his feet were seized. The cords were wound around them, those on his wrists brutally wrenched tight. The bandage was clamped across his face.

He felt himself lifted, manhandled, bundled up. Thrust back into the closet. The door slammed shut.

Darkness. Quiet. Time passed, then he sensed the motor start, his prison vibrate and sway. The nightmare crawled back and took him over. They were on the move again.

Chapter twenty-six

'*How* much?' Vanessa demanded in a tone of outraged disbelief. '*How* much did you say?'

'Fifteen million sterling,' Tony repeated. He took out a handkerchief and wiped away the beads of sweat which had begun to prickle on his lips. They met today in the tropical hothouse at Kew Gardens.

'But who's got that kind of money?' she asked.

His shirt wilted in the stifling humidity and the heat. He felt profoundly uncomfortable. 'Yes, that was rather the reaction of the Board.'

'And *when* do they want it?'

'Friday,' he said and got her started down the path between the dense overhanging branches, headed for the distant exit.

'So what do the police *say*?' she asked. 'That superintendent who came to see us, Nicholas.'

'Negotiate. He says set up a dialogue and play for time. There's *no way* we can pay that amount. We've taken an ad in The Times tomorrow to explain. We're offering one and a half.' He wiped his brow again. He could hardly breathe. 'I've been asked by the Board to put it to you that you might like to cover the other half.'

'Me?' To his dismay she halted, wheeling on him astounded. 'Me? Half a million pounds? What on earth are you talking about?'

'Well, I'm only a messenger of course, but the Board ... Adam's holdings ... '

'I haven't the foggiest notion what those are, or where,' she told him forcefully. 'Besides they're *his*. I don't have the power of attorney, *I* can't dispose of them.'

He restarted her toward the exit. 'Friday's impossible of course,' he said. 'But we're doing all we can to raise the money.'

'Naturally. Every penny *I* have is tied up.' Vanessa said. Her white gloved hand struck at the jungle which surrounded them. 'I've had a word with the Foreign Secretary. I can't understand why *he* can't do something about this Press harassment we're subjected to. They tap our telephones. They picket in the garden and the street, ambush the staff, shout questions through the letterbox. We have to meet in places like this. It's humiliating and degrading.'

They came out of the glasshouse into the clean fresh air. Tony breathed deep. 'They're only doing their job, I suppose,' he said. 'From their point you've got to grant that it's one hell of a good story. Wonderboy tycoon turns drug smuggler and disappears. Is kidnapped and held prisoner by some revolutionary organisation. Now a ransom, demand for fifteen million pounds. It's all front page stuff. Sensational. One can understand the excitement.'

'Fuck Adam,' said Vanessa. 'I'll never forgive him for this. It's all too, too embarrassing.'

Tony agreed. 'Do you want to talk to Superintendent Nicholas?' he asked. 'Before we place the ad?'

'I don't see what that would accomplish. If they tell us to negotiate that's what we do, I suppose. But there's not a hope *I* can come up with half a million pounds. I've talked to Freddy Reynolds about this. Of course we shall do everything, absolutely everything we can to save him but we can't be just too wet and hopeless. It's not fair to Adam. They can't be allowed to get away with this. Also Freddy thinks we should demand proof that Adam is still alive.'

Chapter twenty-seven

The land yacht crept over a desolate plain of raw red rock. Nothing moved except the sun. Below the polished glare of the sky the line of the road danced and quivered in the heat.

The pylons strode across the land, huge legged and black as insects in the vast inhuman scale of things. At Hoover Dam they massed together as an army, gathering in a force of several thousand to suck power from the cateract before marching out across the desert in columns of four and six abreast, bearing out the juice.

The hull of the land yacht shuddered as they crossed the dam; its iron molecules vibrated in that roaring elemental force. On the other bank they passed a sign 'SHADE FOR PETS AT 300 YARDS', and another 'NO SERVICES FOR 200 MILES'. The constant hum of energy remained with them as they drove on, drowning out the radio when they passed beneath the power lines.

Even the prisoner within the closet sensed that ever-present drone though he had no awareness whence it came. In the limbo where he crouched was neither night or day. Time did not exist, there were no landmarks in its passage. The only punctuation to an endless monotony of present pain was the rare sound of his door being banged open and the thrust of a rubber nipple to his greedy mouth through which he sucked and sucked on the sugared milk of life, unutterably cast down by the final slurp of air.

When they next brought him out the vehicle had stopped. The blinds of the motor home were drawn. It was 4 a.m. the spirit's bleakest hour.

In the dim yellow light the same four hooded figures again confronted him. Was Jutta among that grim committee of terror and death, he wondered numbly, was Sheldon?

There was no way to know. Only that same hoarse voice addressed him from the gloom. 'Prisoner, sit! Over there!'

He crawled to where the shrouded arm was pointing. He dragged himself upon a stool.

A newspaper was thrust into his hands. 'Hold it up!' he was commanded.

He raised the page to spread across his chest. A flashbulb exploded in his face, blinded in its incandescence. A scream broke from him as he winced away.

A hand struck him across the cheek. 'Another! Open your eyes!'

A fist gripped in his hair wrenched his head up. Still shaking from the assault he fumbled to obey . . .

Another searing flash stabbed into his eyeballs, infinitely more agonising than that slap across the face.

Sightless, he tumbled from the stool. He was seized, blindfolded and bound, picked up and shoved back into the closet . . .

Chapter twenty-eight

'They are not reasonable,' Vanessa said. 'They are lunatics, they make no sense. If you're bargaining with someone you put the price *down*, not up. Eighteen million pounds - and this demand for *food*, for God's sake. Are they total bloody fools?' She banged her glass down and demanded the question of Freddy Reynolds.

They were dining at the club. Vanessa ate here now on most evenings for she found the empty house oppressive. The table where they sat was permanently reserved for them and their special guests. But it was early now, not yet 10 p.m., and the room was empty. For the moment they were alone.

'Of course they're *Arabs* holding him,' Freddy said and tasted the consistency of the spinach soufflé. 'This food distribution they've asked for to Palestinian refugees proves it quite conclusively. Impossible to deal with, Arabs, hysterical and irrational. That Saudi bill *still* hasn't been paid, you know.'

Tonight she wore a flying suit fashioned of pink, raw silk. Freddy as usual was in a striped suit and polka dotted tie. 'Bloody wogs,' he said. 'Poor old Adam, political matter now.'

'Really?' Vanessa looked up sharply, fork arrested in mid air on its journey to her mouth.

'Rather,' Freddy demolished the remainder of his soufflé. 'Aid and sustenance to stateless refugees, Foreign Office will want a say in *that*. Israelis won't be too wild about it, I imagine.'

'You think that . . . '

'What *we* think is irrelevant,' he said. 'Out of our hands. HMG moving in, their ball. Squarely in their court now, I'd say.'

153

Thoughtfully Vanessa finished her lobster cocktail. 'Poor old Adam,' she remarked. 'Wonder how *he's* coping with all of this.'

'Indeed,' Freddy agreed wholeheartedly. 'Poor old Adam. Must be absolutely bloody for him. Wish we could do more to help.' He gestured to the waiter to serve their second course.

Chapter twenty-nine

A hot wind had blown up in the night, whipping across the desert to crackle against the hull of the motor home. It penetrated the crevices to fray the nerves and flay the skin of all who rode inside with a sticky film of abrasive dust.

Not only for the prisoner incarcerated within but for all those aboard the land yacht, the fourteen days and nights of their aimless voyage had begun to blur. They stopped only to fill up with gasoline, once every two days to take on provisions. They drove in shifts, listening to the radio for the bulletins which concerned them.

Time had eroded for them all. Isolated in ceaseless movement, they believed they had been travelling for ever across this awful land where nothing lived and no birds sang.

The sand scudded over the road and across the windscreen, covering it with powder.

In the last hundred miles they had passed a single trace of man, and that his relic only. Forming from the haze a ghostly heap of litter had reared beside the road, a mountain of wrecked automobiles in the space and desolation beneath the glare of sky.

Jutta sat beside the driver, a map open on her knees. 'Ten more miles,' she said.

The rare townships they went through were identical, a strip of billboards, filling stations, supermarkets and diners which lined the highway. This place where they halted was the same.

They stopped where a picnic area was set up in a parking lot behind the diner. Gemal wrenched on the brake. The sand whipped across the empty lot like spray. He turned and looked at her.

'You tell him,' he ordered.

She saw naked hostility in his horrifying eyes, red-rimmed from lack of sleep.

'There's no risk for Sheldon,' he hissed at her. 'All that comfort and power, he gets off on that.'

She sat quite still, looking ahead. Her nerves were raw.

'Go tell him,' Gemal ordered.

She opened the door and stepped down into the storm of driven sand.

The diner was a one-level concrete building, its windows sealed. The air-conditioning chilled her as she entered the room hung with neon signs. Stools at the counter faced the mirrored display case of desserts, the day's special chalked upon a slate.

She ordered a coke and five dollars worth of quarters and took them to the pay phone. A silent couple watched from a booth wearing matched Hawaiian flowered shirts, he as thin as she was stout.

She fed in the change and dialled the international code followed by the number. Three seconds later she heard the telephone ringing in London. Sheldon picked it up at once.

She said 'Write down this number. I do not have money. You must call me back.'

The His-'n-Her couple were watching her intently, their faces without expression.

The telephone rang. She snatched it up.

'Sheldon, you have to come here,' she said.

'You're having problems?' His tone was light.

'Sheldon, you don't know what it's like,' she told him passionately, 'These are killers you've hired. They want the money and I don't know how to handle them.'

'But don't they understand . . . ' he started.

'No. They don't understand why you want to keep him. They want the ransom and to kill him and get on with what you promised. Please, you have to come.'

'Don't get hysterical,' he told her coldly. 'How can I set up anything from *there* ? How can I come? Be reasonable.'

'No one's taught *them* to be reasonable,' she said. 'They're trained terrorists. The only thing they know is how to kill people.'

He became conciliatory. 'That food condition Gemal wanted. It's been fulfilled, Lupus' company has made a distribution.'

'*Have* they?' she asked. 'There was nothing in the news and they listen all the time. All we hear is the kidnappers are asking eighteen million sterling and his corporation won't pay.'

'It's done. There were photos in the papers,' he protested.

'We don't get the papers. And that's another thing. Gemal thinks you're getting all the publicity.'

'Publicity!' His tone was scathing.

'Also I must have money,' she said. 'I have told you many times and still you do nothing.'

'Gemal has money. From New York.'

'No,' she corrected him. 'They sold none of the coke in New York.'

'Why?' His voice grew sharp. 'Why not?'

'They tried, I think. But Gemal said he was waiting for a better deal.'

'Where is it then?'

'We have it here, all of it.'

'Are they snorting it?'

'What do you think?' she asked.

'Stop them.'

'How?' she demanded, her voice rising in frustation. '*How*? You don't understand what it's like shut up in here. Gemal's crazy and he's used to running things. He rules not because he's smart but because people are scared to death of him. Fear's his thing. *I'm* frightened of him. You must come, Sheldon.'

'I'll come,' he reassured her. 'I'm seeing one of the Libyans on Friday, then I'll fly out.'

'That's not soon enough.'

He snapped 'It has to be. Get it together. They're nothing in this without us.'

'That's not how *they* see it,' she informed him. 'He wants to tell you there's another condition, a manifesto.'

'A *manifesto*? What the hell does that mean?'

'On television. It's boring out here and there's nothing about us on the news. You're having all the fun and Gemal wants in. He wants a manifesto put out on television.'

'It's crazy,' he snapped.

'It's what he wants,' she told him. 'He's ordered me to buy a movie camera here and film him reading it. He's been snorting coke and shouting and rehearsing what he's going to say all day.'

Chapter thirty

'Yes, his luck's run out on him this time, poor chap,' said Freddy Reynolds. He emptied the contents of the ice machine into a silver bucket and brought it to the coffee table. 'I feel desperately sorry for him.' he added, picking up a bottle. 'Cointreau on the rocks?'

It was after lunch and Vanessa had returned to his Eaton Square apartment overcrowded with inherited furniture he could not bring himself to sell. The cleaning woman had left the blinds drawn to protect it from the sun.

'Where was the film found?' asked Freddy. 'A bar you said?'

'A coffee shop, Superintendent Nicholas tells us. Taped underneath a table somewhere.'

'And there was nothing in it? Nothing?'

'Nothing. The film was blank when they developed it. Light had got at it, they said. They had fouled it up putting it in the can or taking it out or something.'

'Who had?'

She shrugged impatiently. 'The police, the Arabs, what difference does it make. There's no way of doing what they want, there's nothing anyone *can* transmit on television.'

'I doubt they'll believe *that*,' said Freddy, picking up his drink. 'How's Prosper taking all of this?'

She frowned. 'He was desperately upset by all that publicity about his father with another woman. It was really fearfully humiliating.'

'Don't you want him with you?' Freddy asked.

'Of course. He's coming up on Saturday, after the match. He's only just made captain of the Eleven. It's the worst possible moment for this kind of thing to happen.'

'I should think it always is,' said Freddy reaching to refill her glass. 'Particularly for Adam.'

Chapter thiry-one

A great raft of macadam had been poured down beside the road somewhere in the desert in the middle of nowhere. On it were toilets, washing facilities and concrete picnic tables with roofed shade.

The camping area could hold several hundred vehicles but as the sun dipped behind the rim of mountains and night shut down, the land yacht was the only one in place. There was no twilight; suddenly it was dark.

A fitted table and two banquettes formed the central feature of the interior. Around this table four people were now grouped. All wore their lookalike sheeted robes but were not yet cowled.

On the table a mirror had been set out, upon the mirror a tiny mountain of cocaine which Gemal was dicing into fine white dust. With a razor blade he detatched a section from the heap, divided and spread it into four long lines.

Setting a straw to his nose he bent forward and noisily sniffed one up. He passed on the mirror. The two Arabs did as he. It was slid before Jutta. After a moment's hesitation she bent and followed suit.

Reaching for the mirror Gemal scraped together the remnants of the powder. 'I say we do it,' he told them.

'But Sheldon . . . ' Jutta began again.

'Our conditions have not been met. The money has not been paid.'

'But Sheldon says . . . '

'He thinks we are fools.' Gemal's voice was harsh, adamant. 'He uses us as his servants,' He ran his finger along his gums. 'We've talked enough,' he said. 'Now we vote.'

He took his hand from his mouth and raised it. 'I say we kill him.'

Beside him Raschid followed suit at once. Boualili, who sat

opposite was smaller and younger than the others. His hand came up, his eyes upon their leader.

Gemal glanced around the table, fixing on the girl.

'So we do it,' he said and turned to the others. 'Bring him out,' he ordered.

Adam's brain was a sea of flame, seething and hot as molten fire. Disorientated and unhinged, there existed no frontier between reality and hallucination in the crazed theatre of his mind.

Recoiling from the smell, they dragged him out. He lay upon the floor and the pattern of the carpet swirled and flowed before his eyes like blood.

It was a scene from the nightmare which confronted him from the gloom. In the dim yellow light the cowled tribunal loomed above, menace and terror flavouring the air as the masked judge leaned forward to pronounce, 'Prisoner, we, The People's Court, have found you guilty . . . '

He saw the expression in the eyes behind the mask; they burned with hatred. He stared beyond the reason into blind resentment and heard the ferocity of the voice as it spelled out the sentence, ' . . . Capitalism, imperialism, exploitation and repression . . . For crimes against the Proletariat . . . DEATH'

Nothing held, nothing was of value. Back in his cell there existed no one solid thing his mind could cling to. Adam Lupus, husband, parent, darling of the business pages, had come apart. His wealth, success, respectability and esteem counted for nothing. The walls he had erected to define himself within the world had crumbled. Their solidarity, their worth, was gone.

In a dark and awful forest he had lost his way and forgotten who he was. The strings which held him together had unravelled, frayed and snapped. There was nothing he could rely upon or call his own. His wife . . . his son . . . the houses which he owned . . . their random images took form then tore away or evaporated into murk. None held, none connected, all were delusive and insubstantial as the flickering of fool's fire.

161

All that specified his life had decomposed. His psyche had fragmented. His brain was mush. Demons crowed and cackled in his skull. As a last effort he struggled to recall his name but it was gone. In the rancid darkness of his cell the shell of flesh once known as Adam Lupus broke down and wept, lifted its muzzle and howled at the surrounding night.

Chapter thirty-two

Seated on its edge, Prosper stirred the water of the swimming pool at Danton Hall with his tanned and naked foot.

'Pretty rough on Dad though,' he observed.

'It's horrendous darling,' his mother agreed, kneeling beside him wearing tennis shorts. 'Utterly ghastly.'

'So what are we supposed to do now?' the boy asked.

'But that's exactly it. The whole thing seems completely to have been taken out of our hands. What *we* want simply doesn't seem to count for anything.'

A leaf floated on the surface of the limpid water. Prosper kicked a wave toward it, failing to make it sink. 'Wonder if *he* understands that,' he said.

'Of course he does,' Vanessa was quick to reassure him. 'He knows we're doing absolutely everything we can. What *they* say though is that you can't give in to this kind of terrorist blackmail or it'll go on happening again and again and again. One must make a stand, show the swine they can't get away with it.'

'It's all very well for *them* to make a stand,' he objected. 'But what about Dad?'

'The Los Angeles police are absolutely confident they'll find them,' Vanessa said. 'They've mounted a huge search in Southern California but what they *do* need is time. They insist we continue to negotiate. That's Tony's job, of course. Even if we give in there's no guarantee they'll let Daddy go because he could identify them, you see. If we *do* pay the ransom now, in fact, it's almost certain that they'll . . . ' She paused. 'Well, kill him actually.'

'Poor old Dad,' said Prosper, kicking at the leaf. 'Not Number One now is he? No one to call up and push around

163

and tell them to fix it. Wonder how he's taking it. I wonder how he's going to get out of this one.'

'We must pray for him darling.' Vanessa answered. Fifty yards away she saw Freddy Reynolds come out of the French windows carrying two tennis racquets. He waved and strolled in the direction of the court.

'The vicar has arranged for Intercessions at the eleven o'clock service tomorrow,' she said. 'I'd like you to come with us. We must remember that we love Daddy very much and ask God to help him.'

She rose and smoothed down her white shorts. 'He needs our prayers just now,' she said 'I'll see you at tea, darling.'

Chapter thirty-three

For all those within the land yacht the voyage had become interminable. The ceaseless travelling had strained and worn away their nerves, taken them to the very limit of mental and physical exhaustion - and beyond that edge. Hysteria and madness saturated the air they breathed.

A sixth passenger in the motor home, Death, rode with them now, with all of them. Courted, solicited by every one, she had come to join them in the vehicle. An invited guest, she graced them with her presence.

The monotony of the desert slid past beyond the windows in the vacant glare. The highway unreeled ahead. They had ceased to speak and the silence grew intolerable, demanding a response. The imposition of Death's company weighed upon them all.

The land yacht had stopped. Somewhere. There was no sound of motor or from outside, no footfall, no whisper, no echo of a distant voice, no breath of air. Stifling blackness hung thick around. Silence was absolute and darkness ruled the world.

Adam's pain had left him and he was calm. In the utter quiet he heard his door click open and Death step softly to join him in the closet.

Death came close. He heard the sharp intake of her breath as she appraised his helpless body. So sharp his senses now, so finely tuned, he heard her thudding heart, the prickle of her nerves, her racing blood.

He heard her, he heard Death's gasp as she looked upon her suitor. He waited, his nerves aflame. He heard the scrape of her clothes as she loosened them. He felt something brush his lips and with infantile response he clamped his mouth around it.

Jutta crouched over him again, her hand wound in his hair,

165

drawing him up to her. Only for a moment was he repulsed, then his whole body thrilled. He strained up avid to obey.

With lewd and desperate greed he licked her hardening nipple and suckled at her breast. He was frantic for union . . .

But it was not to be. Not this time, not like that. From outside the motor home came the sound of voices and of footsteps coming close. The Arabs were returning.

Jutta abruptly pulled away. She closed the closet door and moved toward the table, buttoning up her shirt. When the others came in she was seated, listening to the radio.

He woke from deep long sleep. He felt purged, refreshed and calm. His brain was clear. Hunched sightless in the closet, somehow he knew that outside was morning.

It was 5 a.m. Parked in a grove of sparse and stunted trees, the outline of the land yacht solidified from the dark, taking shape in the pink wash of dawn which seeped into the desert sky.

So fragile is our contact with the natural world that we discount it. The first tendril of green growth and the seasons' cycle pass unremarked within a city. Who cares? Who notices? What is spring but time for a change of dress?

And Adam, a city child sequestered within his mobile prison, had been carried so very far from all it is that composes life. Locked up, isolated, deprived, he could not remember what it was. The thin note of birdsong which filtered through the walls was alien, unknown. He could not identify the sound yet it touched some abandoned place in him, touched and filled it with an ache for something he had forgotten, for some lost paradise sunk and submerged in the unremembered past of the man that he had been. He longed desperately to return.

Only the bare bones of him remained. He had been broken into parts, dehumanised, made mad. There was nothing solid left that he could state with certainty was him. Yet life remained, the primeval spark. As the flame of a candle stirring in a breath of air, it was this in Adam which trembled and flickered in response to the morning chorus in the stunted trees around the camping area.

166

There was life close to him, and it was sweet. Sunlight lay just beyond the walls.

The crystal notes of the bird's call repeated. There was a day beginning, he realised, sunshine and the dear warmth of life itself. Within inches of him it was there, within reach.

He did not fight for life. Jutta's presence lurked around him. She had almost debauched him, the smell of her scent still lingered on his skin. It was her he fought.

He was not ready. It came to him in the clear thin music of the bird's call, he was not ready. Not yet, not now. He would not give up.

So easily snuffed out, the spark of life is amazing in its resilience. It would not be extinguished. There had been no more spirit left in him, yet will and courage surged back to his exhausted body.

He had always been a fighter. All his life he had fought yet Jutta had undermined him. He had been about to melt, to yield. So promising of ecstasy and peace, the bitch had almost tumbled him.

But he would not. Only inches away freedom and life were, here. They were within reach and challenge awoke a force in him, a defiance. He would scheme and he would fight, he was fighting already, snatching advantage from the lull and working out his strategy . . .

The bird called again in the cool desert dawn, three notes ascending up the scale. He would live, he thought. He would.

Chapter thirty-four

The television picture was of the Houses of Parliament by night and the illuminated clock tower of Big Ben. 'The News at Ten' a voice announced.

The identification chords boomed out. 'Deadline for Adam Lupus' execution expires,' the same voice reported and the newsreader raised her face to camera.

'For the businessman tipped for a Knighthood in the Birthday honours,' she began, 'life altered dramatically a month ago when the police intercepted a consignment of drugs sent to him at the London headquarters of The Lupus Group, the company he built up into a multinational corporation today worth a billion pounds.

'Sought by the police, Adam Lupus' disappearance in Los Angeles was rapidly followed by news of his kidnap by a Palestinian terrorist group identifying themselves as the Black June Commando.

'Set initially at fifteen million pounds, the ransom demands posted in London escalated last week to an astonishing eighteen million plus other conditions which the Group has so far been unable to satisfy. Negotiations broke down at the weekend and, early this morning, the deadline set for Adam Lupus' execution finally expired . . . '

Tony Carvel watched the telecast alone in Lupus House. With the excuse that he was expecting a call from Los Angeles, he had left a dinner party to return here.

He went back to his own flat only rarely now. Since Adam's disappearance he had hardly quit the office; often he slept here. The task of managing a diverse and active group of companies in their operations around the globe had

168

required unremitting concentration, the work necessarily interrupted by the hours he had spent in consultation and negotiation for his Chairman's life. The text of releases and all dealings with the Press demanded his personal supervision. Concurrently with every one of these activities, constant vigilance had to be maintained upon the Board for any signs of challenge to his own authority and position in the company.

Alone, Tony watched the News seated on the sofa in that large panelled room. This was the cockpit. Here, surrounded by trained staff, by telex machines, telephones, computer consoles and all the aides to management which a modern enterprise disposes, he had come to feel most comfortable, at home, in charge.

When the item was finished Tony switched off the set. He rose and mixed himself a whisky; he had no interest in the other news.

Carrying the glass he wandered over to the desk, sat in its padded chair, swivelled it to face the picture window and surveyed from this high place all the shining nightime world of London spread out below him.

The view from here was the best in all the building, for Tony Carvel sat at his chairman's desk. He had chosen Adam's office in which to watch the News at Ten.

Shocked by her dismay, Vanessa sat rigid against the pillows. 'God!' she exclaimed. 'God! God! God!'

'One feels so helpless,' said Freddy sombrely. 'I wish one knew what to say.'

'God,' she said. 'Who writes that stuff, and the way she *read* it! Ghouls! I mean photographs of me and Prosper and then saying Adam's estate is estimated at twelve million pounds. Really!'

'Oh I don't think they meant it like that,' Freddy reassured her, reaching for the glass on the bedside table. 'Quite sympathetically done actually I thought. They hardly mentioned the drug charges and the German girl and so on.'

'Of course it's nothing like twelve,' Vanessa said. 'Nowhere *near* it. Nearer five.'

'Yes?' Freddy got up to switch off the television. 'Now, you've got to tell me exactly what you want,' he said. 'To stay here? Shall I drop you home? We'll do exactly as *you* want but I must stop in at the club for an hour or so . . . you do understand.'

'God,' said Vanessa. 'It's just unbelievable the speed things change,' She threw back the sheets and stood up to dress.

The knock upon the study door was repeated.

'Come in,' Prosper Lupus shouted, reaching to turn off the TV set.

A middle-aged man in a tweed suit edged diffidently into the room, his housemaster.

'Thought you might . . . ' he started. 'Probably want to be alone . . . '

'That's perfectly all right, sir,' Prosper said. 'Come in, sir. Coffee?'

His guest waved the invitation aside with the stem of his pipe, at the same time closing the door behind him. 'Gracious no, stops me sleeping . . . very important sleep. Doctor will give you something if you need it.' He looked at Prosper keenly. 'Want to go home tomorrow? Your mother . . . '

'Yes, perhaps,' the boy answered.

'Quite. Stay as long as you like,' the housemaster reassured him. 'Nice if you could play in the Westminster match of course. Entirely up to you though . . . '

'Thank you, sir. I'll telephone.'

'Yes, splendid.' The man sucked at his pipe, removed it from his mouth and tamped it down, his eyes upon the task. 'Dreadful business, dreadful. Bit hard to keep the stiff upper lip, I imagine. Ghastly business.'

'Dad's not dead.' Prosper told him.

The statement was so sure, so positive, it flustered the older man.

'Course not. Didn't mean . . . Just that . . . '

'Not Dad,' said Prosper.

'No, no, didn't mean . . . '

'Not a chance of it, not Dad,' he repeated. 'This is the kind of thing he's tops at. It was never money he was after, you see, it was challenge. It brought out the best in him, made him younger, keener. He *had* to win. Losses, betrayals, setbacks, they only toughened him. It's like an instinct, like drive. Dad can bounce back from anything. Even this.'

The master puffed nervously on his pipe. His eyes roamed the study, unable to meet the boy's level gaze.

'Of course, of course, still ... ' he said. 'Your mother. Ought to be with her ... needs your shoulder, someone to lean on. I've been correcting papers ... Thought you might like to come over. Drink, sleeping pill, you name it I've got what it takes as they used to say.'

The boy did not supress a smile. 'Thank you,' he said. 'There's nothing to worry about. It's quite all right. Dad's perfectly all right.'

Chapter thirty-five

The air conditioning was turned up high and it was cold in the bar. Facing Jutta was a sepia mirror, its glass shelves crowded with postcards, china ornaments, dolls, shells and a single plastic rose. Behind the single rank of reflected faces the room deepened into emptiness and shadow.

Every stool at the counter was occupied. Apart from two wizened males the place was full of women and no one here was less than sixty-five years of age. At Jutta's entry all conversation had ceased. In silence she ordered her drink, placed her call on the wall phone. In silence she had returned to her place in the dim chill room and picked up her glass, waiting for Sheldon to ring back.

'That's a real nice cardigan,' the barmaid said.

Jutta looked up. For a moment she thought the remark was addressed to her.

'My Christmas present from Julie.' It was an elderly woman beside her who answered.

'Yeah, real nice. Warm.'

'No, it's not warm,' the woman corrected her. 'You can wear it winter and summer.'

The barmaid pursed her coral lips. 'They say what keeps the cold out keeps the warm out, too,' she observed and rattled a chunky bracelet on her bony wrist. 'Know what I mean?'

The bar was one of half a dozen permanent buildings which formed the core of this settlement of a thousand people. All around caravans had been wheeled onto site to compose an instant ghetto for the retired. 'The Arabian Nights Trailer Park' a sign on the desert highway had announced somewhere between Devil's Playground and 20 Mule Team Road.

'The brain's a wonderful organ,' one of the old men said. 'Or is it an organ?'

Jutta's eyes located the speaker in the mirror as, 'You should do it,' he told the frail figure perched on the stool beside him. 'It would be a crime not to, a crime.'

Why doesn't he call back? Jutta wondered.

A woman's voice dropped into the silence. 'These kids get everything mixed up,' she complained. 'Even my own sneaking rotten kid, she gets everything mixed up.'

The display of creased faces reflected in the mirror was tanned to antique leather by the unremitting sun. A black man shuffled through dragging a can of garbage. Cigarette burns scarred the carpet. The counter was chipped and dirty. Why the hell doesn't Sheldon call? she thought.

'A crime, you should *do* it,' the man repeated, his enthusiasm undeterred though his friend had not responded. 'A crime not to when you've got it all there inside your brain. Just got to put it down.' His hands dabbed around the pockets of his polyester suit, searching for cigarettes.

'My feet wouldn't reach the pedals,' the other quavered as the telephone rang.

She slipped off her stool and ran to answer it. 'Sheldon?'

'Where are you?'

'Why didn't you call back? Why?' she subdued the hysteria rising in her voice and turned away, conscious that every one of those ancient sepia masks was watching her in the mirror. 'Why not Sheldon?'

'Great news,' he said. 'On television just now. Great.'

'I don't believe this,' she said. 'What are you *doing* to me?'

'They've fixed it,' he told her. 'An informal weekend, it's called. In the South of France. Announced on the news.'

'Sheldon . . . ' She fought her panic. 'Sheldon, you've got to get here.'

' . . . Even the place, Cap Ferrat. A villa belonging to the French President. Next month.'

'Sheldon . . . ' She breathed deeply. 'You've got to come. I can't handle it. I don't know what to do.'

'This is get down time,' he said and his voice from six thousand miles away was jubilant. 'This is it.'

She was desperate. 'They're going to execute him. Tonight,' she whispered.

The door to the bar slapped open and Gemal entered. A handsome dark complexioned man of twenty-eight, he paused, while his eyes adjusted to the dimness and a kind of tremor ran around the room as he stood there, a twitching and preening of dusty feathers, a heightening of awareness. Deliberately he moved closer to the bar and watched them flutter.

Gemal spotted her in the gloom. 'Sheldon,' she said in panic, 'Sheldon ... ' but he was already beside her and reaching for the phone.

'I'll talk to him,' he said. His movements were assured and calm. He was flying high on the stoned certainty of coke.

'You mouthfucker! Where's the money?' he demanded.

'It's on,' said Sheldon.

'The ransom ... '

'A Summit in France. It's on, don't you understand? We have a green light. We move, we do it.' His exaltation, his conviction, flowed down the line.

'The prisoner ... '

'The prisoner,' Sheldon interrupted, 'is our most precious weapon. I'll fly to France tomorrow to set up what we need.'

'You've fucked up the money,' Gemal said.

Sheldon dismissed the point. 'For money we have the coke. I'll come directly from France to join you. In one night I can place that in LA.'

'The prisoner ... ' Gemal persisted.

'The prisoner,' Sheldon told him 'is our wooden horse. We use him to get inside the city walls. A horse - and we break him, you understand. We break him so we ride him and he belongs to *us*. You follow me, Gemal?'

'No!' The Arab answered softly. 'No, *you* follow me. Go to France, *here* we do it my way. My way,' he whispered in the gloom, 'you hear me, Sheldon?'

174

Chapter thirty-six

The next time they brought Adam out it was to clean his cell.

He was too weak to do it himself. Without discussion it was Raschid who undertook the work; the others sat at table.

They had undone the bandage around his eyes and loosened his bonds. Seated propped against the wall he rubbed the circulation back into his wrists and studied his captors.

Homeless Palestinians, Sheldon had recruited them at a training camp in Libya. Three men made shrewd and hard by lifelong deprivation, united by anger and a perverted heroism, their different skills composed an operational unit. A hit squad.

For the first time they were not hooded. Now that they were going to kill him there was no more need for precautions, Adam imagined. He registered Jutta's presence amongst them though he could not bring himself to look at her. He picked out their leader – he knew the reptilian eyes from his interrogations, he recognised the swarthy face he had seen at Kennedy Airport.

Deprived so long and kept in darkness, Adam's visual sense was vividly alert. He took in every detail of his surroundings, bedding heaped in one corner, the trash can overflowing, the dirty plates piled in the sink. They lived in squalor.

Gemal dipped his fingers into the bowl before him and brought food to his mouth. He waved his hand toward the closet. 'These are not the conditions you're used to, I think?'

He tried to answer but could not. The words cracked and broke on his parched lips.

Gemal raised his glass. 'You want?' he asked.

He nodded, dumb. Gemal passed the glass to Boualili who

brought it to him. Adam's hand trembled as he grasped it, the liquid slopped on his wrist. The little Arab slid a hand behind his head and lifted the glass so that he might drink. The taste of the whisky scalded him with a burn like fire. He choked. The heat exploded in his chest and stole out into his limbs.

He reached eagerly for the glass to drink again. Boualili rocked back on his heels and stayed there watching him. In a grimy patterned shirt, white on white, he had the face of a child and body of a monkey. A thief, he could open any window, climb and squirm through the smallest aperture. A knifeman and silent killer, his expression as he regarded the prisoner reflected a mixture of curiosity and concern.

The way Adam looked would have caused anyone alarm. He was unshaven and filthy with the pallor of a corpse. His gaunt cheeks were seamed by lines of strain, his skin had broken out in sores.

Deliberately the Arab lit a cigarette, drew deep, and reached out to place it between the prisoner's lips. Adam sucked hungrily on the burn, he felt its sweet solace melt his nerves. The sudden gesture of companionship was too much for him. Gratitude overwhelmed him. Tears started to his eyes; he shook with the strength of his emotion.

'You are hungry?' Gemal asked abruptly. He gestured to Boualili who rose, filled a plate from the pot which stood upon the stove and placed it before Adam.

Unable to believe his good fortune, at once he grabbed up a handful of the food and thrust it into his mouth. The taste was delicious but the mass of it jammed in his throat. He choked, drank again, then began carefully to pick up and eat in tiny mouthfuls, grasping the plate in case anyone should try to take it away from him.

'In England,' Gemal asked, 'is it a castle that you live in?'

His mouth full, Adam's expression twisted wrily. 'A castle? Of course not.'

'But you are a millionaire?'

He scraped together another mouthful of rice and meat. 'I suppose so, yes.'

'How much money have you?'

'Well ... ' his voice was fragile from disuse. 'It doesn't

176

work like that. I really don't know.'

'How much are you paid for what you do?'

'Paid? I don't know . . . '

'Of course you know,' For a second impatience showed.

'I suppose I have . . .' he calculated quickly, 'A salary of about two hundred thousand.'

'Dollars?' Raschid asked.

'Pounds,' Adam said, and his answer was followed by a moment's silence. The sum was beyond their comprehension.

'How many workers do you employ?' Raschid demanded then.

The plate was empty. 'I don't know,' he said, conscious of how unsatisfactory it sounded.

'No?' Germal snapped. 'Tell me prisoner, how do you justify this exploitation?'

The food and alcohol had revived him; he felt a sort of strength flow back. 'It's not that,' he protested. 'Not exploitation. We provide work, jobs. Jobs for many thousands.'

'And what was your job?'

'We are a management company,' Adam explained. 'I ran it. Someone had to.'

Raschid had stopped swabbing out the closet and was watching him with the others. Only Jutta's eyes were turned away as she fiddled nervously with a pack of cigarettes.

Adam was dismayed by their questions and the impossibility of explaining himself. He realised how callous and reprehensibile his life must seem to them, how far removed he was from all that they believed.

'But what do you *want* with me?' he pleaded. 'Why me? Who are you?'

'We are Palestinians,' Gemal said. 'It is regretted that you are held like this . . . ' Again his hand waved toward the closet. 'But this is war. It is necessary.'

Adam finished the last golden droplets in his glass. 'For God's sake, I won't cause you trouble. I couldn't walk, far less escape or run.'

Abruptly Jutta rose. Picking up her cigarettes she moved to the door. 'I'm going out,' she announced.

Adam dropped his glance. He would not look at her. He

could not face her, nor she him. Gemal ignored her. 'You have children?' he asked.

'One, a boy.' Adam told him, and his son's face was very clear at that moment. 'And you,' he asked. 'You have a family?'

'My family are dead.' The voice suddenly was harsh. 'Killed by your allies the Jews.'

'Not my allies . . . ' Adam protested.

'How do you *justify* it?' the Arab demanded bitterly. 'This Zionist imperialism and privilege with your comfort built on others' misery?'

Boualili and Raschid were listening closely to Gemal's words, sharing his passionate resentment.

Adam said carefully, 'I am as much a product of my birth and circumstance as you are. We are what we become. We do not question it.'

'And here,' Gemal persisted, 'This America where you do your business, where five per cent of the world's population consumes fifty per cent of its goods . . . How is that just?'

He agreed at once. 'It's not, but . . . '

It was just the way it was. Adam had never tried to alter it; the world's wrongs had not come within his frame of reference.

The gulf between them was enormous, the vast unbridgeable chasm which divides the planet's heirs from its disaffected. Even the country which they spoke of was a different place for Adam. He had never glimpsed that America they knew, those shabby streets strewn with refuse, torn paper, smashed toys, bottles, cans, plastic debris and blown dirt scattered by the wind, those gutted hulks of cars without wheels rusting at the filthy kerb; that vandalised and ruined landscape.

'I know how you live,' Gemal accused him. 'I have seen the fascist pig swilling at the trough. But why should the poor crouch at your feet, waiting for the crumbs to fall from your table, insulted and dismissed? You eat, they starve. What is left upon your plate is thrown away.'

Adam said tiredly, 'I can't justify it.'

He understood their resentment, understood it all too well.

178

His confidence was gone. He felt ashamed; he had no pride in what he was. He was afraid of his captors but they impressed him, he almost envied them. They existed outside the role of order and all law yet their lives had a terrifying simplicity. Their way was straightforward, the enemy was clear, passion coursed in their veins. He had never felt passion for anything except his own advancement.

'But what do you want of me?' he asked. 'A ransom? Why haven't you got it?'

'Our conditions have not been met,' he heard. 'Negotiations have broken down.'

'Why?' he demanded. 'Why?'

'Because your family and your business partners do not care about you,' Raschid said. 'They do not want you back. It is they who have condemned you, not us. They do not care.'

The answer had the sting of truth. It rocked him though he did not show it.

'You are a criminal,' Gemal told him. 'A drug dealer and adulterer and they will not pay money for you. Even our manifesto they lied about. They would not transmit it.'

Adam sipped his drink. 'You frighten them,' he said. 'This ideology, this jargon, they've heard it all before. All that comes through now is the violence and terror of its message. It threatens the very basis of their lives. You have a case, of course, but it is inaudible behind the threat. It is a pity,' he added, 'that your people do it so very badly.'

Gemal went white with anger. His lips curled back. He was about to shriek . . . and then he did not. He said almost gently, 'There is only one way.'

'No,' Adam disagreed with him. 'That is not the case. Communication is a science and you flout its rules. In the States and Europe, politics are products now. They have to be packaged, packaged by experts who understand the market and the people they are selling to.'

'Go on,' Gemal said quietly. 'Tell us, Lupus.'

'I don't know,' Adam admitted, confused by the direction his thoughts were moving. 'But hate is answered only by hate, violence by violence; the reaction is automatic. You have to

179

woo hearts, not scare them . . . I don't know.'

His confidence was shot but his brain was working . . . and Adam had always possessed considerable presence. Waiters and barmen sensed it; however crowded a place he could summon attention by the slightest movement of his head. Of late immured within his cell, that psychic gift had stood him in poor stead. It was a skill which could not operate in solitude or in the dark, but it was working now.

People had always been attracted to Adam. The force of intelligence and will which came off him drew them, as to a light. And, for all their alienation from the world, Gemal and the arabs were not insensible to its radiance.

His kidnappers shared a state not so different from his own, shared the same capsule of the land yacht travelling through a hostile world where fear and boredom ruled hand in hand, shared its discomforts and its isolation. For the first time they treated him as a human being. He became a person to them.

That night Adam won his first precarious concession. At the rear of the motor home and halfway up the wall was a bunk which pulled down. It formed an attic space, low roofed and windowless, but it measured eight feet long by four feet wide. A man could lie flat and stretch out in it. For someone whose cell had been an upright closet it was a place of the utmost luxury and the most significant improvement in his life. And, that night, Adam slept in it.

Chapter thirty-seven

A prisoner's world is rigorously contained. His life is measured out in tiny details; in the time which followed, Adam became intensely aware of every one.

The highlight of each day was when his cords were loosed and, under supervision, he was allowed to wash and shave.

The cold water cleansed and renewed him. To stand under the tiny shower was a voluptuous delight. It became an essential ritual whose performance restored him to the world of men. He was haunted by the fear that the concession might be snatched away.

In time Adam experienced other major improvements to his condition. His hands and feet were still secured, yet he could stretch out upon his bunk; he could change position. The bonds which held him there were largely symbolic.

He was properly fed now. He shared his captors' diet. Poor though it was, his pleasure was greater than in all the five star meals he had ever eaten.

Also in this new regime was human contact and conversation. For an hour in the evenings he was taken down and permitted to join his kidnappers at table.

He was an object of curiosity and wonder to them, an entertainment, though frequently he was insulted and reviled. They resented him - less for what he was, which they took for granted now, but rather because of the inconvenience and discomfort which his captivity imposed upon them. Gemal's attitude to forward him was mercurial, the instability of his mood exaggerated by cocaine. He could shift in seconds from familiarity to raw hostility and rage.

Jutta was never present during these periods of conversation. Always she found excuse to absent herself on whatever desert site it was where they had halted for the night. He was grateful for her absences. If she had stayed all his resolution and control would have come apart. He could not bring himself to speak while she was there or even look at her. She, too, appeared equally troubled by their encounters and cut them short. She never addressed a word to him.

Adam's greatest enemy was boredom. Twenty-three hours of twenty-four he passed alone within his curtained space. A transistor radio tuned to an all music station played constantly by his head, isolating him from the life and talk within the motor home by its screen of noise.

Boredom and fear were ever present. Always there was the threat that they would kill him, but routine composed his day. Routine enabled him to survive it.

He found himself looking forward to his evening period of conversation. 'Children's Hour', he termed it to himself, for to talk to them was like dealing with unpredictable and dangerous infants in a nursery which Gemal dominated with all the authority of a capricious tyrant.

But he was grateful for this daily necessity to talk and negotiate with them, profoundly grateful. It saved him from his greatest fear of all; if he were returned to the closet he knew that he would not be able to endure it.

He gained experience of the men who held him. Boualili, the child-faced thief who brought his meals was the most gentle, almost feminine in the softness of his touch. He seldom spoke and passed his evenings endlessly stripping down and reassembling his gun while listening bright-eyed to everything that was going on.

Raschid, dressed in plastic sandals and blue trousers which daily grew more soiled and shapeless, was technician to the group. An expert in binary explosives, he boasted once of how he had blown up an ambassador's car. 'The largest piece to come down was a foot long. It was just beautiful,' he said.

And Gemal. He was the dominant and scary force in 'Children's Hour'. At times his nerves ran ragged with claustrophobia and tension. Adam would be exposed then to the essential ferocity of his captors, that core of envy, hate and anger which made them what they were. Impregnable to argument or reason, their fury was a sort of madness. At any moment they might flip over the top and shoot him on a whim.

But other days were different. Gemal would be rational and articulate and Adam could negotiate with him.

He came to know the man he dealt with. Not fully, not in depth, but he knew what made him. An essential element of Adam's success had lain in his assessment of those he opposed or who might work for him. He recognised a part of Gemal, recognised it instinctively.

He was a man unencumbered by guilt or sympathy. A capacity for ruthlessness fused with intelligence and imagination and the sheer terror he could inspire, rendered him formidable as a leader. He had the singlemindedness, the dedication of a religious zealot. He burned with energy. In the confinement of the motor home he was never still. Restlessness and dissatisfaction lay behind the habitual fury of his expression, its twitch informed his every movement.

This was the man whom Adam bargained with. All Adam's skills were focused on Gemal and 'Children's Hour'. This was the most important deal he had ever been involved in, the most critical. He was negotiating for his life.

Chapter thirty-eight

In Zurich, Dr Liebl was always at his desk at Credit Suisse by 8.30 a.m. There was nothing unusual about this, in Switzerland it is normal business practice.

His small private office was neatly, meticulously arranged. There was no sign here of the panelled elegance and discreet opulence of the bank's conference rooms where the investment managers met their clients. This was a place of work, functional, stark. All papers and documentation were filed away in metal cabinets. The desk top was bare of everything except a computer console and two telephones. At 8.35 a.m. one of these began to ring.

Dr Liebl picked it up. 'Ja?'

'Mr Adam Lupus on the line,' his secretary announced.

Dr Liebl was fully aware of his caller's recent history, as indeed anybody who read newspapers in the western world could not fail to be, for, until ten days ago, the news had dominated the front pages. Since then, the story had hardly featured for the simple reason that its principal character was considered to be dead.

'Good morning, Mr Lupus,' said Dr Liebl, and not a hint of emotion or curiosity showed in his voice. He was professional from the toes of his sensible Swiss shoes to the tips of his short finger nails.

'Dr Liebl?' the caller asked.

'Indeed, Mr Lupus. What can I do for you?'

'I need to liberate some funds.'

'Of course,' said the banker. 'What do you wish to sell?'

'I'd better leave the choice to you. I have not been studying the markets.' The speaker made a short sharp noise which sounded like a laugh. 'Of late I've been rather out of touch.'

'Of course I shall be pleased to attend to that on your behalf. What amount do you wish to liquidify and when?'

'For the moment 60,000 dollars,' Adam said. 'As soon as possible.'

'Of course . . . ' Dr Liebl's fingers were already tapping for a record of Adam's holdings on the computer. He was studying the screen. 'The easiest will be to dispose of bullion.'

'How long will that take?' Adam asked from a public telephone booth in Tucson, Arizona with Gemal's gun resting loosely against his belly.

'I shall have this clear to you at noon,' the banker told him. 'Do you wish to give me your instructions on the funds?'

'They are these,' said Adam and studied the grimy scrap of paper in his hand. '£10,304 to the London *Times*, $18,770 to the *New York Times* and $15,233 to the *Los Angeles Times*. The money to be telexed as soon as possible.'

'No problem,' the banker reassured him. 'How should I reference these transfers?'

'With my name,' said Adam. 'They will know what they are for.'

'Of course,' said Dr Liebl and rang off. Picking up his other telephone he issued the necessary instructions within the bank.

When he replaced the receiver Dr Liebl made no further calls which related to Adam Lupus and his affairs. He did not telephone his client's family or company in London, nor did he telephone the police. The job he had been asked to do was done. The rest of it was not his business.

The first that Tony Carvel heard of it was three hours later, London time.

He took the call from Ernest Chapman in Adam's office in which Tony was now installed. With two secretaries and all other necessary equipment in its annexe it was more convenient than his own.

'I thought now was the time to remind you that you owe me a good turn,' said Chapman, a financial journalist well known to him.

'Indeed we do, Ernie. As I told you we were all very happy

185

with that piece you did. Sensitive and sympathetic.'

'And reassuring, no? I noticed your share price nudged up a shade.'

'And reassuring,' Tony agreed. 'How can we help you?'

'Not we, old boy,' said the journalist. 'You.'

'Of course. But how?'

'I hoped you might give me an exclusive.'

'Willingly, but aren't you a bit late? There's been an awful lot done on Adam.'

'Well, in my trade,' Chapman told him cheerfully, 'being alive is what we call a new angle. Are you free for lunch?'

It was a moment before Tony answered. 'It would suit me better to chat about it over a drink tonight, in fact.'

'Have to be earlier than that. I want this for tomorrow. How did you manage to keep it so quiet?' he asked. 'Full page ads in *The Times* and two dailies in the States! What is that costing you in real money?'

'Well if *we're* not, who *is* paying for them?' Vanessa asked.

'I've no idea,' Tony told her. '*The Times* received a transfer from Switzerland shortly after they got the ads. I spoke to the editor.'

What do the ads say?'

'I have their texts here. There's a statement by Adam that he's alive and in good health . . .'

'Alive!' She interrupted, startled and incredulous.

'That's what it says,'

'My God. I must call Prosper, he always believed it. What amazing news. What else?'

'"I'm pretty desperate to be free",' Tony read, '"But I'm being well treated and the food is good. I have books to read and adequate living facilities with a shower. It's only fair to say that my treatment has been very good indeed."'

'God, it's unbelievable. Any more?' she asked.

'Not from him. The rest of it's a manfesto from the Black June Commando.'

'What's that about?'

'Well . . . ' Tony bent forward to the sheets of typescript. 'It talks about the West Bank and the Palestinian homeland . . .

about greed and Zionism ... the power of multinational corporations ... It's the usual sort of stuff, but ... ' He paused.

'But what?'

'But it's rather well-written. Quite persuasively argued in fact. There's an apology for the methods used by "The revolutionaries" who "stand in solidarity with the poor peoples of the world" ... their methods are justified and legitimate ... they expected no personal profit from Adam's ransom, it says, then goes on to accuse us – quite savagely – of hypocrisy and deceit and condemns us for not paying it.'

'But ... ' she began.

'Of course,' Tony said, cutting her short. 'Of course it's unreasonable.'

'What are you trying to tell me?' Vanessa asked. 'I can hear it in your voice.'

'Well ... it's an offensive document, but the fact is it's well argued and very well-written. Quite unlike the earlier communiqués we've had from them.'

'Oh my God,' Vanessa said. She looked for an ashtray to extinguish her cigarette but could not see one. 'You mean ...?'

'Yes,' Tony answered. 'I recognise his style. Fortunately I don't think the papers will be able to do the same – yet. They don't know him as well as we do but it's not exactly a *help* to a public company that its Chairman should be assisting terrorists in drafting their revolutionary manifestos. I don't think it would exactly make the stock go up in value should it become known.'

'God, no!' Vanessa said as the cigarette scorched her fingers. 'How can he *do* this to us?' she demanded. She looked round once more for an ashtray, then dropped the burning end onto the carpet and ground it beneath her heel. 'How *can* he?'

The English newspapers arrive in the South of France on the daily British Airways flight which lands at Nice at twelve noon.

The editions reach local newsstands in the early afternoon

but it was 4 p.m. when Sheldon picked up a copy of *The Times* in Antibes and came upon the manifesto of The Black June Commando which occupied the whole of page five.

He had been on the Coast for three days, and when he bought the paper he had already completed his business there which was to charter a 60-foot yacht for one week, the period of hire to start in one week's time and coincide with the Summit Weekend to be hosted by the French President on Cap Ferrat.

Sheldon had not been idle in the south. Though the summer weather had been excellent he had had no time to sunbathe. He had stayed at the Voile d'Or, the only good hotel on Cap Ferrat and, apart from two visits to Antibes to arrange the yacht, he had spent the time in the guise of an ardent American tourist and photographer.

There was as yet no security force around La Fiorentina, the villa where the Summit Weekend was announced to take place. Protection of the palatial house – at that moment empty – was restricted to a middle-aged guardian plus two ferocious Alsatians and his son.

The first day Sheldon passed with his camera on the rocky shore and the two adjacent beaches to the house. The next morning he donned a bathing suit, rented a pedalo and examined the place with binoculars and telephoto lens from the sea. That afternoon he costumed himself again as the camera-slung crass American – a role as an actor he excelled in – and called upon the guardian of La Fiorentina.

He was already familiar to the man from his ostentatious photographic activities in the environs. To enter the grounds of the villa and continue his studies was achieved by a simple bribe. The guardian found a banknote crumpled into his hand with fulsome but inarticulate goodwill. On glancing down he saw to his astonishment that this fool in a cabana suit had misunderstood the local currency and pressed upon him a note of 500 francs, more than $100.

The banknote disappeared with swift contempt. The dogs were called in and the crass American received grudging permission to enter and photograph the gardens of La Fiorentina.

When Sheldon picked up *The Times* and settled down on a café terrace in Antibes to relax with a drink and catch up with the news, he had just finalised and paid for his charter of the yacht. The negotiations had not been entirely satisfactory for, though he had obtained the boat, he had failed to convince the owner that he and his guests were competent to run it without help. The skipper had insisted that he must accompany them and only agreed to forego his normal crew on assurance that Sheldon's friends were experienced yachtsmen, and that the entire charter was paid up immediately in cash.

This Sheldon had reluctantly done. The transaction left him remarkably short of funds. His entire liquid fortune now amounted to less than $4000. The rest of Sheldon's substance was tied up in one and half kilos of ninety-eight per cent pure and a kidnap hostage. These unusual assets were both of them aboard a travelling motor home in California.

Sitting on the café terrace in the afternoon sunshine Sheldon opened his copy of *The Times*. The manifesto was a rude, unpleasant shock. How the advertisement had been paid for and exactly what had occured to make it possible he could not fathom. One thing was clear though, he thought as his eyes scanned the text, and that was that the situation out there had got totally out of hand. Control of the motor home had gone from his grasp. Also it struck Sheldon with painful clarity that he was a long way from his money.

He stood up abruptly, moved to the bar, and asked to use the telephone. After two failed attempts he managed to get through to Air France and someone in Reservations who spoke English.

When the direct flight to San Francisco took off from Nice airport at ten o'clock that night Sheldon was aboard it, travelling economy class on a one way ticket.

He was a general whose final battle plan was perfectly prepared. Everything was ready for attack and victory, except two elements that were missing. His army and his cash.

For Sheldon it was a sleepless flight.

Chapter thirty-nine

For those in the motor home another day was ending. Adam had only recently been returned to his bunk, his hands and feet secured and the curtains drawn to close him off within his cell.

The land yacht had logged over 4,000 miles in its desert odyssey, a vast loop across the states of Nevada, Arizona and Utah. Now it was moving west again across a treeless terrain of rock and scrub.

The land was flat and featureless, bounded by a distant line of ragged mountains. By the road reared the tortured scarecrow shapes of huge cacti-like spectral figures skew-limbed and broken-armed, flayed by the desert wind.

The interior of the motor home was a putrid sty whose, atmosphere stank of sweat and decaying food, for the air-conditioner was not working. The Arabs were careless of their surroundings and possessions. If something broke they made no attempt to repair it but let it lie, to be thrown away or not.

Since the publication of their manifesto their attitude toward Adam had softened remarkably. At times they seemed to accept him as an equal who shared their discomfort. For much of today he had ridden with them at the table while Jutta drove. From where he had sat he could see no more than the fall of her hair and outline of her head silhouetted against the windscreen in a frame of glaring sky. He was glad not to have to look her in the face. The emotions he felt for her were ambivalent and fierce; the sight of her disturbed him profoundly.

Now as he lay in his bunk and sweated in the heat, the drone of the engine formed a background to his thoughts of her, along with the insistent pop music of the transistor radio.

190

Today, however, its volume was lower than usual and he remained aware of movement and desultory conversation.

He identified the click of metal as Raschid stripped down, cleaned and reassembled his pistol in the endlesss and obsessional activity which was his only relaxation. When the vehicle stopped for several minutes he knew what was happening. They were changing drivers. He heard the slap of the door as they went outside to relieve themselves and stretch their legs. He heard them come back and Boualili move into the driving seat and start up the motor while the curtains rattled as Jutta climbed into the bunk below Adam's for her spell of rest.

He heard no more conversation in the vehicle for Raschid had also retired to his bunk directly above the driving compartment.

Only Gemal remained at the table where he poured himself the last drops of whisky which remained in the bottle and lit a cigarette. After a few moments he pulled toward him the package of cocaine. Unwrapping it, he spooned out a small pile upon the mirror which remained a constant item among the litter on the table . . .

For a long time Adam's ears distinguished nothing as the motor home droned onward at a steady fifty mph toward the setting sun. Then he heard Gemal's harsh snort as he sniffed up a line, a pause, then the strike of a match as he lit a cigarette. He heard him rise from the table, the sound of his footsteps as he approached. Adam closed his eyes and pretended sleep.

But it was not he whom Gemal was visiting. Adam heard the rattle of the plastic slide as the curtain below was slipped open. He heard the creak of the bunk as Gemal entered the compartment. He heard Jutta's startled exclamation as she woke from sleep and the mutter of the Arab's voice.

Adam tensed as he listened to the noises from below. The meaning of them was too plain to misinterpret. He could distinguish nothing that was said but he burned with jealousy and resentment.

Jutta's voice rose in fear or anger. There was the sound of a blow, a cry followed by a confused scuffling from below

191

and thuds against the wall. The noises were growing louder and more frantic when Adam sensed that the vehicle they rode in was slowing as Boualili applied the brakes, unaware of what was going on behind him. The automatic box shifted to low gear as the land yacht turned off the highway into the neon forecourt of a filling station with its row of pumps.

Boualili clamped on the handbrake, wiped his palms upon his shirt and stretched. Edging between the seats he opened the door and stepped down and out, letting it swing wide behind him.

A boy of about seventeen in overalls and yellow baseball cap came out of the office and hurried toward him with a smile.

'Fill her up,' Boualili ordered.

'Sure thing,' the boy said and Adam stiffened as he over-heard the words. Normally he was gagged when they stopped for fuel and the door was always closed. But on this occasion they had grown tired or forgetful and only Boualili, the least swift of mind and least effective, was on duty. If he cried out, whoever was there certainly would hear him and come to investigate. Or would they? Who was out there? Most likely just one man, and even if he heard Adam's call for help what would he do, what *could* he do alone with four armed terrorists in some isolated filling station in the middle of nowhere?

Adam stifled his shout while, outside, the boy moved toward the pump, passing the vehicle's open door and the reeking gust of torrid air which poured out.

His eyes widened in amazement. 'Man,' he said. 'Sure is hot as hell in there. You could die there, man.'

Boualili nodded. 'Conditioner no work,' he said.

'Yeah? Them things is always shorting. I'll fix it for you.' He turned and put his foot on the metal step which led to the interior.

Raschid was asleep, but the exchange was clearly audible to the others in the motor home. They heard the boy's words. The felt his weight upon the step as he came to enter.

Gemal tore back the bunk's curtain and leaped out.

The boy stopped short as he entered the vehicle. For

someone unused to the atmosphere it was akin to entering a foul and stinking furnace. So appalled was he by the filth, disorder, stench and the apparition of a near naked man bounding at him from the gloom that he stepped back, missed his footing and almost fell as he stumbled down onto the concrete.

But, even as Gemal moved, so had Jutta. Adam's curtain flapped open. As the boy came through the door she was in the bunk with him, her gun in hand.

'Get out of here,' Gemal shouted. 'Fill her up. Do what you're told.'

Quite slowly the boy backed toward the pump, unhitched the nozzle and unscrewed the petrol cap. His glance flicked toward the doorway, met Gemal's hot and angry gaze then dropped to the task he was engaged upon.

Her shirt ripped open in the struggle, Jutta lay tensely upon Adam, the pistol thrust beneath his chin. Their faces were inches apart. They lay absolutely still, looking full into each other's eyes.

The boy said nothing as he filled the tank, but visibly, a slow puzzlement and dissatisfaction spread across his open face. In silence he completed his job, took money from Boualili and gave change.

Grabbing it from his hand, quick as an agile monkey the little Arab sprang up the steps and slammed the door. He jumped into the driving seat and started up.

The bulky vehicle jerked away in a squeal of tyres, accelerating down the interstate highway which disappeared into the settling dusk. For a long time the boy remained standing where he was, staring after it thoughtfully and wiping his fingers on a rag.

Inside, Jutta prised herself off Adam, lowering the gun. Sliding across him she swung her legs over the side and dropped from sight. The curtains swayed back into place. He was alone, shocked to discover that he was hard.

Bearing its inhabitants, the land yacht rushed onward down the long straight road. The sun had set and they travelled beneath a black and looming sky, under a cloud the colour of a bruise into a foreboding mouth of darkness.

193

It was 3 a.m. when they had the accident.

This was the dogwatch of the night and Raschid had replaced Boualili as driver. Beyond the windscreen the country was the same, flat and desolate and ghostly in the moonlight. The straight, empty road flowed into his headlights as he straddled its centre and the white line unwound hypnotically between his wheels. He blinked his eyes to clear them. He had been driving for over four hours. The others were all asleep.

Normally they never travelled at night. There had been a weary monotony in their unvarying routine and a boring sameness to all their days - but this one was different. They were headed for their destination.

Raschid blinked again. He yawned and felt for his packet of cigarettes.

The Yamaha 1000 at first was no more than a prick of light rising dead ahead from the fringe of night. Initially no bigger than a star, it strengthened till it became a beacon.

The Arab groped beside his seat for cigarettes. He found the packet and felt it for the two which remained inside. In practised blindness his fingernail slit the foil; he fumbled out a smoke and raised it to his mouth. His hand dropped and resumed searching for a lighter . . .

The nightrider crouched over his bike, burning up the road between them. His headlamp swelled in size and power as he hurtled toward the land yacht.

Feeling for a light, Raschid had driven so many endless miles. His eyes were gritty, his mouth stale, his muscles ached with weariness. One hand upon the wheel he started to haul over toward the verge to give room.

At an impact of 140 mph the Yamaha smacked into the offside fender of the motor home.

It felt as though the vehicle had been hit by an explosive shell. The noise was extraordinary. All aboard were wrenched awake to feel the place they lay in cant at a crazy angle and slide sideways down the road. It skidded up onto the verge, spun, bumped back and swaying, came to rest.

After a stunned moment of silence the inhabitants grabbed for their clothes and tumbled out.

194

There was no sign of anything behind them. The road gleamed empty below the moon. Silence lay across the world.

The wing of the motor home was brutally stove in. Its hull was split by a long and ragged gash; the bike had struck and cartwheeled down the side, opening it up like a tin can. On impact the rider had lifted from his seat, his body straightening as it rose, his head aimed like a torpedo to smash into the side pillar of the windscreen, ricochet, bounce into the road thirty yards beyond and slide.

The little group stood shocked and irresolute beside the land yacht. 'We have to find him' Jutta said at last.

She set off. They followed in a group, tramping down the road, fearful of what they would discover. For yards they found no sign of him then they came upon a long smear of pinkish mush spread along the highway in a sticky trail. It led off toward the verge and a shapeless figure huddled in the sand, his leathers ripped and tattered and half his head rubbed away and the brain exposed like something on a butcher's slab.

They stood around the corpse unable to think or act, a tableau of four figures in the silence bathed by the eerie wash of moonlight, aimless, disconnected and afraid. It had been so swift and arbitrary, the way this unknown man had been pasted across the road. The suddenness of it dazed them.

A sudden rattle startled them and broke the quiet. Raschid was shaking uncontrollably, his teeth chattering with shock, a high keening moan escaping from his mouth. Gemal moved then. He stepped forward and struck him sharply across the face. The noise ceased as abruptly as it had begun.

'We must bury him,' Gemal said. The voice was dry and distant. 'They will find him. We can't leave him here.'

Wreckage of the motorbike strewed the verge. Its shattered hulk lay embedded in the sand. Gemal kicked sand over it and then they dragged the leaking body into the desert, laid it down and set to scrape a shallow grave, clawing dirt out with their hands.

Adam lay within the ruined motor home, secured and cut off behind his curtain with no idea of what was going on outside. Rudely woken, his mind churned with speculation.

In the distance Gemal saw the headlights of an approaching car. They lay flat until the automobile had passed. Fifty yards beyond the motor home its brake lights flared on as it slowed. Gemal felt for his gun and calculated what he would do.

But the car did not stop. At once, in a shriek of rubber it accelerated away. This was just too desolate a place to halt for a lightless vehicle slewed across the verge. The silence and lack of movement presaged only terror and the unknown.

The men and girl were panting like dogs as they crouched and scrabbled away the dirt. Their breath came short and harsh and their eyes stung with sweat. They worked fast, filled with a desperate hurry to be done with it and gone.

At last they scraped out a shallow trough. Gemal rolled the body in. It flopped into the hole, settling and spreading as it took its contours from the earth. They gathered rocks and piled them over it, and kicked back the sand.

They moved off at once. Their pace quickened. Boualili began to run. The others hurried after but they were still twenty paces behind when he entered the motor home.

Gemal urged Raschid up the step. Jutta followed and was about to close the door when the others' absolute immobility caused her to glance round.

They had left the darkened vehicle so precipitately they had not registered the extent of damage which the accident had caused within.

The entire side of the motor home was sliced open. Night showed through the rent which split its hull. The banquettes and table sagged loose, ripped from the fixtures in the wall. The once crowded table top was bare and angled down. Everything that had stood upon it had whirled out through the gap.

Gemal let out a sharp cry, a gasp of grief and pain. He spun about and pushed past them to the door. He leapt down and started to run back down the road.

Jutta did not follow him at once. Coming so soon after the accident, it was a moment before the sheer enormity and implication of the disaster penetrated her brain. Then she and Boualili moved as one as they ran after him.

196

The glasses and crockery which had cascaded from the moving vehicle had shattered into fragments as they hit. The newspapers had blown off to the side, but the plastic satchel of cocaine had struck and burst and flung its contents in a ten yard swathe. The white powder was spread into the sand and grit which formed the surface of the road.

Gemal moaned. Dropping to his knees he dabbed his fingerstips on the rough surface, raised them to his lips and thrust them up his nose. Even as they watched, the dry desert breeze whirled away the residue from the cracks and crannies of the macadam.

In a single moment nearly a kilo and a half of coke at a street value of $150,000 had been blown away. The loss was so devastating that the little group lost for a while even the will to move. They could hardly speak. Nearly an hour passed before they gathered themselves to lever away the shattered wing and try the motor to discover it still worked.

The sagging hull creaked and grated as Gemal eased the engine cautiously into gear and inched off. The wind whistled through the broken side. The structure threatened to tear apart.

At a grinding thirty mph the motor home crept away from the wreckage of their fortune toward its final destination.

It had not gone from sight before the coyotes closed in upon that other thing they left behind and started to dig up the corpse. A few hours later in the light of dawn the black winged birds of carrion came flapping in for the remnants of the feast.

Chapter forty

The sun rose behind the slow moving home to illuminate the ancient slopes of hills, sprawling rounded and bare like a woman sleeping. Coming toward Bakersfield the desert yielded to yellow grass beside the road and sparse fields cropped by cattle. They saw the plume of smoke rising from a distant asphalt factory. The hillside behind was scarred by strip mining. As the morning advanced the awful emptiness they had lived in was left behind and the country grew more human.

Palpitating and complaining at a speed of twenty-five mph the motor home toiled up into the hills and lipped the crest. All at once the view was different. The enormous coastal plain stretched away from them to the limit of the morning. Below was black earth and fertile farmland dotted with homesteads, vines and orange trees. In the distance where the land merged into the sky the horizon was blurred with smog.

They were back in the world of men. A light plane was spraying fields, flying beneath the powerlines and pivoting upon one wingtip to turn around. The pylons had gathered here in strength to serve their human masters with the energy they required. There were thousands of them sprouting together in a steel forest with undergrowth of condensers and tracery of metal filaments for leaves.

It was 10 a.m. and the Highway Patrol car cruised the arrow-straight desert road at seventy mph, its windows sealed against the heat. Shaded by dark glasses the driver's eyes scanned the featureless corridor he knew so well; this was his beat.

Each night yielded its crop of wrecks, their cause

198

invariably the same. A man did not need to be drunk or even sleepy to fall victim to the dulling sameness of the route luring him to look inward while his speeding car edged imperceptibly closer to the sandy verge which lay in wait to trap his wheels, somersault him into the desert and snuff him out.

But the State Trooper had found no accidents since he had come on duty two hours before. He had encountered no incident of any kind and no traffic.

It was the birds that told him what to expect. It was always the birds. A mile ahead a whole flock of them turned slack-winged in the sky, wheeling endlessly around the same patch of ground.

He slowed, glancing beside him to check the First Aid box was in place.

The State Trooper braked and brought the patrol car to a halt beneath the cloud of carrion. They showed no fear when he stepped out, swooping low above his head as he squatted to examine the road. The skid marks and dried trail of blood and brains, now thick with insects, told their story. He did not linger but walked that smear till it reached the verge where the sand was trampled and marked by a smooth track as if something had been dragged from there into the mesquite.

Gorged on food, the dense crowd of carrion flapped away heavily as he came near. Their shining feathered pall had rippled and shimmered with the twitch of beaks and what was revealed below, as the covering dispersed, did not nauseate the State Trooper as it would another man. He was used, too used, to the sight of this gory dismembered skeleton pecked out of flesh.

He felt in the blood-caked wreckage of its clothes for the wallet, then walked around its scattered bones, examining the ground. In places he dropped to his knees to study the sand more closely, though he never touched for fear he would disturb the detail of those human footprints mixed in with the coyotes'. Four people, he calculated, and one of them a woman. Four – apart from the victim.

The State Trooper stood, dusted himself down, and trudged back to the patrol car. He did not hurry for the air temperature was 110° and a few minutes made no difference now. There was no wind to fudge the prints before a car could come from Bakersfield with the expert to preserve the marks in plaster. The size and weight of those who had been here then could be determined. The colour of their vehicle and its type would be reconstructed from the scraps of wreckage which lined the highway.

It was unlikely that those people went far in the time the State Trooper took to plod back to his car. It was unlikely, he thought, that they could travel either far or fast in a vehicle which must be badly damaged.

Thankfully he stepped into the patrol car and savoured the blessed cool of its interior. He slammed the door and reached for his radio microphone to report manslaughter and a hit-and-run.

The ruined land yacht clanked on into the day through a lush country where settlements grew few, at noon faltering up the Temblor Range past the township of McKittrick, one gas station, one hotel, one post office, one store, two ruined shacks and all around upon the slopes the dipping bills of oil pumps like prehistoric birds pecking in slow motion at the earth. A sign: NO SERVICES FOR 75 MILES.

The sun lowered from its meridian and slanted into their eyes as a haze settled upon low hills of wheat with not a house in sight but silos, oilpumps, pylons, birds and rabbits. The radiator leaking now and steaming, they lumbered through fold after fold of hills, coming down toward the sea.

They ground through the last curve and the ocean was revealed. Impossibly blue, the Pacific spread to the horizon. Their weary spirits lifted as they looked upon it. Even Adam immured within his bunk sensed that change of mood as, for a moment, all again seemed possible.

They joined the coastal highway and turned north. To their right was rich pasture and bold hills drawn against the sky, their shadows lengthening; on the left, dunes and surf and fishing boats riding on the ocean. The green land sloped gently to the beach and the warm sea came boiling in.

They pressed on through forest of pine and eucalyptus,

past dark sand beaches spread with tangled skeins of kelp, under the drooping shade of trees drowsy and aromatic in the thickening dusk.

Their wrecked, steaming vehicle staggered by unremarked – or at least unquestioned – though there was traffic here. The road carried automobiles, campers and gaudy customised vans with outsize tyres and personal licence plates. There was a feel of holiday. The sea's white fangs gnawed at the rocks and hang-gliders soared from the mountain in the last flight of evening. Surfers bobbed off the beaches in the setting sun, waiting for the perfect wave.

This was Big Sur, the place where they were headed. The place where Sheldon awaited them.

Chapter forty-one

Adam woke to an unfamiliar ceiling. His hands and feet were tied but he was no longer in the motor home. There was space around him.

He lay in a large and airy room, furnished in stripped pine. The blinds were drawn but morning sunlight gleamed behind them. There was the sound of birds and, beyond, the crash and rustle of the sea. The air was cool and fresh.

The land yacht had reached its destination but Adam had been blindfolded when he had been brought here the night before. He had been aware of conversation outside the vehicle and voices raised in altercation. Then Boualili had tied a bandage around his eyes and he had been taken out. It had been done quite gently. Hands had grasped his elbows, he had been helped solicitously on his stumbling walk here. He had heard the creak of a screen door, felt a wooden floor beneath his feet and sensed the silent dimensions of a house around him. He had been assisted to a bed and laid upon it. The blindfold had been removed. Boualili brought him milk to drink. Exhausted, he had slept.

He woke to a new world. He, together with his captors, had grown so weary of the stifling capsule they had inhabited; the frenzy of that claustrophobia at times had made them mad. Now, despite his bonds, the bed he lay in afforded Adam the keenest satisfaction. This was a proper room, carpeted and well-appointed, graced by the sound of the sea and freshness of the air.

Blindfolded on arrival, he had not identified the hands which led him here. The move had been effected in total quiet, but, though no words had been exchanged, he knew that Sheldon had stood among that group. He had smelled his enemy. He had sensed him to be near.

It had taken strength of will, but he maintained his silence and precarious dignity. Adam smiled wryly now, recalling that once he had been described as a man who used silence well.

He heard footsteps approach his door. As the lock turned, his heart jumped in expectation, but it was Boualili who entered, carrying a tray, followed by Gemal.

Both looked different. They were shaved and wore clean clothes.

Boualili busied himself untying Adam's wrists. He fetched cushions and set them behind his back so that he could sit up. It was done with a nurse's care.

'Today you have real coffee,' Gemal announced.

Adam had smelled it the instant they came into the room. His juices flowed as the tray was laid upon his lap, cornflakes, toast and scrambled eggs.

'Thank you,' he said, profoundly grateful. 'Can you undo my feet?'

'I'm sorry that is not possible,' Gemal told him. He moved to the window and edged aside a blind to look out. 'I'm sorry but for the moment your liberties must be restricted.'

Adam took up his spoon and ate. For a while sheer enjoyment of the food drowned out all other consideration. Gemal watched him thoughtfully. 'It is regretted,' he said, 'the way you have been kept. For us, too, these conditions have not been pleasant.'

'Can I have a bath?' he asked.

Gemal nodded. 'I can permit that.'

Boualili untied his legs and helped him up. He staggered as he crossed the room, leaning heavily on the little man for his muscles were weak with disuse.

He almost wept with pleasure as he eased himself into the water. He saw Gemal staring at his thighs and looked down at the sores which marked his pallid flesh.

'We shall get you medicines,' Gemal assured him.

The blissful heat soaked away the pain and stiffness from his body. The two Arabs watched while he soaped himself and luxuriated in the water.

'What happens now?' he asked at last, knowing the answer.

'You will talk to Sheldon. We shall be with you.' Gemal answered and threw him a towel.

Boualili had laid out clean clothes upon the bed, briefs, a shirt and trousers recovered from his case. He put them on and the sensation of their laundered crispness against his skin was extraordinary. Distantly he remembered a time when he had dressed like this every day.

'A cigarette?' Gemal held out a pack.

'Thank you.'

The Arab gestured to a chair. 'You may sit.' He nodded to Boualili who left the room.

Adam drew deep upon his cigarette and waited.

'Do not be afraid,' Gemal said. 'It is I who am in charge. But do not trust him.'

A strange turbulence shook through Adam as Sheldon came in. He hated him. This devious villian had brought him low, had been the cause of his humiliation and so great a torment and a terror. Yet Sheldon's open face was not the devil's. He looked disconcertingly as he always had in his lightweight suit.

'Hi!' he said cheerfully. 'Sure am sorry to see you here.'

Adam stared back in silence.

'This was not the game plan,' Sheldon said. 'But the operation went wrong on us. The police busted your office - you knew that?'

Adam looked back stonily yet the other seemed unconcerned. 'You gave us a problem,' he explained. 'I'm truly sorry it worked out like this. I can understand if you feel sore about it.'

'*Sore*?' The word burst from Adam's mouth. 'Are you out of your mind? You've wrecked my life and you ask if I feel *sore* about it. You set me up!'

Boualili sat upon the bed, toying with his gun. Gemal lounged by the window, his eyes fixed upon the American.

'To be absolutely accurate,' Sheldon answered, 'you set yourself up.'

Fury choked Adam. He could not speak.

'You did,' Sheldon maintained. 'You wanted excitement, change.'

'You call *this* change?' Adam demanded bitterly.

Sheldon laughed. 'And how! Don't you?'

'That stuff about our shared birthday,' Adam asked, 'The horoscope in Zurich. That was all invention?'

'All of it,' Sheldon admitted cheerfully. 'I figured you as the perfect drug smuggler. To photograph your suitcase you even gave me your address.'

A thought struck Adam. 'I was introduced to your Ambassador. Is *he* part of this?'

'Like you, I only met him once,' Sheldon answered. 'Frankly I don't think he'd be up to it.'

'So how did you arrange *that* charade?'

Sheldon glanced at Germal and Boualili as though to make sure they were listening. 'You were an honoured guest. I know a girl who works there; she added our names to the invitation list.'

'And I suppose it was her I delivered the Tehran blueprints to?'

'No, she's nothing,' Sheldon said. 'And you forget. You kindly sent those round by chauffeur to the Embassy. I was waiting on the steps.'

Adam tasted the bitter gall of his own naivety.

Sheldon said, 'It wasn't personal. In politics the end justifies the means.'

'Politics?' demanded Adam. 'What's *politics* to do with it?'

'Everything,' Sheldon answered. 'I understand you've done a deal.'

'With Gemal,' Adam told him coldly. 'Not with you.'

Leaning against the wall, watching both of them, the Arab smiled.

'It's the same,' Sheldon said. 'One million pounds from your personal account in Zurich telexed to a bank in Tripoli . . .'

'In Gemal's name.'

'And when will it arrive?'

'Tomorrow,' Adam answered. 'The bank must sell bonds. It takes time.'

Gemal said, 'I fly tonight. I shall wait to receive it.'

'Yes, I hope so,' Sheldon remarked. 'It's cheap, one million.'

205

Gemal bristled 'It is enough. *You* got nothing.'

Sheldon just looked at him. 'Yes. Since that unfortunate accident with the coke I agree we do need the money.' His look flicked back to Adam, 'Your family and corporation won't come up with a single cent to set you free. They don't appear exactly *wild* to have you back.'

Adam held his gaze while a noise intruded on the room. Distant at first, it penetrated the charged silence as a clatter which mounted rapidly in pitch and loudness as it approached till its racket rebounded from the walls and the whole house shook with sound.

Sheldon stepped rapidly to the window and twitched the blind aside. Gemal moved to join him. Both were appalled by what they saw.

Only two hundred feet above the ground a pair of Highway Patrol helicopters fluttered down the line of coast toward them.

Chapter forty-two

That night, Sheldon, Gemal and Raschid left to dispose of the motor home on their way to San Francisco airport.

Its usefulness was finished now. Possession of the vehicle with its crushed front still spattered with blood and brains, its side gashed open, had become a bane to them. The helicopters had not paused as they clattered above the house that afternoon. Their dipping insect flight had continued down the coast but clearly it was this which they were looking for together with its owners, the perpetrators of a hit-and-run. It was necessary to get rid of it.

It was a clear night. There were no lights visible anywhere as the battered vehicle pulled out from below the trees and clanked down the driveway to the coastal highway, following Sheldon's rented Mustang.

The moon rode high. The hills reared upon their right as they followed the winding road above the ocean.

Raschid drove the land yacht. In the Mustang with Gemal beside him, Sheldon led at twenty miles an hour, the maximum at which the motor home could proceed. Even at that pace it rattled and banged like a wrecked tin drum; they could hear it from fifty yards ahead.

Their headlights swept the road in front, at curves beaming out across the ocean. Twice they halted, only to discover that the lie of land prevented what they had to do. They pressed on looking for the spot where it might be staged . . .

In his dark room Adam lay restlessly awake. An hour ago Boualili had checked the ropes which bound his wrists and ankles to the bed and turned off the light. But Adam could not sleep.

He had heard the racket of the motor home as it started up and drove off down the drive. Since then, nothing. The house was quiet.

A faint sound reached him from outside and his eyes flicked toward the door. The lock turned. It opened. He saw a figure slip into his room.

'Adam?' It was Jutta's voice.

He did not answer. She approached the bed. 'Are you awake?'

'What do you want?' he asked and his voice was cold and hard.

'Quiet!' she whispered. 'He is asleep.'

'Where have the others gone?'

'To get rid of it.'

'What do you want?' he demanded.

'Listen.' The bed creaked as she sat down. 'Be quiet and listen to me. You are in great danger.'

'*Now* you tell me.' he mocked.

'No. Listen. The Arabs, do not trust them.'

'Trust? I don't trust *any* of you,' said Adam, his tone rising.

'Quiet!' She listened intently to the silence. 'I gave him a pill. In his coffee.'

'You have such charming tricks,' he said.

'Do not joke. Listen, when Gemal has your money they will kill you.'

Moonlight filtered through the blind. Her face was a pale blur suspended above him. The curve of her shoulder and her breast was outlined against the window.

'So? What do you suggest?' he asked.

Below the Ventana Wilderness, on Point Sur, Sheldon found the perfect place.

The highway cut short across the headland but, where it curved away, a thirty yard slope of turf rose gently to the cliff's edge.

He pulled over and cut his lights. Like some monstrous carnival machine the motor home wheezed and clattered to a halt behind them, its split radiator throwing up a cloud of steam.

The three walked to the rim of land. The cliff dropped fifty feet to a narrow ledge, from there plunged sheer into the dark water swirling round its base.

Gemal glanced up and down the empty highway. 'We do it now,' he said.

The house creaked. Jutta stiffened, listening.

'So what do you suggest?' Adam asked again.

She bent close to whisper in his ear. 'They have to kill you. What else can they do?' she asked.

He felt the pressure of her body. He felt her warmth.

'What Sheldon wants is very important to all of us,' she said. 'To do it will be the one most important thing in all our lives. We cannot risk that you betray us.'

'He is your lover?' Adam asked.

'No!'

'You sleep with him.' It was not a question but a bitter accusation.

She sat up abruptly. 'No. My lover's neck was broken by the police. He was in a wheelchair, now he is dead. It is from those days, from Germany, that I know Sheldon. He was in the army. He got us weapons.'

'So now you are his partner in kidnapping and terrorism? To do what?'

'No!' The question frightened her. 'No, don't ask! How can I tell you? Already you know too much and will set the police to find us. They like you yet you think we are your enemies, but all we want is a kind of justice in the world. Just one act of justice.'

'It is *you* who acted as *my* enemy,' said Adam.

She grasped his shoulders. Her voice was desperate. 'No! You happened. I did not want to. How could I know what you would turn out to be?' she asked him miserably. 'How could I know?'

'Untie me,' Adam told her.

The motor home lurched from off the road. It mounted the verge and jolted across the grass.

As it ground toward the cliff Gemal flung himself from the

209

open door, rolling over to regain his feet at once. The three men stood together as they watched it topple from the edge.

It was strangely slow, the way it fell at journey's end. It somersaulted down, turning in the air. Up-ended, it struck the ledge and ruptured. On the bounce an explosion ripped it through. It became a ball of flames arching in a lazy curve and plunging to the sea. As it hit the water its gas spattered wide. A rose of flame unfolded on the ocean, sizzled and went out. The water closed above it.

Gemal glanced at his watch. 'To the airport,' he told Sheldon.

Adam pleaded, 'Let me loose.'

'*No*,' she whispered back. 'How can I?'

She was straddled across him. He struggled to be free. 'Untie me!'

'Quiet,' she hissed. 'don't wake him. Quiet.' Her tongue invaded his mouth.

He tore away. 'But . . . '

Her mouth clamped on his to silence him. Her hand slipped between them to undo him.

For a moment he felt trapped, both excited and repelled by his own desire which, despite himself, betrayed him and showed him up.

She rocked back upon her thighs, impatiently hitching up her skirt. She gasped with pleasure as she sank onto him. She lost all restraint, it went from her on the instant.

For so long she had tried to exorcise him. She had wanted to hate him, had longed at times for his death to deliver her from the embarrassment which he represented. But nothing had freed her. She moaned and drove down upon him, exulting in the fever and abandon of her release . . .

210

Chapter forty-three

The house stood upon a saucer of flat land below Big Sur between the mountains and the ocean, on a coast scrubbed bare by the wind and scoured by the sea.

Here, next evening, Adam regained the freedom and beauty of the world.

He had passed his day alone and tied upon his bed. At the end of afternoon Boualili brought a summons to join his remaining captors at a meal. He had been released and escorted to the living room.

The open windows overlooked the ocean. The effect upon Adam as he hobbled stiffly in and saw the view was overwhelming.

Light and space were everywhere. The sky was huge, the ocean infinite. A wild storm-tossed sea leaped below the cliff. The breakers came pounding in, the air was fogged by spray. The sun was sinking toward the ocean in a blood-red stain. The headland stood black in silhouette against the shrouded crimson ball and the churned light breaking through the clouds. He tasted salt upon his lips and smelled the scent of growth and herbs. Birds were singing in the pine trees. He saw every leaf, every blade of grass. Below, a pelican took off in ungainly lumbering flight. He was filled by a kind of rapture, as though a miracle had occurred. He felt so full of life he could have hugged the earth.

Jutta had prepared a meal. They ate steak and salad and fresh bread. There was wine to drink. It was the first proper fare those from the motor home had tasted in a month but there was an hysteria to this meal independent of the food and wine.

Tonight was the end of the affair. Tonight, if all went to

211

plan, would come the call to say the ransom had been received. This feast was celebration.

All around the table were infected by the festive mood. Enmity was forgotten or laid aside.

Sheldon played host and did it well, expansive, talkative and in top form. Vitality and excitement crackled from him. In a previous role Adam had known Sheldon for what he chose to be, here he was what he was and glorying in it.

Adam's own state of mind was very strange. He was caught up in their atmosphere. He drank glass for glass with them and shared their mood. It was as though he, with them, had outwitted the opposition and got what *all* of them desired.

The meal was finished when the telephone rang with the expected call.

All went rigid. Utter silence fell. After a moment Sheldon stood up to take it.

Adam watched him, saw the tension in his eyes, saw it melt away and the expression change. Sheldon spoke briefly then, holding the phone, turned to the silent table with manic joy pinned across his face. 'We've *scored*!' he shouted. 'Gemal has the money.'

Boualili screamed with laughter. He flung his glass against the wall. Jutta threw her arms around Adam and embraced him and at once he was possessed by that same hilarity. A rush of madness swept through them all, a kind of triumph in the victory they shared.

Sheldon drew the cork from another bottle. Refilling all their glasses, he raised his own, 'To success,' he toasted.

Only Adam did not join in. 'May I go out?' he asked when they had drunk. Boualili sobered up at once. All his training clicked back on line. 'No!'

Sheldon was more indulgent. 'Sure why not? I'll join you.'

'No!' said Boualili.

'Don't worry,' Sheldon told him. Drawing his hand from his pocket he showed his gun. 'All right?' He opened the screen door and ushered Adam out.

The sun was low. The dark sea came rolling in to smash upon the rocks. The air was filled with the crashing of the surf and a salt mist of spray. The wild coastline stretched away into the settling dusk.

'What success?' Adam asked, standing on the deck.

'For the Arabs,' Sheldon answered 'it's getting back the West Bank. It's a homeland. It's justice.'

'And now,' said Adam calmly, 'Having delivered on my side of it, how does the deal go now? You shoot me?'

'You don't believe that,' said Sheldon. 'But Gemal would if I hadn't got rid of him.'

'They're *your* soldiers,' Adam murmured. 'Can't you control them?'

'No way,' said Sheldon crisply. 'They're high on the idea of martyrdom. Blowing you away don't mean a fuck to them. These guys march to a different drum and the name of it is Islam. To die for the cause is a straight door to paradise.'

Still gazing out across the ocean, after a moment Adam asked, 'What cause?'

'Cause?' Sheldon laughed abruptly. 'Did I call it that? You want to walk?'

Adam nodded. Together they stepped off the terrace and onto the narrow strip of turf above the cliff. By them stood a grove of Monetrey Pine with trunks bleached to whiteness by the spray and tortured limbs. They looked like ghosts fleeing from the wind.

The two had gone a few yards before Sheldon spoke again. 'What are you going to do?' he asked.

Adam shook his head. 'I'm trying not to get used to the idea that I may live.'

Sheldon protested. 'I'd never let you *die*. Surely you know that. I've changed your life, so what are you going to do now?'

Adam stopped and looked him in the face. They stared directly into each other's eyes and for a moment it was as if each gazed clear into the other's soul and shared a perfect understanding of what he was.

Adam blinked. 'I don't know,' he said.

'*I* know.' The claim rang out, an affirmation.

Adam struggled to restrain the beating of his heart. He kept silent, waiting for the other to continue.

213

Sheldon's exuberance shone from him like a light. 'All that shit,' he said and grabbed Adam's arm tightly at the shoulder. 'It's *shit*,' he repeated, shaking the truth into him. 'The West shuffling toward its end gorged on luxury and human blood. Its institutions are rotten, its governments corrupt. They're not just unworthy of survival, they're doomed and crying out to be exterminated. You know it Adam . . . '

The rising wind whipped around them. The spray beat upon their faces. 'You know it,' Sheldon shouted at the crashing sea. He turned on Adam, his face exalted, streaming water. 'And *you* want to go *back*?'

They stood together on the headland. The waves thundered at their feet.

'Let it come,' Sheldon cried. 'The sooner the better, let it come. Let's have the bang of it and the fire to clear the shit away. Let's burn up all the rubbish in its hot bright flame. Let's have chaos and a wilderness till creeping from the holes and crannies in the desert come a stonemason and a farmer and a miller to rebuild the fucking world. Let it come,' he shouted at the raging sea. 'Let it come down.'

The clouds parted. From the setting sun a path of fire raced to where they stood. The sunset was like a huge explosion, like a dawn, a golden dawn when the world was young and Man had only just come upon the earth.

'No,' said Adam. 'Of course not. I can't go back.'

It was as though he stood apart and heard his own voice speak the words. He was free. He knew what he must do.

Chapter forty-four

The four of them quit the house two days later in the early morning.

Sheldon headed the Mustang north on the coastal highway and they drove on empty roads through a bright world as yet without traffic. The bluffs were bare and buildings few. A wooden farm in a fold of hills, a hawk perched upon its gatepost. On their left they passed dark beaches with the tide gone out, the wet sand trailed by kelp and thongs of maidens' hair. Seals basked upon the rocks and giant gulls swooped in the flat leaden light above a flaccid ocean.

Boualili sat beside Sheldon, next to Jutta in the back Adam rode with them, no longer a prisoner.

They were all possessed of that same euphoria which had fired them in the house when they learned the ransom had been received and the project so long planned was feasible and immediate. Adrenalin scorched their veins. They felt they could do no wrong and that providence was their right, that cosmic will sustained them. Mad they were, for that is the nearest word.

And, as for the blessed whose way is the light, all obstacles dissolved before them. They crossed into San Francisco from San Mateo across the green slope of the hills, below them a jumbo jet drifting in white and easy on the middle air toward the airport which was their own destination, the blue bay and the shimmering of the sea, music on the radio and the hoarse yearning of Rod Stewart's voice singing of dirty love.

They sailed through the airport without check. No deference attended them but American civility, automatic and efficient in the daily processing of 15,000 passengers who took planes from here with the same unthinking facility as others

215

step upon a bus. Even Adam's passport – one of the three which Sheldon carried for his own use – attracted the barest glance. 'Have a nice flight, Mr Littman,' and they were aboard.

The whistling rush of the big jets boosted to a roar. The aircraft barrelled down the runway and lifted off. The shape of the wing tipped across the geometrical gridwork of San Francisco, banking east. They were away.

At 8 p.m. local time, they landed at Kennedy, waited for the plane to be refuelled then took off on the transatlantic haul.

They drank a little, watched the movie, ate and slept. They looked like tourists, friends travelling on vacation. When they talked it was lightheartedly, about matters of no consequence.

The operation all were engaged upon was not discussed in Adam's presence. They trusted him, it seemed, and he had justified that trust for, had he wanted to escape, he could have done so in the airports of San Francisco or New York. They trusted him but they were wary. He was of their number but not yet privy to the detail of their plan.

They landed at Paris de Gaulle early next morning, then headed for the Coast. At 11 a.m. they touched down at Nice.

Gemal and Raschid were waiting for them in the airport. They saw them beyond the barrier as they came up to the immigration desk in single file.

The others went through without delay. Adam handed his passport to the uniformed official who flipped it open, the stamp held poised. He hesitated, glanced closer at the page and frowned. 'Monsieur . . .'

Adam stood there with arm extended. His fingers twitched. 'Monsieur, this passport . . . '

Adam's mouth went dry. 'Yes?'

'There is a problem,' the official said. 'Your passport . . . in one week it will expire.'

Adam breathed out slowly. 'Indeed, I know,' he said in perfect French. 'I am only here for three days. For a meeting,' he explained.

216

'This is a time for meetings,' the man observed. 'You are part of your President's delegation perhaps?'

'Not exactly,' Adam answered.

'Many of your compatriots are already here,' the official told him. 'Many people from the Press. Enjoy your stay,' he said, handing back the passport.

Adam thanked him and walked through to join the others.

The Arabs who met them here were different creatures to the unshaven terrorists who had been Adam's jailers in the motor home. In white suit and black shirt open to the chest, a gold medallion hanging from a chain around his neck, Gemal had become scented and sophisticated. He reeked of money.

They followed him and Raschid to a rented Pontiac which glittered beneath the palm trees in the open parking. He led them to its trunk. With a glance to check they were unobserved, he reached in to unzip a canvas grip. 'Look!' he invited them.

It was stuffed with 5,000 French franc bank notes. A thick dense pack of them. As if hypnotised, they stared. Not even Adam had ever seen so much in cash before.

In the bright sun they drove the expressway which sweeps around the Baie des Anges, and everywhere they looked was holiday and money, the gleaming facades of apartment blocks and hotels, the coast road a solid line of expensive automobiles, the private beaches dense with tanned bodies, the warm blue sea beyond, the speedboats and the yachts. This was the summer playground of the rich and, with a million pounds riding in the trunk, they were paid up subscribing members of the clan.

They coasted toward Antibes, the car's windows open, its radio playing at full volume. This was the hit and rush of crime, its frenzy and its joy. Their spirits soared with exhilaration, their nerves stung and tingled and their hearts beat swiftly. None there had ever felt so sharp or so alive.

At the *capitanerie* in Antibes marina they asked for *Xanadu*. The yacht was pointed out to them among the bigger power boats.

Captain Barrie greeted them on board in white uniform and yachting cap, a tanned middle-aged Englishman with a ready smile and manner between the professional and obsequious.

'Welcome to *Xanadu*, Mr Sheldon.' he said thrusting out his hand.

All shook hands and were introduced. The glance Barrie cast Adam was bright with welcome; it contained no hint of recognition or that faint start, impossible to conceal, upon spotting a face in some way – perhaps a newspaper – familiar and known. Thin to the point of emaciation, with long dark-dyed hair and a moustache. Adam resembled not at all the plump clean-cut English businessman whose disappearance had roused so much attention only a few weeks before.

The members of the charter party were shown to their cabins. They washed and changed then assembled on the stern for the champagne which Captain Barrie had already set out in a silver bucket.

It had all gone so well till now, without a single hitch. As they raised their glasses they felt they could walk on water and come through. The operation was underway. They toasted, high on excitement and on themselves. The countdown had begun.

Chapter forty-five

Next day Sheldon and Gemal drove off in the car together. They returned from the rail freight depot with a heavy suitcase.

Gemal kicked the yacht's cat from beneath his feet and set the case down on the deck. He was sweating from the effort of humping it up the gangway.

'What've you got there?' Captain Barrie Asked. 'Gold?'

'Practical models,' Sheldon answered easily. 'I told you, this is a working holiday.'

After lunch they took the *Xanadu* to sea for the first time.

The manoeuvre was stage managed from the bridge by Captain Barrie who already had complained to Sheldon about his lack of crew.

'That was the deal,' the American reminded him. 'When I paid for the charter that's what we agreed.'

'I know it was, but why?' Barrie protested. 'You're making work for yourselves.'

'They *want* to crew,' Sheldon said but the skipper looked sceptically at Boualili and Raschid standing by the stern mooring in bare feet and gaudy resort clothes, both of them smoking.

'Without an experienced crew I can only take you up and down the coast,' he said. 'This boat's insured for half a million pounds.'

'It's insured, that's the point,' Sheldon informed him shortly. 'I explained, we want privacy. We're here to work.'

'But . . . '

Captain Barrie was not happy with his charter. The conditions were unusual and this ill-assorted group, half Arab, half Caucasian were not the sort of party he was accustomed to.

219

There had been none of that easy cordiality of yachting life, the charterers dining in town and returning well oiled to invite the skipper to join them for drinks in the saloon.

They had made it plain that Barrie was not welcome in their group. Though clearly wealthy, they had not eaten ashore but subsisted on take-out food which Boualili fetched from a hamburger bar in town. Sheldon showed no interest in examining the charts and planning a cruise. The Arabs had reacted blankly to the proposal; Barrie had the impression it was the first time any of them had been aboard a yacht. They lacked the rudiments of civilised behaviour. They scattered cigarette ash everywhere and had already broken the tape player.

But there was no one on the bridge to whom the skipper might confide his dissatisfaction. He set his hand to the gear lever and leaned out. 'OK, cast off aft,' he shouted irritably.

Both the Arabs were talking at the time but Raschid threw off his line at once. Boualili had neither heard nor understood. The yacht snagged and swung as it eased forward, scraping the fenders of the craft beside it.

'Bloody fool,' Barrie muttered, nosing his bow out into the lane of water.

Passing below the citadel they came out from the harbour mouth and he eased the twin engines up to half speed. The boat angled minutely and set back on the water, scudding across the surface at fifteen knots.

Xanadu headed obliquely across the Baie des Anges.

Sheldon had moved to the stern and sat beside Gemal. Both of them were studying the shoreline through high powered binoculars. These were not part of the yacht's equipment. They must have brought them, Barrie thought, recognising the glasses as US Army issue, or maybe they had come in the suitcase . . .

Against the backdrop of the Alps, even from here the town of Nice looked jammed. The beaches were packed, the Promenade des Anglais immovable with cars. The usual throng of holidaymakers down for the season had been augmented by the entourages of the heads of state here for the 'informal' conference plus an international contingent of correspondents, camera teams and media men who had assembled to cover the event. Not a single hotel room was available anywhere. The town overflowed and was teeming with policemen.

Captain Barrie put the wheel over, cutting past a sailboat as he swung south to clear Cap Ferrat. Sheldon came up to join him on the bridge, carrying a map.

Two hundred yards offshore they skimmed by a coast of rock and crystal water and tiny secluded coves, the roofs of big villas half hidden among the pine trees.

'Can you come in closer,' Sheldon asked as they approached the point of land.

'No can do, old boy,' Barrie answered. 'Not today. They've closed the water to shipping on the other side. That's where it's all happening, the villa where the French President is staying.'

As they rounded the Cap both house and shoreline were revealed to sight. But land and sea had a very different aspect to the way that they had looked when Sheldon had effected his reconaissance. Three naval patrol boats were now anchored in the deep water below the villa, inflatables with divers were at work between them.

Through his binoculars Sheldon examined this activity, then raised his look to the shore beyond and went white. It seemed that every rock was occupied by an armed marine in combat uniform. A force of three or four hundred men had been deployed between the tip of the Cap and the large hotel which formed its base. Sheldon lowered his glasses and hurried to join Gemal in the stern.

'Allah,' the Arab murmured, turning from the sight appalled. 'You never said it was going to be like *this*.' Bracing against the movement off the boat he raised his glasses and looked again. 'There's no way we can get through that,' he stated.

'We don't have to,' Sheldon told him. He moved forward and called up to Barrie to cut the engines.

'You want to swim?' Barrie shouted back.

'Yeah, sure,' Sheldon answered.

'I'll put the ladder over.'

221

'You do that,' Sheldon called, returning to Gemal.

Hardly had the *Xanadu* lost momentum and begun to drift before a police launch came racing toward them, a man in the bow energetically waving them away.

On the bridge Barrie raised his arm in acknowledgement, restarting the engines. 'Where now?' he shouted down.

Sheldon gestured ahead. 'Keep going,' he ordered.

Twenty minutes later they anchored off Cap d'Ail.

The sun had slanted into afternoon and, in the heat, the faint scent of resin wafted to them from the land. The shore was without movement. It looked deserted until the eye distinguished the brown forms of men and women out-stretched upon the jetty beside a speedboat stacked with skis. The clear water slapped against the hull of *Xanadu*, stirred by tiny waves.

'All right,' said Sheldon, seated with the others in the stern. He glanced forward to check that Barrie still remained upon the bridge. 'All right,' he repeated quietly and looked to Adam, 'You want to hear it now?'

'Of course,' Adam said.

'You've been holding out on us,' Sheldon told him. 'We'd be happy if you'd set it right.'

'How so?' Adam asked, conscious that the eyes of all were on him.

'In Israel,' Sheldon said. His voice was flat.

'In Israel?' Adam was confused. 'Israel? What are you talking about?'

Gemal lunged toward him. 'You lied! Why did you lie?'

'What is this?' Adam demanded.

'You lie,' Gemal answered furiously. 'All the time we're discussing the West Bank and the Arab State. Even when you are agreeing and working on the manifesto you are lying, lying so you may live.'

Adam looked him back between the eyes. 'I don't under-stand,' he said.

'Missiles, neutron warheads. Construction of silos by *your* company and . . . ' Gemal mimicked him savagely ' . . . you don't understand.'

Adam felt himself turn cold. 'I don't,' he answered. 'You're

222

saying that missile silos are being constructed on the West Bank and *my* company's doing the work?'

'Exactly,' Sheldon said. 'Your company, International Construction.'

Adam said, 'The only work Intco's involved in in Israel is the construction of several schools.'

Gemal jeered, 'Schools!'

'With deep shelters?' Gemal added.

'I think so,' Adam answered struggling to remember the details in one of the contracts of one of the forty-eight companies the Lupus Group controlled, 'Yes, I think so.'

'If I had known,' Gemal told him, 'I would have shot you.'

'They are certainly not missile silos,' Adam protested,

'You want to see the photographs?' Sheldon asked. 'I'll fetch them. The rigs have already been installed.' He leaned back against the cushions of the stern banquette. 'Don't know why you got so sore at *us*, you're anyone's.' he said. '*Anyone* can have you dancing on a string.'

Adam stared at them, dismayed. Was it true? Had all of them including the Foreign Secretary and his own government betrayed him? Was the invitation which – a lifetime ago – he had received to attend the conference now taking place ashore the reward for his passive unquestioning complacency. Had *everybody* merely used him for a fool?

'I don't believe this,' he said.

'You'll have a chance to find out,' Sheldon told him. 'You're going to talk to him.'

'Who?'

'Sir John Doff, the Foreign Secretary of your tinpot country, flunkey to the United States. *You*, of course, will perform for anyone who pulls your strings.'

Adam fought to control his anger. He stood up abruptly. 'I shall swim,' he said. He stripped down to his underpants and stepped onto the transom. Jutta's eyes were lowered. The others all were watching him. He saw Gemal start forward as though to stop him, and then he dived.

He went down deep, cleaving through the water, relishing the shock of it on his overheated skin. The light was green and misty, the detail of the bottom clouded. He curved toward the surface which splintered as he rose. He put his head down and reached out. Half a dozen strokes took him from the boat. He stopped, trod water and glanced back; they were still observing him from the stern. Boualili had risen to his feet and was looking on enviously.

'Join me,' Adam shouted, but the little man shook his head. 'Me no swim,' he called back.

Flung by Barrie who had come to life upon the bridge, a lifejacket flew through the air to land at Boualili's feet. Shedding his clothes, donning the lifejacket, he jumped into the sea with a shout of joy. Since landing on the Coast he had been agog with wonder at all he saw, a child gazing on a world-become-real which exceeded his wildest imagination. Of all the Arabs he was the only one for whom Adam felt the least affection; he alone had prepared his meals and been attentive to his welfare. The little man bobbed in the water, splashing and waving.

Adam dived again. The hull of the yacht floated above him, stained and trailing weed. If he swam for it, he thought, what would they do? Shoot? Hardly. Start the boat and come after him? He could make it to the rocks before them. But then – what? He trickled the breath from his mouth and kicked up toward the surface. No, he had to win.

And what of Jutta? he asked himself. She had shown no reaction to this new and terrifying accusation that Sheldon had come up with. They had found no moment alone together since the night when the others had disposed of the motor home. Since her warning then there had been no chance to speak.

He swam back toward the boat. Boualili was clinging to the ladder. 'Nice,' the little man grinned, climbing back on board.

Adam followed him up and stretched out to dry upon the deck.

Captain Barrie had watched the exhibition with scorn. They were bathing in their underpants. What sort of people *were* these, he wondered, not for the first time. He glanced toward the shore and frowned; the outline of the rocks suddenly had blurred, a patch of view became opaque. As it stretched toward him it took Barrie several seconds to realise what it was. As soon as he did, he acted instantly, hurridly sliding the bridge window shut.

'Look out,' he shouted aft, slamming the door.

The horde of wasps was so numerous and so dense they formed a speckled shadow on the air as they swarmed toward the boat in a buzzing, see-through cloud.

Borne upon the breeze they swept across the yacht's bow, darkening the sun; in a throbbing hum they flowed on down the deck.

Adam lay naked and outstretched and Boualili sat beside him eating a cream pastry he had fetched from the saloon. Sticky fragments adhered around his mouth. Passing over Adam, the cloud of wasps checked, veered, and whirled upon the Arab in a mass. His head became enveloped in fuming yellow casque. He screamed and beat at them with his hands. They clung around him as he ran across the deck. He was wrapped in a furry pelt. Blinded, his arms flapped like wings.

Adam looked around him desperately for some weapon he could use. He snatched up his shirt and ran to help as Boualili stumbled and fell upon the deck.

Adam lashed out at the squirming carpet of them clinging to the body. A few detached and flew at him. He felt the electric pricking of their stings. He beat at the rolling figure in a frenzy. Their buzzing shrilly mounted to a whine. All at once the whole mass of them took off, soaring up, dense and thick, sweeping away together over the stern.

Several had stung him but, mindless of his own pain, Adam bent to Boualili. The others formed around them as the little Arab lay writhing and kicking on the deck, clawing at his eyes and screaming in agony.

Barrie dashed up with a medicine chest, in his haste spilling its contents at their feet. They groped through the bottles, tubes and packets, flinging them aside, not knowing what they were looking for.

Adam grabbed Boualili's hands and gently prised them from his face. His eyes were closed and the lids had already begun to swell, leaking milky tears. The skin was flushed and mottled. His face was twisted, the mouth wrenched back in a

225

rictus which bared his teeth. He shook in paroxysm and foam bubbled and dribbled from his mouth.

Jutta held his wrists while Adam sponged his face with water. He struggled to be free of them, jerking and thrashing. The red weals across his face were smearing into purple. Behind their lids, his eyes swelled out. His whole body was distending as they watched, and changing colour.

He tore his hands from their grip and thrust them to his mouth, trying to tug it wider. His tongue, stung all over, was dilating. Huge and black it lolled from his mouth. His screams stifled as he fought for air, sucking the breath down his thickening throat.

His limbs convulsed. Tightening and snapping like a spring they threw him up. His body crashed back, shuddered and lay still.

They stared, stricken and appalled. Captain Barrie, first to recover, was feeling for the pulse. 'Got to get to shore,' he said and leapt up, going for the bridge.

He had not moved three steps before Gemal's voice cracked out, 'Stop!'

So sharp was the command he halted, looked around.

Gemal was crouched there, holding a gun on him.

Captain Barrie blinked in disbelief. 'Now *come on*, old chap,' he said in a voice of extraordinary reasonableness, stretching out a hand and starting back.

Gemal fired.

Barrie felt something strike his chest. There was no pain but his legs failed and slowly he crumpled and kneeled down, a look of astonishment on his face. He touched his hand to his chest. 'I'm bleeding. I've been shot,' he said, bewildered.

His limbs were burning. He thought he was going to faint, he felt so hot. He did not understand what was happening. He saw the startled faces of the others, for whom the scene had the logic and inevitability of a dream. They stood powerless. He saw Gemal move toward him and raise the gun. 'No . . . please,' he begged and then the blast exploded in his face and flung him over . . .

On the jetty, the bathers rose languidly to their feet and began to gather up their towels and books. The sun was gone.

226

With a last glance at the white yacht anchored off shore upon the wine dark sea they strolled up toward the house to bath and change. The day was ended.

Chapter forty-six

The yacht *Xanadu* did not return to Antibes that night.

It would have been madness for those aboard to take her back to berth there. The crews and skippers of the marina formed a small tight knit fraternity. It would have been impossible to conceal Captain Barrie's absence. Another reason was that no one now on the boat knew how to sail her.

They learned by trial and error, most by error.

At length Sheldon managed to get the engines started. With Adam by him, he cautiously guided *Xanadu* to sea while both attempted to decipher the array of dials and instrumentation which equipped the bridge.

Two miles offshore they idled the motors while the two bodies were slid over the side. Weighed by the toolbox and spare parts they were committed to the deep.

All were party to that act and, in the strain and strangeness of the moment, Jutta's eyes lifted to Adam's face. For a second she looked at him in sudden fear. Instinctively he reached to her but she had pulled away, turned, and was going to the saloon.

The exchange went unnoticed. He returned with Sheldon to the bridge. The *Xanadu* set course for Nice.

Sheldon steered, narrowing his eyes against the low evening glitter on the waves. Locked in his private thoughts, he did not speak.

Adam's gaze too was trained ahead on the darkening line of coast and the mountains reared behind. He held himself carefully in check but his mind boiled in turmoil.

He was sickened by Boualili's end, horrified by the arbitrary fashion that Barrie had been disposed of. Their deaths had literally nauseated him, following so swiftly upon

228

the shock and dismay at learning of his own deception and what was now expected of him in redress.

His unwitting guilt had been explained to him, so also had his role of spokesman. The Americans and British were using his company to construct missile silos upon the West Bank. Unless these sites were at once dismantled and a joint statement issued by these two countries endorsing the creation of an Arab State, evidence of their perfidious collusion would be exposed to the Russian delegation, to all present at this Summit, and to the media. The conference would be scuttled, the cause of détente irrevocably destroyed.

Adam was the messenger who would lay these terms before the British Foreign Secretary.

Light evaporated from the sky as *Xanadu* approached the twinkling shore. On the eastward edge of the city, the harbour lay beneath the chateau, protected by the long arm of a breakwater. They rounded its fist and Sheldon cut back the motors.

'Hell's shit,' he exclaimed to Adam as both scanned the rows of craft which occupied all the moorings. 'So where do I park this mother?'

Adam pointed to a single empty space.

'Fetch the others and move up front,' Sheldon ordered. 'Get fenders and stuff and stay good and ready.'

Turning her on the wheel, he misjudged the sheer weight and stopping distance of the yacht. *Xanadu* came in much too fast, slewing sideways to bash into a Riva speedboat and cannon off, grazing a sailboat on the other side, finally to ram bow first into the dock and shudder to a stop.

A party of tourists on the quay had paused to watch the manoeuvre. Now they were laughing and one of them was reaching for his camera.

Sheldon scowled over the side. 'I want you to stay aboard and out of sight,' he said to Adam. 'There are probably a whole gang of people wandering round this town who know you.'

Adam shrugged. 'You're the boss.'

'Not enough it seems,' the other answered. 'It should never have gone like that out there. I should never have allowed them to get at the case to arm themselves but those guys feel naked unless they're carrying guns. They're goofed up and crazy and coming off the ceiling but it's taken me years to set this number up and *no one's* going to blow it for me now.'

'So now?' began Adam as Jutta stepped up the companionway onto the bridge.

She was looking hard at Sheldon. 'They want to go ashore,' she said abruptly.

Sheldon exploded. 'He's out of his mind!'

'Then *you* tell him,' she snapped back.

'I will.' He pushed past her roughly and clattered down the steps into the saloon.

They heard him shouting and the mutter of Gemal's voice in answer. 'No, *I* go,' Sheldon stated loudly, then silence from below and the slam of his cabin door as he went to change.

Sheldon showered and put on clean clothes. He dressed in white trousers, shirt and casual jacket, when he had finished studying his appearance in the full length mirror. Fashionable, composed, he was satisfied by what he saw. His irritation and first-night nerves were gone. He was ready.

Just before he left the cabin he took his suitcase from the closet, set it on the floor and kneeled to open it. He felt underneath a pile of shirts to remove a towel-wrapped package. He undid this with great care. He took out a small square bottle labelled St Laurent Aftershave. He looked at it fixedly and the inch of clear liquid it contained.

The power and the glory lay within his hand. Here was the occasion, here the place. The time was so close now.

Meticulously he repacked the bottle and slid it back into his case.

Sheldon went ashore alone.

No one gave him further argument, not even Gemal. The Arab's usual cockiness and defiance had been subdued by the events of the afternoon but, beyond that, there was a force coming off Sheldon now which cowed dissent. A side to him was showing which Adam had not seen before, a fervour and the resolution of commitment.

His manner commanded obedience and no one disobeyed.

230

They waited for him in the saloon, drinking whisky and hardly speaking. From time to time Adam stole a glance at Jutta but she would not meet his look.

When Sheldon did return they thought at first that he was drunk. He was filled with wild intoxication, his eyes ablaze with sparks of madness flickering in their depths.

He jumped down from the quay and burst into the saloon, his face ecstatic. 'I've got it!' he announced triumphantly.

They stared, blinded by the light which shone from him.

He paced to the table and spun round as if he were upon a stage. 'There's a banquet, tommorrow night.' He looked at Adam, 'Given by your country's delegation at the Carlton where they're staying.'

He surveyed his audience and graced them with a dazzling smile. 'Tomorrow,' he proclaimed. 'We're going to do it then.'

He was radiant, charismatic. He was all glitter and energy and excitement, like a star. He was a hero whose day has come.

Chapter forty-seven

Sir John Doff, Foreign Secretary in her Britannic Majesty's government, entered his hotel suite and collapsed onto the sofa, elaborately exhausted by the lunch he had just returned from in the company of his Prime Minister.

'My dear, too strenuous. How the old thing does go on,' he complained to the well-suited young assistant who, unasked, brought him a glass of Alka Seltzer and his pill. 'Dear boy, what calls?' he enquired and, even as he asked, the telephone rang again.

The young man picked it up, 'Yes.' He listened, 'Who?' An expression of extreme puzzlement came upon his face. '*Who* did you say?' he asked again.

'Whoever,' drawled the Foreign Secretary, 'deal with it, do.'

'It's Adam Lupus,' his assistant said.

Astonishment startled the minister from his pose of lethargy. He rose at once to take the call. 'Yes? who's speaking?'

He listened in blank surprise. 'Adam, is this really you? Where are you?'

He listened again, after a few seconds interrupting, 'Adam, I simply do not comprehend. In Nice? Why, what's happened to you? What are you asking, meet? Meet you? I can't possibly.'

And then he listened, at greater length.

Whatever it was that Adam Lupus said to the Foreign Secretary the words were not audible to his assistant busy rearranging the papers which lay upon his master's Empire desk. And, in fact, the message Adam communicated to the minister was not specific in its menace. He did not talk of the

232

West Bank, or of missiles or détente, indeed anything beyond the fact that it was vital that they meet. The two of them, privately and at once. Vital for Sir John.

And Sir John recognised it as such. For all his plumpness, his affected languor and proclivities, he was an animal of the keenest political instinct. He could identify an imperative when he heard one. All men have something to be ashamed of; whatever Adam referred to, he knew it to be a threat.

'Where are you?' he asked. 'The Majestic? Now? Yes, I suppose so if it's quick.'

When he set down the receiver he stood, thinking deeply. 'Where's my security man?' he asked.

'Downstairs sir,' his assistant answered. 'Are you going out?'

'Briefly, yes. Lupus has surfaced, here of all places. I suppose I'd better see him.'

He did not seem happy at the prospect, his assistant thought. 'Shall I come?' he offered.

The Minister recoverd his normal mien. 'No, dear boy,' he told him, heading for the door. 'I'll take my minder. You hold the fort. I'll be back well in time for the reception.

The couple did not look out of place in the lobby of the five star Hotel Majestic.

Gemal wore a Palm Beach suit, beside him Jutta was in wide shorts, lace t-shirt and spike shoes. She held herself with perfect ease, sexual and self-assured in the certitude that she was dressed as she belonged. Young and handsome, the couple were an asset to the lobby.

As the Foreign Secretary entered the hotel accompanied by his bodyguard, the two came up to him. 'Sir John Doff?' the girl asked.

He stopped short. 'Yes?'

'Mr Lupus has asked us to take you to him.'

Pink-faced, perspiring slightly, the minister looked down upon the girl with suspicion and distaste. 'No, I don't think . . .'

But Gemal stepped forward, offering something. 'There is a letter . . .' The Foreign Secretary glanced at him – and held

233

his stare, hypnotised for a moment by those extraordinary eyes which burned with such intensity in the lean brown face. He blinked, dropped his look, tore open and read the note. 'Very well,' he said, 'Take me to Mr Lupus.'

His armed bodyguard a pace behind him, the Foreign Secretary left the Hotel Majestic and followed the young couple onto the croisette, hot and bright in the heavy lull of afternoon.

The waterskier shifted balance, pivoting on his rearward foot. Abruptly changing course he cut across the speedboat's wake, leaping airborn as he went over. Braced against the tension of the rope, his tanned body leaned almost parallel to the water as he made the turn. A curtain of spray fanned up behind him in an iridescent rainbow screen against the sun.

In the stern of *Xanadu* Sheldon, Raschid and Adam watched the display with varying reactions, the last of these keyed tense by what he must do now.

The skier dropped his tow. Cut free and balanced delicately upon his single ski he sped back toward a yacht moored fifty yards from them in the channel between the islands offshore from Cannes. Still dry, he reached the ladder, grasped it and stepped aboard. The speedboat came alongside and was secured. Its driver joined the group on deck. As those upon *Xanadu* observed, they heard the pop of an opening bottle of champagne.

Sheldon snapped open another can of beer. 'I guess this is all old hat to you,' he remarked to Adam.

The other shook his head. 'Not so, I was too busy. All *I* ever did was make money.'

'Come *on*,' said Sheldon. 'You were right up there swilling the goodies with the rest of them.'

Adam shook his head. 'Not me. I worked too hard.'

'Then you were a fool,' said Sheldon shortly.

An open Riva rounded the headland of the island and sped toward them. Sheldon set down his beer and raised his binoculars. 'It's them,' he said.

One of the many boats available for hire off the croisette's beach, swiftly the Riva drew close. Behind its driver they identified Gemal and Jutta with two other figures in the open cockpit.

'Your friend,' Sheldon murmured to Adam with a sour smile as the craft cut speed and bumped alongside. The driver reached across to steady his boat so his passengers might climb aboard.

In the striped blue suit, Sir John Doff came up the ladder onto *Xanadu*.

The tutored behaviour of all Englishmen of a certain class, when faced by crisis or the unexpected, is to suppress all demonstration of emotion. The more dire the circumstance, the more vital it is to act as though nothing untoward is taking place.

'My dear Adam,' Sir John said as he stepped on deck, 'how delightful to see you again. One had rather given you up for dead.'

Adam smiled tightly. 'Well ... yes,' he answered, 'at one point I did myself.'

The two behind him and his bodyguard followed the Foreign Secretary aboard. The driver of the Riva made fast then stretched out upon his cockpit in the afternoon's last sun.

'Shall we go inside,' Sheldon suggested.

They entered the saloon. 'Well, Adam,' said Sir John, looking around him, 'introduce me, do.'

Incongruously Adam found himself performing the civilities. And, even while he did so, Raschid came up to the Minister. 'Tea?' he enquired softly.

'Thank you,' Sir John said and addressed himself to Adam. 'I could not be more happy to find you in good health. Now ... you mentioned that you needed to speak to me.' He looked around him, again, quite pleasantly.

'These people are with me,' Adam said. 'We can talk in front of them.'

'As you wish, of course.' Sir John seated himself in a white plastic chair. 'The problem is that I am somewhat involved ashore. I am dying of curiosity as to how and why you're here, but time is short.' His easy smile embraced them all,

'I'm sure you understand.'

'Your tea,' said Raschid, offering the tray. The minister took it with automatic hand. Standing in the doorway his English bodyguard gazed with longing at the single cup.

'Vanessa must be overwhelmed to hear you're free,' Sir John remarked, 'and enjoying so salubrious a situation.'

'I have spoken to nobody but you,' Adam told him.

The Minister sipped his tea. 'Gracious, I am agog. But why exactly?'

'Because you have lied to me,' Adam answered. 'You have deceived and cheated me. In any other sphere but politics the way you have behaved would be judged criminal.'

Sir John did not blink. 'My dear, what fervour! I am totally confused.'

'Oh *please*,' Adam responded wearily. 'You said *you* were short of time.'

All his accumulated resentment found focus in the spectacle of the plump figure lolling in its chair, a bah-bahing caricature of hypocrisy and complacence. Animosity and accusation spewed from Adam's mouth in indictment of this man who had duped and used him, exploited his company in Israel and his own good nature in a gross and cynical political manouevre.

Finishing his tea, the Minister set aside the cup and heard him out.

'Are you finished?' he asked at last.

White-lipped, Adam nodded.

'I do not know what pressures you are under,' Sir John began, 'Or if conceivably you believe what you are telling me, but every single word that you have said is total bloody balls.'

It was spoken with conviction and Adam felt a sudden chill. Goose pimples raised across his skin.

'Total balls,' the Minister repeated.

Adam saw Jutta flush and drop her eyes. His own nerves crackled into life.

Adam moved then. As it all came clear, an unstoppable hot rush of fury rose within him and he went for Sheldon.

He did not move fast enough. Gemal's hand flicked out quick as a snake's tongue, gripped his wrist and swung him round. With surprising agility the Minister threw himself sideways from his chair, calling out an order as he fell. His bodyguard shocked alert and reached inside his jacket.

Without taking the gun from out of his pocket Raschid fired.

The noise was tiny, a muffled crack. The bullet struck the bodyguard in the chest. Its impact flung him against the wall. An expression of bewilderment upon his face, he slid down till he was sitting on the floor. Blood spurted from his chest.

In the sudden quiet. 'Don't do it!' Sheldon said to Adam. Jutta held a short automatic rifle. It was aimed at him.

With a grunt the bodyguard folded forward till his face rested on the floor. His eyes rolled up, showing white.

'Take him out,' Sheldon snapped at Jutta.

She gestured at Adam with her gun. Like a sleepwalker he moved toward the door. He passed through. She came after, closing it behind.

'Put your hands behind your neck,' she said. 'The cabin on the right. Don't cry out, don't try anything!'

Like a sleepwalker, he obeyed.

Lying upon the floor of the saloon the Foreign Secretary stared at his own hand splayed upon the carpet. He stared as though it were an object he was seeing for the first time. He could still taste the bitter sweet acid of the tea beneath his tongue.

'You can get up now,' Sheldon said.

He scrambled to his feet. With careful dignity he regained his chair. 'Very well, what do you want?' he asked. 'What . . .' His voice cracked.

The toxin of insanity began to dribble into his brain. The three men stood there watching him. A terrible multiplying anxiety groped through the flesh and marrow of the Minister. He was seized by a sense of dread so acute that his vision dimmed. His heart pumped out blood and terror as the world turned black.

A photograph was thrust before his eyes. 'Look at it!' Sheldon ordered.

He was staring down a dark tunnel at a face. The likeness

was unmistakable. It was the President of the USSR.

'Look!' commanded Sheldon.

His gaze faltered and fell away, vacant and confused. Gemal stepped behind his chair. Grasping the Minister's ears he jerked his head up. He squealed with pain.

'Look!' said Sheldon and thrust it closer. 'Look!'

The face of the Russian President bellied and swayed before him. It was expanding, growing. The pressure swelled so full within his head he thought his skull would burst. His head was going to explode like a rotten egg, his brains spatter across the ceiling . . .

'Look!' said Sheldon, 'Look and listen, for tonight you kill him.'

He looked and saw it plain. Saw the man for what he was. The horror and the terror went away. His vision cleared as the mirrors of his mind clicked to final angle and the madness which had awaited the Minister for fifty-seven years reached out and took him over.

It was late afternoon. The light was failing. Yet to Sir John Doff the world looked calm and clear and beautiful as on the first dawn of the world.

Chapter forty-eight

Adam and Jutta stood in the cabin. She held the gun on him. The low beams of the sun reflected through the porthole and dappled their bodies in dancing light.

They heard the clatter made by those in the saloon as they went on deck, the noise of the Riva starting up. The Foreign Secretary, accompanied by Gemal who substituted for his bodyguard, were headed back for Cannes.

The sound of the speedboat faded as it pulled away across the waves and unwanted memory returned to Adam of the hours he had spent with Jutta in their hotel room in Cartagena, her bare knee raised in silhouette against the window and moonlit ocean; the warmth, the langour and the peace of that dark world of flesh. He had been used and betrayed by everybody, by her not once but twice.

He said, 'I can't begin to express the disgust I feel for you. Of all of them you are the lowest and the most contemptible.'

'You've wrecked my life too,' she said.

'Your life!' His voice was scathing.

'Yes. Everything I wanted, everything I believed in. You've wrecked it for me.'

He said coldly, 'I despise you more than anyone I've known.'

The gun jerked in her hands. 'There isn't time,' she answered. 'Not now. You know what's about to happen. I'll tell you how I feel about you. I love you more than any man ever in my life.'

He faced her down, expressionless. Deceived so often he struggled to remain immune. Yet his stomach lurched, his heart began to thud.

She came close to him, the gun hung loosely in her hand.

'You don't hate me,' she said. 'It's not important now. And I've lost all my hate because of you, I want life. I want nobody to die but there's so little time. He's on his way ashore and Gemal's given him a gun.'

She stood against him. Her body gave off heat. Her face was tilted up to his, waxy and luminous in the reflected light. 'We have to stop it happening,' she said. 'We have to stop them. Now.'

Sheldon was with Raschid in the stern. Both were smoking. They turned as Adam stepped out on deck followed by Jutta. She wore a pistol in a belt around her waist. The stub-barrelled automatic rifle in her hands was pressed into Adam's back.

'I'm sorry,' Sheldon said, 'I'm sorry that it had to be like that but I couldn't trust you.'

Adam looked back at him stonily.

'Don't you understand?' Sheldon asked. 'I couldn't trust you with the truth. You might have blown it for all of us.'

'You were lucky,' Adam told him. 'In Zurich, you were lucky to find me.'

Sheldon nodded. 'Yes,' he agreed, 'It was the right time and you were right for me. For us. For you too,' he added. His voice dropped, intense and low, 'Surely you see now that it *has* to happen, that this is the only way that it will change. They're creatures of the past,' he said and his hand lifted toward the distant mainland shore where the Foreign Secretary was heading. 'They're greedy, indolent and self-centred men and we're fools to have tolerated their mis-management so long. They rule in comfort and dignity perpetuating their immense conceit, but they hold the power and they'll stick to the controls like barnacles. This is how it has to be, they will discredit and destroy each other. They'll bring the end upon themselves.'

Adam looked at him sombrely. From fifty yards away, where the speedboat bobbed beside the anchored yacht, there stole upon their ears the sound of music. The group aboard had switched on a record player. A mindless disco beat thudded across the water.

'What then?' Adam asked. 'Chaos, reprisal? Barbarism? Anarchy?'

'A holy war,' Raschid said. The words were uttered flat side up. 'The return of Islam.'

From behind Adam Jutta stepped away, putting space between them. Her back was to the sea, her gun pointed unwaveringly at Sheldon and Raschid. Her voice cracked out.

'Don't move,' she ordered 'Not a hand, not a finger, or I fire.'

Adam turned and ran toward the bridge. He came up the steps three at a time. He grasped the wheel, he turned the key. His finger stabbed at the starter button. The twin engines churned and burst to life. He gunned them up in a roar of noise. He glanced back to where the others still stood in the stern. He rammed the motors into drive.

Under full power the yacht leapt forward like a racehorse bursting from its cage. Accelerating, it travelled fifteen yards before the anchor chain drew tight. From sand Adam would have succeeded to wrench it out, but it lay in rock. The chain pulled solid. Crystal droplets sprang into the air along its rigid length.

The yacht crashed to a stop as brutal as if it had run into a wall. Adam was thrown against the windscreen. Sheldon and Raschid were flung headlong to the deck. Jutta's feet swept from under her and she somersaulted overboard, the gun spinning from her grasp.

Motors screaming, twin screws churning the sea to white, *Xanadu* surged and lashed against its chain. Those on the nearby yacht were staring in astonishment at the sight and the figure of the girl swimming who had surfaced and struck out toward them.

On *Xanadu* Raschid was the first to recover. He came up gun in hand, staggering to his feet on the heaving deck, lurching for the bridge.

Adam did not wait. He went off the side in a flat racing dive as a bullet whacked into the combing just behind him.

He hit the water, came up at once, kicked out. He set his head low and reached forward with all his strength.

241

Raschid fired again. Sheldon was clambering past him to the bridge, screaming at him.

Adam drove on, cleaving through the water. He was halfway there.

The party on the other yacht had risen to their feet. The music was still blaring out. Wine glasses in hand they watched bemused as the two swimmers churned forward in a racing crawl.

Adam gulped air, forced on. He was beside Jutta. Together they reached the speedboat moored to the yacht. He stretched up, gripped its cockpit edge and hauled himself in. He reached for Jutta and pulled her from the water. He leapt forward to throw off the mooring line, regaining the padded cockpit and twisted the ignition key.

It had taken the party in the yacht above a moment to comprehend what was happening. Only feet away, their ski boat was being stolen. The owner was leaning from the rail, 'You! Stop! How dare . . . ' He was puce with rage.

The engine fired. Adam slammed it into gear. The speed-boat exploded forward, toppling him back and tearing his hands from the wheel. He scrambled up, reaching for it, grabbed and hauled, fighting for control. Canting level, the boat shot below the bow of *Xanadu*, scattering spray.

As he clambered into the seat by Jutta, Adam caught a single glimpse of Raschid above him on the prow, frantically hauling up the anchor. Their eyes met. It was like a photograph, a frozen second, and then they were accelerating away and he was gripping the wheel and steering down the channel between the islands.

Sheltered from the wind, the water had been calm. Coming out of the passage they hit a rougher sea. He wrenched the wheel to head obliquely for the distant line of coast. Jutta stared out behind. Within a minute *Xanadu* roared into sight, burning at full throttle in pursuit and gaining.

He waited as long as he dared. When *Xanadu* had come so close she reared above them he flung the wheel over and skidded in a turn. Much faster than he, the big boat was less manoeuvrable. He came round in a curve tighter than she could make, straightened, and roared away.

242

In Sheldon's hands *Xanadu* was after him at once. Adam snatched a glance at Jutta, her wet hair streaming in the wind.

Xanadu's bow was only feet behind when he spun the wheel and jinked away again. The Isles de Lerin passed by. They were in open sea now and the waves came crashing at them. They slammed across the crests, a V of foam spraying from the bow. The hull vibrated as if about to shake apart. It felt as though they were racing over cobbles. Half a mile ahead, a dozen fishing boats chugged toward Nice.

Again the *Xanadu* came scudding up behind, but Sheldon had learned and angled off the overtake in a wide sweeping curve. He came about and headed directly at him.

Both boats hurtled toward the collision. Adam held the course unflinchingly, knowing if he chickened early they would have time to get him. Only at the last second did he fling the wheel across. The speedboat slanted as it swerved, hit the other's bow wave and leapt clear.

Fighting the leather-cladded wheel, Adam raced toward the land. The fishing boats were way behind. The sea was rougher here.

Sheldon threw the *Xanadu* around and straddled Adam's wake. On full power he roared up on him. Adam jinked again but, this time, Sheldon was wise to him. As the speedboat banked in a hard tight turn Sheldon thrust one motor into full reverse. The gearbox shrieked, stripping cogs. *Xanadu* reared up like a hard-reined horse and spun, pivoting on her stern. Her bow smashed down. She shuddered on the impact. While Adam was still struggling to correct his turn she was thundering down on him.

The moment before the crash was endless. Adam hauled upon the wheel. The speedboat twitched and veered . . . but it was too late. At an impact speed of fifty mph the bow and knife-edged keel of *Xanadu* rammed down on her, slicing her in two. The big yacht drove right over her and roared on.

Behind, the two halves of the speedboat sprang apart, glissading down opposing slopes of wake as one section exploded in a boom and sullen flash of fire. A dense cloud of oily smoke billowed upward from the sea.

Sheldon cut back his speed. He and Raschid stared and

243

turned to look behind. One of *Xanadu*'s engines was screaming as if in pain, choking on splintered metal.

The sun was going down behind the Esterel. A brilliant dazzle slanted across the waves, marred by the column of black smoke and islands of blazing wreckage scattered across the sea in the path of the approaching fishing boats. In that destruction nothing lived.

Sheldon turned away. As he checked his course against the darkening lie of land an engine clanked and failed. Misfiring on the other, at quarter speed the disabled motor vessel *Xanadu* crept into shelter of the night toward the coast.

Chapter forty-nine

By 7.30 p.m. the growing crowd had jammed the croisette and stood immovable and densely packed outside the ornate facade of the Carlton, Cannes.

Since the start of the century this had ranked among the world's half-dozen top hotels. It was this distinction which saved the town from bombardment during the Allied landings in 1944; the same enduring reputation had caused its choice by the British Prime Minister to house the country's delegation for this internal conference.

The Carlton was where the PM, Foreign Secretary and other British delegates were resident. This was where, tonight, they were to entertain the Russian, American and European Heads of State to dinner. The occasion, and the Summit all were engaged in had been described as 'informal', yet this fact had in no way lessened public and media interest in the event.

From early morning the armoured personnel carriers of the CRS had rumbled in to find parking in the side streets where they remained, each containing a platoon of highly-trained, crack troops. The police presence was heavy and operational. By 4 p.m. the whole area had been closed to traffic. Armed men stood thick upon the croisette and adjacent streets, their radios crackling in non-stop flow.

The crowd had started to assemble in late afternoon, augmented by sunbathers as they came off the beach. It was the banquet which drew them here, of course, and the imminent arrival of the leaders of the world but, even more seductive there existed everywhere the surrounding high profile presence of the media.

The flaring lights, the photographers and reporters, the TV cameras high on rostrums and the roofs of OB trucks, the

245

jostling press of people, the brusque commands and hyperactivity of the police, the massive armed detachment of the CRS lining the croisette, all made for a potent and heady mix. Hustle and anticipation ran like a current through the crowd gathered outside the Carlton as the time drew close to 8 p.m.

The atmosphere built and thickened in the wait. Just before the hour the Prime Minister and Foreign Secretary of Britain were seen to come out of the hotel and position themselves to receive their guests. They stood beneath the ornate portico at the source of a river of red carpet which flowed down the marble steps to the croisette. Two solid lines of CRS were ranked either side of a pathway through the crowds.

From the distance came a wail of sirens, sweeping close. Preceded by motor cycle outriders, first to arrive was the cavalcade of the President of the United States. The second of six black Cadillacs drew up precisely opposite the entrance to the hotel.

The doors of the two flanking cars sprang open. A phalanx of dark-suited men debouched and fanned out in a protective screen. The President stepped from his car, closely followed by his Secretary of State. Dark-haired and vigorous despite his age, he paused to acknowledge the crowd's cheers then strode up the wide red carpet. Flashbulbs dazzled the night as he was welcomed by the PM and Foreign Secretary and passed through into the hotel.

A second cavalcade could already be heard approaching. The Foreign Secretary remained in place beside his Prime Minister.

Though portly, Sir John's pink face belied his age as did his posture, stance and bearing. He stood there proud and upright, canonised by office, mantled by success. Self-doubt was a stranger to Sir John, but he had never felt more sure or confident than he did tonight. The events of the afternoon and that traumatic and hallucinatory half hour when his entire personality had shattered and split apart was behind him and forgotten. He had emerged from chaos into clarity and peace. Everything around him was etched in a light so sharp and cool and pure it looked as though it had just been created and

246

placed upon the earth.

The second cavalcade of limousines glided to a halt below the Carlton entrance. The President of West Germany escorted by his delegation and security men came up the red carpet to be welcomed and pass inside.

Again there came the roar of motorbikes and scream of sirens, the approach of a line of fast black cars. This had to be the President either of France or Russia. And in those few moments while the great mass of people craned to determine which, at the periphery of that dense mob where the croisette was bounded by a wall beyond which was the sea, at the limit of the lit area of his vision, the Foreign Secretary observed a ripple and disturbance, a sudden shift among the throng, a jostling and upheaval. In the far distance he saw two tiny figures who had emerged from the darkness which lay beyond and were shouldering their way into the crowd.

And then his hand was out. He was smiling graciously and speaking French in welcome to the President of the Fifth Republic.

The clapping and the cheering died away as the French delegation disappeared from sight into the hotel. The crowd fell silent though a rustling remained in anticipation of the last guest due to arrive.

And then from far off there built upon the air the note of sirens, the growl of motorcycle engines. The Russians were coming.

The column nosed into view. The black-uniformed outriders, then the first car closely followed by half a dozen others.

Though they remained quiet a tremor rippled through the crowd. The man approaching was mythic in the power and threat he represented.

The black cars drew level, halted. Men dismounted, burly men in thick unfashionable suits who grouped around their leader's vehicle. Only then did he step out. Someone cheered, but his reception was muted. All stood uncertain and in awe of this short thickset figure who now, surrounded by his entourage, was moving up the carpet to where his hosts awaited him beneath the portico.

247

The Foreign Secretary saw his man. The image and his purpose lit up his brain. He started down the steps toward the Russian President.

He moved quite slowly, stepping down toward his country's guest. Unchecked, largely unremarked, his hand going to his jacket pocket, he stepped forward into history.

He was on the red carpet, striding forward, that hand coming from his pocket. The two men advanced toward their meeting down the corridor which split the crowd, an aisle bounded by uniformed policemen ... one of whom staggered suddenly, stumbling forward. A man burst through the human wall, was on the red carpet, was running toward the British Foreign Secretary ...

What happened then occupied a space in time of no more than two or three seconds, yet for those who watched it seemed to stretch into slow motion. They saw the running man. They saw the Foreign Secretary. They saw his hand come clear. They saw the gun.

That other running figure looked like nothing human. Charred clothes clung to him in rags, he looked like wreckage cast up by the sea, a ruined scarecrow.

Eyes fixed upon the Russian President, Sir John's target was suddenly hidden. A figure blocked his aim, was coming at him. Sir John saw the black streaked face which had the familiarity of a dream. It was Lupus. Lupus was coming at him, shouting something. Lupus was about to stop him.

Sir John's hand raised. His gun pointed at Adam's heart. He fired.

The sound was shocking. The running figure jerked. Carried by its own momentum it came on two paces, then it staggered and it fell, spilling to the ground.

In the uncertainty and surprise which followed the guards around the Russian President had begun to move a full instant before anyone else. They had closed around their leader, had turned him and were starting back toward the car ...

There was screaming in the crowd. Those behind pressed forward, those in front pushed back. A policeman had grasped the Foreign Secretary, was grappling for his gun. Its

248

doors were open and the Russian President was being bundled into his car . . .

. . . The sight of it was too much for Gemal. He, Sheldon and Raschid stood within the crowd. They had come to witness the climax to their plan. And Gemal saw that it had failed. Only they in that whole multitude were still. In the tumult and hysteria which had fallen on the crowd only these three stood unmoving, stricken and short-changed.

And that was how Jutta spotted them from the steps. By their stillness.

For Gemal the disappointment was too much. Reaching to his belt he jerked loose a grenade. In one trained movement he ripped away the tape, drew back his arm to fling it. His hand shot forward . . .

In the clamour Jutta's silenced pistol went unheard. Her shot took him in the face. His skull exploded as his moving hand shook loose of the grenade which sailed away and up. While his body tumbled it soared to the limit of its arc, held, and slowly started to descend. It thudded into the mass and burst.

The hotel's facade was lit by a brilliant flash. The crack of the explosion was strangely dulled by the walls of human flesh around it. At the same moment all the floodlights in the area detonated and went out.

Instant darkness fell. Like a curtain. One heartbeat of the world followed, one pulse of silence, and then the summer night was sliced apart by voices screaming in agony and terror, the shrill blubbering of humanity ripped open and torn apart.

Again the night split open with a roar as Raschid flung a second grenade. A car heaved up and burst into orange flame. A swathe of people went down as if their legs had been scythed from under them. The blast boomed along the seaside buildings. The dry rattle of shrapnel splattered through the palm trees. Raschid fell beneath a mob, trampled to the ground.

The carpet where Adam lay was soaked in blood. Around him was soot, flames, acrid stench, the hysteria of the crowd.

Lit by yellow flame the macabre scene lay beneath a pall of smoke. Dazed he struggled to sit up. He spat something soft and dreadful from his mouth. He wiped away the gore which had sprayed his eyes.

Sheldon was kneeling opposite, he swayed, bringing up his gun. His scalp was half ripped off and blood was spilling down his face but he was shouting.

It was as if time stopped. Silence fell upon the earth. All Adam saw was the gun wavering to bear on him and Sheldon's face beyond, maimed and shrieking.

'You *bastard*!' Sheldon screamed. Then he squeezed the trigger.

Just beside him Adam heard the crack. He stared and saw it happen. The hate on Sheldon's bloodied face was wiped away by shock. The eyes flew wide, the jaw sagged down, the mouth dropped open. In slow motion, the figure rose to stand and pirouette, its arm stretched out and reaching for the sky. It posed there for an instant like a statue, then the body crumpled and twisted to the ground.

It happened in silence, then the glass wall shattered. The screaming crashed back like an avalanche of surf. Jutta had thrown herself upon him, the gun still smoking in her hand. She flung it from her, with her hands she was trying to staunch the blood flowing from his chest.

He could not speak. A roaring thundered in his ears. Tasting blood, smelling sulphur, he drew her to him. All around was chaos, yet great wings wrapped them, gathering them together. Their sanctuary lay in the core of horror. Death had raged, this surrounding carnage was its aftermath. But the holocaust was spent. Sheldon, Gemal and Raschid were dead, Adam and Jutta alive. The guns of the police trained upon them as they lay in a lake of blood, they were together and they were alive.

Chapter fifty

It was morning, ten days later. Full summer lay upon the land. Overnight the streets of Nice had been hosed down and now were drying in the sun. Waiters were busy setting out tables on the sidewalk. The air was fragrant with the smell of flowers and resin and ambre solaire, the scent of holiday. Inches apart the striped mattresses lay in ranks upon the raked sand of private beaches. The temperature was 85° in sunny skies and everywhere you looked were the oiled curves and tanned geometry of naked flesh.

In the hospital room the slatted blinds had been closed against the sun. The place was cool with sterile air.

The room's sole occupant, the man was set up against the angle of the bed. His nude torso was wrapped in bandages. A drip was still plugged into his arm but the oxygen mask which at first had sustained him now was hooked back on the wall.

A nurse entered. She said something. The patient nodded and she hurried out.

A few minutes later she returned with two visitors. Seeing them come in the man in the bed made a token effort as if to rise. A pale hand acknowledged the gesture, waving him back against the pillows, 'Please, we do not wish to tire you.'

'I am honoured, Prime Minister,' Adam Lupus said.

Chairs were offered but the visitors declined them. 'We shall not be staying long,' the Prime Minister announced, 'But I wanted to meet you, Mr Lupus. To meet you and to thank you ...'

'SAVIOUR OF THE WEST'. That is what one of the headlines had named Adam; one of the more sensational admittedly, though in every newspaper in Europe and the United States there had been little else to read about for

251

several days. Extensive film coverage of the drama which had taken place outside the Carlton had monopolised the news. Having experienced notoriety, Adam achieved fame. For a while the curiosity of the world focused narrowly upon him; briefly he had become a hero.

'I beheld, and lo a red horse!' quoted the Prime Minister, 'And power was given to him to take peace from the earth, and that they should kill one another. There was given unto him a great sword . . .'

'Perhaps,' Adam answered, for a moment set aback, 'but Drury Sheldon was not the antichrist.'

'No? It was a Holy War he wanted. The return of Islam?'

It was a moment before Adam answered. 'No, I don't think so. Islam, the Arab cause, those were for him only another instrument. He used everybody, he was brilliant at it. No, he wanted to run the world. He thought he could do it better and he wanted to see his dream come true.'

'The dream of madmen and of tyrants,' said the PM.

Adam nodded curtly. 'Yes. What of the girl?' he asked.

'That creature,' the PM answered with distaste, 'you've received her letter?'

'You know about that?'

'Of course. It was smuggled out, but naturally our people read it. She seems to feel . . . rather warmly for you.'

'And I for her,' said Adam defiantly. 'Apart from other things, she saved my life. Where is she?'

'For the present we're holding her in a safe house in England. There is no cause to disturb yourself. She is comfortable and well treated.'

'Will she come to trial?' he asked.

The PM made a show of mild surprise. 'In Britain most definitely not. Apart from casualties within the crowd, the incident resulted in the deaths of two Arabs with Libyan passports, and an American citizen. It took place on French soil and was perpetrated by a German national. In international law certainly we have no jurisdiction over the affair.'

'Who does?'

'Actually,' answered the Prime Minister in a distant tone

252

'no one seems too keen to assume that role. We have not been deluged with demands for Fraulein Metz's extradition.'

'And the Foreign Secretary . . . ?' Adam questioned when a few seconds had gone by.

From the expression elicited by his enquiry it was clear the Premier found the subject embarrassing. 'Poor man. He's in the London Clinic.'

'And is he . . . ?'

'No,' the other answered shortly. 'He is the same. Still, deeply distressing though the whole thing is, the assassination with its truly dreadful consequences was prevented. But for you . . . '

'But for the girl,' Adam interjected.

'Yes. But it is you who have undergone the worst. When will you be up?'

'Next week they tell me,' Adam said.

'And then?— You'll return to London?'

'I don't think so,' Adam answered.

'But your company, The Lupus Group?'

'I've checked on it,' said Adam. 'Even in my absence the share price seems to be holding up.'

His visitor had strayed to the window and was peering through the slatted blind onto the sunlit street. 'Your decisions are your own of course. I came to thank you. If there's anything we can do for you . . . ' The words had become indistinct. The PM appeared to have developed an acute interest in the view outside.

'Well,' Adam said carefully, 'There is the matter of the girl.'

'Goodness, why on earth would you want to throw away your life and all you have achieved for a woman like her?'

'She saved it,' Adam replied. 'In another culture that would mean it belonged to her. I do not approve of her, I do not even like but, inconveniently, I love her. I don't really have a choice.'

Still staring at the street his listener considered this explanation for several moments before turning to remark, 'That is neither rational nor prudent.'

'No,' Adam agreed at once. 'But I have come to believe

253

that all change is desirable, even change which may be for the worse. What can be done about her?'

'Yes,' the Prime Minister answered, 'yes, we were rather afraid you were going to ask that. Possibly something can be arranged . . . '

It might have been thought by some that Adam had gained wisdom from the experience of all that he had gone through. By others it was not. To their judgement Adam remained indifferent.

He did not return to London. Within a month he had resigned from his position as head of the Lupus Group. There, Tony Carvel emerged victorious from a boardroom battle and retained title of Chief Executive. Under his on-going management the company continued to expand, the share price rose to record heights.

A year after Adam's kidnapping, Vanessa Lupus was granted a divorce by reason of the breakdown of her marriage. Her intention to marry Freddy Reynolds was announced by Nigel Dempster together with the opening of their new club in Gstaad.

In the company of Jutta, Adam set out upon a journey shared. He was happy that she bore his child. The knowledge heartened him on the path he had chosen. It was not the road of renunciation; though he had no interest anymore in the trappings of money and power, power itself again excited him. It was a lever which could move the globe. He had a conviction, a certitude to light his way, and nothing, not even death, could frighten him again. He was rich in his resolve. His life was filled with a passionate intensity; he did not brood unduly on what had happened to him.

He did not seek the memory yet, sometimes, late at night when they had made love and Jutta slept beside him but he could not, while he lay wide-eyed and wide-awake with the window open to the silence and the dark outside, his thoughts returned to those times that he had lived through.

Then he would feel a chill, goose pimples prickle down his skin, his mind fetch back to terror and loathsome flapping shapes crowd into his skull.

254

He would remember how it had been in the desolation of his prison, cut off from life and sanity under the constant threat of death ... his thoughts calming only as he then recalled that bright day which was like the first in all creation when he knew that he was free and walked with Sheldon below Big Sur in the mounting storm when the long green Pacific breakers came thundering in to hurl upon the rocks and drench them with their spray. He thought of the sun going down like a vast explosion behind the clouds and the sight of the American as he stood upon the headland with streaming face and blazing eyes and shouted out his dream above the howl and buffet of the wind ... and of how he, Adam, had felt at the offer of its mantle.

His mind would move forward then to the way that it had ended. Recollection would come back to him clear and sharp of the summer night, the crowd, the leaders of the West arriving at the banquet ... the moment when history itself was poised tip-tilted and hung upon the edge. And then inexorably his memory would wind on to include his own part in the affair as the man who had foiled the dream, he who had become a hero by keeping things the way they were, and are, orderly and safe in what passes for civilisation.

And then Adam would begin to wonder how it might be now if the impossible dream had succeeded and the world had changed ... and who could be running it now.